ONE OF A KIND

JANE LOVERING

Boldwood

First published in Great Britain in 2024 by Boldwood Books Ltd.

Copyright © Jane Lovering, 2024

Cover Design by Alexandra Allden

Cover Photography: Shutterstock

A CIP catalogue record for this book is available from the British Library.

Paperback ISBN 978-1-83533-222-1

Large Print ISBN 978-1-83533-218-4

Hardback ISBN 978-1-83533-217-7

Ebook ISBN 978-1-83533-215-3

Kindle ISBN 978-1-83533-216-0

Audio CD ISBN 978-1-83533-223-8

MP3 CD ISBN 978-1-83533-220-7

Digital audio download ISBN 978-1-83533-214-6

Boldwood Books Ltd
23 Bowerdean Street
London SW6 3TN
www.boldwoodbooks.com

For all the wildlife volunteers and workers out there, who suffer appalling conditions, low wages and career instability in the interests of helping animals that basically just want to bite them and run off into the undergrowth. Also for the red squirrel unit at Castle Howard, which is the closest I can come to seeing reds these days.

Also, for my family, who have had to put up with my mutterings about this book. I am not a natural plotter and making this storyline work involved far more walking up and down and talking to myself than usual, and they have borne it manfully. As has my dog, who has now just stopped looking up every time I shouted something aloud. Sorry, guys. I won't do it again. No, really.

1

The man lay on his back, eyes wide to the sky, as though death had taken him by surprise and the afterlife was proving something of a disappointment. Nearby, the trees that lined the path shivered their leaves as the last breeze of spring ran through on its way to summer, but nothing else moved. The darkness was blanket-thick, air chilly and still, and beginning to be filled by the smell of death.

Deep in the recess of the man's pocket *something* twitched, terrified, in the corpse-silence.

This was not proving to be a good day for anyone concerned.

* * *

The phone rang and woke me. 'Hello?'

'Cress? Is that you? You sound weird.'

I sighed. This level of enthusiasm was too much when my head was pounding and my pillow was covered with what could have been a modern art installation: tissues both used and unused, old Vicks inhalers and a couple of gel cool pads. 'What is it, Ivo?'

'Are you at work?'

I sniffed outrageously and hauled my aching body upright in the bed. 'No. I'm ill. I'm wallowing in my sick bed.' Then, more curiously, 'Why?'

There was a rustling noise, as though Ivo were moving, and then his voice again but quieter, almost a whisper. 'I'm on a job and I need you in a professional capacity.'

I would have laughed but I didn't have sufficient snot-free lung space. 'Don't be bloody daft. I work in a wildlife sanctuary and you're a reporter. There is absolutely no point of contact, unless you need to know whether a grown man can actually have his arm broken by a swan. I *keep* telling you, just stay a respectful distance away and you'll be fine.'

There was a pause and I could hear voices in the background. Ivo was, presumably, listening too, because he'd gone very quiet. Then he was back. 'No. No, this is something else, Cress.' His voice was urgent, fast and excited, which was typical Ivo. His default position was just above the surface of the planet, full of potential energy, like an asteroid hurtling towards Earth. 'And I really need you.'

There was a pause. I felt the tug that was our friendship trying to pull me out of bed to go to him, but then the equal and opposite drag of feeling wretched and wanting my bed. 'I'm ill!' I pleaded again, wafting some vapour rub under my nose to keep my passages open for long enough to be comprehensible. 'I've got this stonker of a cold that's been going round and I've had to phone in sick for the week.'

'Good. Means you're available for me,' he replied.

'I'm not "available", I'm in bed. Poorly,' I added, and then went into a round of coughing, just to prove my point.

'But you wouldn't want an animal to suffer, would you?' There was a sweetness in his tone that said he *knew* this would be the way to get to me. 'A poor, fluffy creature that's all alone?'

I narrowed my eyes, although he couldn't see so I didn't know why I was bothering. 'Is it injured?'

'I don't know. Probably. If it means you'll come I'll poke it with my biro.'

'Ivo!'

'Joke! Of course I wouldn't. You know me, Cress.'

Ivo and I had met at university, eight years ago. Although we'd grown up geographically in the same area, when it came to social circles we'd been a universe apart so we'd never met beforehand and during our time at Cambridge we'd orbited one another at varying distances. However, since we'd left, he always seemed to be not far away, a satellite in velvet bell-bottom jeans and embroidered waistcoat. A bit like having the 1970s on speed dial.

So I did know Ivo. And I knew he was as capable of hurting an animal as I was of dancing the can-can right now. He was, in fact, the person least capable of any injurious activity in a five-hundred-kilometre radius. Impetuous, yes, Ivo tended to act first and think far too deeply about his actions afterwards, but he couldn't deliberately have caused pain, particularly not to an animal. People called him 'wet' or 'bonkers', and I knew him to be neither of those things; he just wasn't your typical macho Yorkshireman. The flared velvet trousers and rainbow-coloured cravats were just one of the giveaways. My feelings for Ivo were as complicated as his fashion choices: fondness and exasperation layered over something hotter and deeper. Feelings I denied and concealed as hard as I could.

'All right, all right. To save a poor fluffy creature from your wicked machinations, I'll come.' Then, after a moment's thought, 'It's not dangerous, is it?'

'You just *will* not let that drop, will you! One time. One time I get involved with an international venomous reptile dealer!' He sounded half amused and half exasperated, which didn't seem fair. It hadn't been *me* trapped in a flat in Leeds by a cobra in the heating vents. 'And no. This time it's nothing like that.'

I felt my shoulders drop with relief. 'What is it, then?'

'What's what?'

'The animal, Ivo,' I said, patiently, sticking my foot out from under the covers to stir through the discarded clothing on the floor of my bedroom. Fortunately it was my work uniform; I'd come home from the rescue centre two days ago feeling so wretched that I'd torn it off and fallen into bed and I hadn't got dressed since. I'd been flopping from bed to bathroom and kitchen wrapped in a fleecy blanket, and my housemates had taken one look at me and gone away for the weekend.

'I want to surprise you,' Ivo said. 'Look, you know that bridleway above Helmsley that runs out onto the moor?'

I propped one bleary eye open for long enough to focus on my underwear. 'Yes.' Bending down made my nose run, so I had to crouch while keeping my head perfectly still to pick up my knickers.

'We're about half a mile out along the track past the trig point.'

'We?' I tucked the phone under my chin to pull clothes on, but this made my nose stream again, so I had to take it out and hold it up.

'Oh. Yes, the police are here as well,' he said, and hung up on me, leaving me wedging tissue up my nose in order to put a jumper over my head without leaving little wet trails down it.

I stared at the phone. 'You absolute bugger, Ivo.'

This wasn't totally new. The first time he'd called me in a professional capacity it had been the escaped and hidden cobra, and there had been several incidents since. Once, when he'd dashed over to report on a woman who had found a tropical spider in some bananas she'd been unpacking at the supermarket. The spider had re-emerged when they'd been looking at the bananas in question and I'd had to go over to capture it. It had been holding Ivo at bay in the supermarket's disabled toilet, where he had been standing on the seat whilst the arachnid waddled sleepily across the tiled floor. Then there had been the time he'd been trampled by a herd of deer – yes, Ivo and wildlife were an accident actually happening.

The exasperation had won out, emotionally, on that occasion.

With this in mind, I hurried myself into an assortment of clothing, my wildlife rescue centre sweatshirt and a pair of fleece trousers, work boots and my beanie hat with the centre's logo on, and, pausing only to grab a fistful of tissues, I dashed off to Ivo before he could meet his end at the paws of something hopefully about as menacing as the average earthworm.

It wasn't a long drive before I was out on the stretch of moor that Ivo had described, while the sun was still stretching its morning light across the tops of the trees and lightly touching the tips of the high hills. I hadn't even thought to look at the clock when he'd rung me, and it was evidently very early.

I left the car on the road and, hunching my shoulders against the cold shivers, I set out along the path towards the trig point. In the distance I could see a group of people, presumably Ivo was among them, a small tent, with tape delineating an area just off the track and flapping in the morning breeze. I couldn't work up any curiosity. I could barely work up the energy to trudge down the path. Bloody Ivo. Bloody, bloody Ivo.

The track was peaty and held the mark of every hoof from the horses that were regularly exercised up here and tyre marks from the quad bikes of the farmers who rode across to check the sheep. I had to tread carefully to avoid plunging into dank puddles, but as I was wearing my work boots, which Ivo described as 'a cross between Doc Marten and SS Officer', I wasn't too worried. Besides, I had a headache and my nose was still running and I was concentrating more on blasting Ivo for raising me from my sick bed as soon as I saw him than I was on the state of my footwear or the ground beneath.

I was also concerned for the safety of any animal involved in the activity going on in the area. Why was there a tent? I was pretty sure they weren't providing accommodation for wildlife now.

I reached the blue police incident tape and stopped. Beside the track the little white tent bulged with activity, like a seaside changing cubicle, and then Ivo popped out of one side with his blond hair awry and his face alight with excitement.

'Hi, Cress!'

I shook my head. 'This had better be good,' I said, hoarsely. 'I'm not well.'

'Yeah, you look rubbish. Have you got make-up on? Your eyes...'

Well, at least he'd noticed. 'No. I just haven't slept properly for three nights. Why am I here? I can't see any animals in obvious distress.' I dug my hands into my pockets and hunched my shoulders a bit more. Even though the sun was climbing high into the June sky, my cold-ridden body was feeling the last of the night's chill in every fibre.

'There's a body.' Ivo pointed with an elbow. He, too, had his hands in his pockets. Although he wasn't wearing a sturdy double-knit work jumper, today he was positively channelling the seventies in an embroidered coat with a manky-looking fur trim. With his classically handsome face, his tousled blond hair and his long legs, he looked ever so slightly like 'Acid Trip Ken'. The Barbie movie missed a trick, I thought, fever-ridden. 'In there.'

'A *body*?' That knocked my temperature down a few degrees. He hadn't mentioned *that* on the phone. 'A *human* one?'

'Well, yes, but it's all right, he only died last night so he's not too smelly or anything. They think it was an accident. Fell and banged his head, it looks like.'

I sighed. 'Well, I didn't trip him up. So, again, why am I here? Where's the animal? Unless you are about to conduct a Hercule Poirot-style accusation, with all the suspects being accused in turn, and they're all in there...' I looked at the tent. 'And I'm here to referee.'

He rolled his eyes. 'I told you, you're here in a professional capacity.'

The sun shone a particularly well-aimed beam that struck me full in the face and made me squint and wince in equal measure. My hair was unwashed and on end, my skin prickled with the sweat of several sleepless nights and, in short, I was not feeling up to Ivo's twenty-questions conversational technique. 'Just tell me,' I sighed.

Ivo's eyes twinkled. He was enjoying this. I wished he'd tell me *what* was such fun about being up at the spark of dawn in the middle of nowhere with – his words percolated through the fug in my head – a *dead body* in the vicinity, and what it had to do with wildlife rescue, and, more importantly, me. But his wiggling eyebrows and manic grin were indicative of a story. And one thing I knew about Ivo and stories was, he liked to take his time.

'Come over here.' One hand came out of his pocket and took my elbow to tug me further down the path. Behind his shoulder the tent bulged again.

'Are there people in there or is the body dirigible?' I asked, curiosity getting the better of the sniffing.

'Oh, the police are still here,' Ivo said, vaguely.

'And letting you trample over their investigation?'

We sat on a convenient rock that jutted from the moorland like a broken rib. Birds scattered skywards as Ivo pushed me gently down. 'Rufus gave me a call over. I don't think it's really an investigation, more of a puzzle. I'm staying out of the way. Mostly.'

Rufus was a police sergeant. We weren't supposed to know, but he was Ivo's contact with the police, feeding him information about various crimes and incidents in time for them to get onto the local daily news site. He was also, incidentally, Ivo's brother, so the secret was fairly open.

'Mostly,' I repeated.

'They're having a quick poke around but it's not looking suspicious. Bloke falls over, cracks head, dies, is found by someone walking their dog. Only, not a dog walker in this case,' he added quickly. 'Horse rider.'

'I don't need to know the details, Ivo, I just need to know why I'm here.' I rubbed a hand through my hair. It was plaited into scouring pad texture at the back of my head where I'd tossed and turned on the pillow. A tiny waving corner of my vanity protested that I ought to have had a wash and tidy-up before I came out, but Ivo had seen me in worse states. I was also wondering a little about him noticing that I looked rubbish. Ivo rarely said anything about my appearance, which was just another nail that kept the lid on my secret crush on him. Not one 'you look nice' or 'cute boots', and yet he could tell me that I looked awful. Yep. That was our relationship in a nutshell.

'Okay.' Ivo's blue eyes were sparkling. 'Well. Dead body reported, police attended, yada yada. Here he is, up on the moor, very early morning, not really dressed for hiking, but that's not the point.'

I dropped my head into my hands. It felt like a concrete block. 'What *is* the point, Ivo?' I asked, wearily. 'And could we get to it fairly swiftly. I want to go back to bed.'

'Guess what they found in his pocket?' Ivo grinned hugely, clearly very pleased with himself. 'Go on. Guess.'

'A rocket launcher.'

'Nope.'

'Four hundred million pounds in forged currency... I don't know!'

Ivo looked at me steadily. 'That's a surprisingly specific amount, Cress.'

I sighed again. 'Look. I've had to ring in sick to work and you know I hardly ever do that, so please, for all you hold dear, just tell me why I'm here so I can go back home.'

'A squirrel.'

I dropped my head even further forward so that my forehead was resting on my knees. Obedient to gravity, my nose started to run again. 'What?'

'That's what he had in his pocket. A squirrel.'

'Maybe he was out here squirrel hunting? There's a forest down there.' I waved a hand behind me, without looking up. 'And people eat squirrel. Some people do, anyway. Weird people.' I raised my head and caught his eye. '*You'd* probably eat squirrel,' I finished, pointedly.

'It's sustainable.'

'Not right now it isn't,' I muttered darkly. 'Nothing about this is sustainable.'

'And it wasn't just a squirrel, Cress.' Ivo sounded really excited now. I hoped he wasn't getting carried away. Ivo had dreams of being what he called a 'proper investigative journalist' and, as we lived somewhere where a bike being stolen from a shed made the headlines for three weeks running, things that needed proper investigative journalism were thin on the ground. Squirrel poaching was hardly the topic for the next conspiracy theory.

'What, then?' I asked, tiredly. 'Two squirrels? A squirrel uprising? Are they banding together to take down their human overlords?'

Ivo looked at me solemnly. Without the usually present twinkle and effervescence, I could see the outline of the person he really was. Driven, conscientious. More than an Afghan coat and open-toed sandals. Ivo's single-minded focus made him good at what he did. And a spectacularly irritating friend. 'Red squirrel, Cress,' he said.

I mopped my nose and rubbed the back of my hand across my aching forehead. 'Don't be silly. There aren't any red squirrels for a hundred miles. The Cumbrian border would be the nearest colony – it's probably just a brown-coated grey.'

Ivo jiggled closer. 'How many hours have I spent listening to you lecture me on wildlife?' he asked. 'Roughly?'

'I wasn't lecturing. I was informing.'

'You went on that course and then came back and told me all about it. And you think I can't tell a red squirrel from a grey? *Seriously*?' He put a hand on my forehead. 'Wow. You're hot. You've probably got a temperature.'

I leaned, for a second, into the cool of his palm, soothing my headache. He smelled, predictably, of incense and patchouli oil. Ivo didn't do anything by halves. The velvet of his coat sleeve was soft against my skin and I closed my eyes for a moment before I jerked up and away. This was *Ivo*. I wasn't going there. Leaps into the unknown were not my thing, I was all about the reliable and the dependable. Those two words could not be applied to Ivo in any way, and I'd take what I could get of his company without risking my neck, my affections and my clean driving licence. He was attractive, but with an edge that made me wonder if it was sometimes kept sharp with chemical help.

'So, hang on. You're telling me that there was a body found, up here in the middle of nowhere, and he had a *red squirrel* in his pocket? An animal that is not found anywhere even close to here? And – in his *pocket*? Reds are really shy, there's no way he was carrying one around in his pocket, not without it going ballistic and escaping!'

Ivo took my shoulders and pulled me around to face him. The spark was back in his eyes now, his face, sculpted like a stonemason's best example of his art, was almost rippling with the constant emotional feed. 'That's why I'm here. It's weird, you agree? Why was he here? I've seen the body, he wasn't dressed for hiking – besides, the attending doctor reckoned he died about midnight – and he *definitely* wasn't dressed for walking in the dark.'

I sighed again. 'That's the police's job, Ivo. You know that. Nothing to do with us. You go back and put the story on the website, I – well, I guess you've got me here to pick up the squirrel? Is it still about?'

Ivo looked over towards the white tent, bulging and wobbling, like a tiny windbreak on a gale-ridden beach. 'They're just waiting for the van to come and take him away.'

'And the squirrel?'

He shrugged. 'They think it climbed into his trouser pocket once he was dead. Hiding, or something.'

I gaped at him. 'But, where from? Like I said, no—'

'Red squirrels for miles, I know. I *did* listen, Cress.' He shook my shoulders lightly and I was sure I heard my brain clattering around inside my skull. 'But I've just got a *feeling* that there's something not right.'

'Apart from there being a dead body and a squirrel, which isn't exactly normal.' His enthusiasm would have been infectious, if I weren't already so full of infection that it was leaking out of my nose.

'Yeah.' He almost breathed it. 'So. You in?'

His hair caught the wind and blew out behind him and made him look like a photo shoot for a retro magazine. Ivo. My friend. The only reason I went along with half of his schemes was to keep him from making a complete tit of himself.

'All right,' I coughed now. 'I'm in. What do you want me to do?'

'Have you got those cages still, in the back of your car?'

As a wildlife rescue person, all I'd had to do was turn up in the police tent, in my uniform, carrying one of the small-animal cages, and they'd looked at me with relief.

'You here for the squirrel?'

It briefly crossed my mind to say, 'No, I'm here for you; here, climb into this really *tiny* little cage,' but I didn't feel it would be a good way for me to establish my credentials, so I didn't. I just nodded.

'Okay. Where's it gone? Tom?'

Tom, who was in a uniform that looked as though he'd put it on very hastily in the middle of the night, and who was looking about as cheerful as someone called upon to wrangle a squirrel on not enough sleep, pointed. 'We stuck it in that box.'

I tried not to look at the plastic sheeted shape on the ground, from which a pair of scuffed and dirty trainers were poking. I'd worked with the police before – normally it was ferrets that needed removing when poachers got caught – but I'd never been this close to a dead human body before.

At least they'd had the sense to cover the cardboard box. Someone had flung their jacket over the top, and I hoped that the squirrel hadn't climbed into an armhole or something.

Carefully and gently I removed the jacket. The squirrel was a tiny ball of red fluff huddled deeply into one corner of the box, nose tucked in so far that only half of one tufted ear was visible. I held the travel box down in front of it. The squirrel didn't move.

Obedient to my training, I gave it a quick visual once over. There were no wet streaks in the fur that would indicate bleeding. No limbs held at odd angles, no shivering or other indicators of pain. It was small, and round and much redder than even the most auburn of the greys, most definitely a red squirrel. Uninjured, apparently, and not sick or starved – what the hell was it doing here?

Prepared to initiate emergency measures should it panic, I touched it, very gently with the tip of my finger. A head emerged and a beady eye rolled upward, then, in a flash of auburn, the little creature had fled into my nicely enclosed, dark and safe-looking transport box and I closed the door behind it with relief.

'You don't need it?' I asked the two sleepy looking detectives in the tent with the body. 'For evidence, or anything?'

They looked at one another and I could feel the sarcasm building. 'Well, we don't reckon the squirrel did him in,' said one.

'But if you could hold onto it until we need it for questioning,' said the other. 'We need to know what it might have seen.'

I sighed. 'Right. I'll take him back with me then.'

Then, moving carefully so as not to tread on the body, I carried the little box outside, where the sun was now shining blindingly across the top of the moor and highlighting the white-painted trig point like a pimple on a rolling purple buttock.

Ivo was vibrating with anticipation. As soon as he saw me

emerge from the tent, he held up both arms in a Victory gesture and shook his fists at the sky.

'No good pretending to be macho now, Ivo. I know you, remember?'

'Shut up. I'm happy.' He bent his head to look through the wire of the cage door. 'Is it in there?'

There was still some left-over sarcasm boiling inside me, clearly, because I managed to snort. 'No. I left it in the tent. These things are the new "must have" accessory, didn't you get the memo?'

'Shut up. Right. What do we do now?'

'*I* get this poor creature to somewhere more secure and then go back to bed.' I started clumping my way back along the peaty track, trying to forget the covered body I was leaving behind, and that the decorative Ivo was wriggling his way out of a hot coat at my side.

'Great, great. The police don't know who he was; did they say that to you? No idea. No identification.'

I held the little box higher and peered inside. The squirrel had taken itself into the darkest recesses and was nothing but a bright eye of suspicion and a curled tail. 'What were they expecting, a driving licence?'

'Of the bloke, not the squirrel.'

'Oh. Okay.'

Ivo grabbed the arm not holding the squirrel box and pulled me to a standstill. 'Have you no intellectual curiosity *at all*?' he asked, tugging me around until I faced him.

I sighed again. Deep, steadying breaths seemed to be a feature of any conversation with Ivo. 'Right now I am wondering whether I'll get home before my paracetamol wears off, why you came up here before dawn in such unsuitable clothing, what to do with this poor animal when I get back seeing as I'm not supposed to go into work because I am ill, and whether my housemates have left enough hot water for me to have a nice warm bath as soon as I get in. Is that enough for you?'

He let go of me and dropped his face into his hands. 'God, yes, I'm sorry, Cress. Not your problem. A mystery body on the moor with a squirrel in his pocket. It's more an intellectual exercise than a story, isn't it?'

I felt a momentary pang of shame for upsetting him and patted his shoulder. 'It's fine. I'll go home, make this chap comfortable in the emergency housing in the shed and go back to bed for the rest of the week. I might see you next weekend? Isn't Jamie having a party that we're invited to in Doncaster?'

Jamie was another university friend. He'd gone into the civil service but we still spoke to him.

'Yeah, yeah.' Ivo sounded tired. 'I just thought – no, you're right. Course. I'm just getting carried away again.'

But then I looked at the box in my hand. 'Ivo,' I said, steadily. 'Look.'

The squirrel had uncurled. It sniffed its way up to the wire door and poked a nose through the narrow gap, then splayed itself across the wiring, giving us a lovely view of a fluffy white stomach. Tiny paws gripped the wire.

'Probably hungry,' Ivo remarked, after a quick glance. 'God knows I am. Might try to catch a fry up before I head back.'

'No, you don't understand.' I was still keeping my voice level. 'This is a red squirrel. Noted for their aloof behaviour and shyness. They don't approach humans, they hide away, that's why we have such trouble keeping track of the populations and their spread or decline; they're really hard to count.'

Ivo looked down at the cage. The squirrel was snuffling its way around the entire hinge side of the door, seemingly unconcerned about our conversation. 'There's one,' he said. 'Definitely one. Not making it difficult at all.'

I could feel the fizzling coil of query deep in my stomach, like a fuse burning through. 'You still don't get it. The only reason for a squirrel – a *red* squirrel – to behave like this, would be if it had been hand-reared. Or, at least, kept domestically. And that's illegal, you can't keep them as pets, can't keep them at all unless you're properly licensed.'

Ivo dropped his hands and the gleam was back in his eyes. 'So, we have a man, with no identification, dead on the moor in the middle of the night, with an illegal *tame squirrel*?' He bent lower and his hair brushed against me. I ignored the goosepimples this raised and concentrated on the squirrel. 'And you're not even a *bit* curious?'

'It's edging towards *Scooby-Doo* territory,' I said, simultaneously annoyed at his persistence and caught in the backwash of his enthusiastic excitement. This might not be a mystery, but it was rather enjoyable to see Ivo treating it as though it were.

'I suppose he could have been – what? Taking his squirrel for a walk?' The sound of a vehicle on the road beyond made us both look up. 'It's the body wagon,' Ivo carried on. 'Come to take the poor bloke away.'

I stood up. I didn't particularly want to see the removal of the corpse; it had been bad enough making its acquaintance under the circumstances as it was. 'I'll take this chap home then,' I said, watching the squirrel's continuing antics. He, or she, didn't seem in the least fazed by being in a cage with the enormous faces of two humans staring through the bars, and was now scuttering through the straw bedding. 'And go back to bed,' I added, to drop a little more guilt on Ivo for dragging me out, even though I had to admit that a lovely early morning on the moors with the sun and Ivo hadn't been the chore I was making it out to be, and the presence of the squirrel had added a piquant touch.

'I have to go and put this up on the online page.' Ivo curled his lip. He pined for the days when reporters had to dash to the nearest payphone to call in a story, and had always longed to be able to say, 'Hold the front page!' With online editions updated hourly, and only the best stories making the weekly print edition, this was unlikely to happen and he clearly felt it in every centimetre of his patchwork-and-velvet coated heart. 'And you really don't think there's anything weird about it?'

I took the cage in my arms, unwilling to risk swinging the squirrel too much. 'Oddest thing is him having the squirrel in his pocket, to be honest. I mean, you couldn't carry it any distance like that, it would just climb out and run away.'

'Trust you to be practical.' Ivo led the way out along the path, where we passed four burly men in black carrying what was obviously a collapsible stretcher and a body bag. We all smiled early-morning smiles built of too much tea and not enough patience at one another as we jostled through. 'You're *always* so practical, Cress. Can't you just admit, this once, to a tiny tingle of curiosity about what the hell was going on up here last night?'

I thought for a moment. *Practical?* Was that how Ivo saw me? I felt a momentary stab of disappointment that he couldn't see me as something a little more... anything but practical. Although, compared to Ivo, I was as sensible as lace-up brogues and as down to earth as a lawn mower, so it wasn't a ridiculous description, but, just for once, couldn't he see me as what my mother would have called a flibbertigibbet?

'Maybe,' was all I said.

'Ru said he wouldn't put this out on the police Twitter until I'd had chance to update our site,' Ivo said, conversationally.

'That's nice of him.'

'Yes. They're going to do fingerprints to try to identify our body.'

'Oh. Good.' I really didn't want to think about the body any more. I wanted to go home and back to bed.

In my hand the box twitched as the squirrel moved from side to side.

'And I thought I might beat them to it by going round the B&Bs.'

'What on Earth for?' We reached our cars, my poor battered old Land Rover and Ivo's totally out-of-character Volvo V90. His was electric though, so not quite so out of character as all that.

'I've just got a *feeling*. Reporter's intuition.' There was a suppressed excitement about Ivo again now, as though, under that 1970s fashion-victim exterior lay steel-tipped ammunition. His gaze was focussed and that slight tension that made him stand straighter felt just a wee bit dangerous. 'Plus something else.'

'Tell me,' I said as sternly as I could.

He wiggled his eyebrows at me and his precarious piercing fell out. 'Well. When I got here and the police were all "what the hell is he doing with a squirrel in his pocket" and everything, I had a quick squizz along the track where they found the body. And I found... this.'

I bent down and picked up the eyebrow ring, handed it to him, and looked at what he was holding out. A piece of paper. A printout of a receipt, on cheap paper in faded blue ink.

17 June
One night accommodation, no breakfast. £75.

The rest of the receipt had been rendered illegible by damp and having been screwed up into a ball.

'Ivo, that could be *anyone's*! Loads of people go walking up and down here every day, anyone could have dropped that.' I looked at the sad and tatty bit of paper. 'Why do you think it's relevant? It might not even be 17 June this year!' I unlocked the Land Rover, although I didn't know why I ever even bothered to lock it in the first place seeing as you could open the doors with a hefty thump on the roof and a kick.

Again that feeling that Ivo was a mass of repressed energy; he almost crackled. 'Because *yesterday*' – he leaned an arm against his car roof and his overly embellished shirt blew in the breeze, making him look like an illustration of anachronism in an edition of *Vogue* – 'I was over here doing a quick piece on litter pickers. They did the whole of this stretch, Newgate bank to Cowhouse. Cleared it of everything. I interviewed them when they got to the car park and they were taking bag loads of stuff off to the recycling point – this path was as clean as a whistle last night. So the chances are' – he held the tiny scrap of paper up and it fluttered like a flag of surrender – 'this came from our man. It's dry, it's not been out here for long. And 17 June was yesterday, although you won't know that as you've been wallowing about in your sick bed like a poorly hippo, so it must have been left *after* the clean-up, and they didn't finish until six.'

I stared at him but he was avoiding my eye and fiddling with the crumpled paper, as though it held the secrets of the universe. 'I have *not* been wallowing. And comparing me to a hippo is not the way to go about getting me to co-operate with your crazy schemes, you know.'

'Sorry. You're nothing like a hippo really,' he said, vaguely. 'But look,' and now I was getting the fully focussed gaze again, as though he were trying to will me to understand. 'This is important. It just *is*.'

'Then you should show it to the police.' I put the squirrel in the boot. It continued its unflustered examination of its cage with no notable signs of terror.

'What, and give them a heads-up?' Ivo widened his eyes in shock.

'Please, Ivo, please tell me that you aren't going to try to make a mystery out of this!' I pointed to the tiny coil of paper still flapping between his fingers. 'It could have blown here from the road. It could have been carried by one of the litter pickers who dropped it right at the end of the pick. It might have come out of the pocket of the horse rider who found the body. It could be—'

'Yes, yes, all right, no need to labour the point.'

I opened my driver's door and was about to get into the Land Rover, which smelled rather too much of fish to be comfortable, and I remembered that I still hadn't given it a good fumigation after the rescue of a seagull that had got itself tangled in wire. Ivo put a hand on my arm to stop me. 'But what if,' he said, suddenly serious. '*What, if*, Cress? Because, if it's a receipt from last night, he stayed somewhere, he must have booked in, so someone must know who he is. And what about the squirrel? You can't pretend that it's normal to go about with a tree rodent that close to your bollocks.'

'Maybe not,' I conceded. 'But it's a police matter, none of our business.'

He waved dismissively. 'Them? They're just treating it as a bit of a bizarre accident. Bloke with a weird pet goes out for a midnight stroll and leaves his wallet and driving licence behind...'

'And maybe that's just what happened.' My head was aching again and I wanted to climb back into my cool bed, where I could cough and sniffle into tissues and feel miserable without Ivo's relentless attempts to invoke Miss Marple in me, masochistically enjoyable though they were.

There was a clonk from the boot as the squirrel rattled around in the little cage.

Ivo moved his hand onto my shoulder and pushed, until I had to turn around to look at him properly or risk a dislocation. 'I *know* it's not, Cress,' he said, his voice hard with a quiet urgency. 'I can *feel* it. Something really strange went on here last night, something that I need to...' He stared off over my head in search of vocabulary, but all there was was the metallic blue of the sky and some swifts whistling low above us. 'I *know* it,' he repeated. Then his eyes came back down to mine and one eyebrow wiggled. 'And, come on, you can't let me go off investigating by myself. It will only end in trouble. Besides, all good detectives have a sidekick, and you're mine!'

I drove away, leaving him with a promise that I'd come along with him when he 'investigated'. I had to; Ivo could get himself into untold amounts of danger just reporting on an escaped bullock. He had ideas of in-depth reporting that would leave him halfway up a sixty-foot tree while the bullock in question prowled around below making threatening bellowing noises, so there was no way I could leave him looking into an unexplained squirrel. He'd probably end up in police custody and I'd have to bake a cake with a file in it or something.

Sometimes, being Ivo's friend was worse than being his enemy. And a lot, lot harder.

2

At least the house was quiet when I got back. I shared the little cottage with two others, my friend Lilith and her partner Dix, who were, as I should have been on this Monday morning, at work. I parked the Land Rover in the resulting big space right outside and relaxed. I'd just got to make the squirrel safe and happy in the temporary quarters of the garden shed and I could collapse back into my bed and wallow away another day feeling sorry for myself.

The house was mine. Bought with an inheritance unexpectedly bequeathed while prices had been spiralling, it was slightly too small for three people. I needed the extra money to cover the bills, so I'd invited Lilith and Dix, whose landlord had decided he wanted to reclaim their flat, to share. It mostly worked, although the bathroom could be a bone of contention. Owning the house meant that I could afford my job, which paid so little as to almost constitute a hobby. But it was secure – chiefly because nobody else wanted a job where you were on call almost continually, for pocket money – and it involved being useful.

As I got out of the Land Rover and opened the back door, I

had a resurgence of the passing irritation that had been haunting me through the night. Annoyed with the sticky back-door handle, the lack of space, my lack of funds, in the darkness of the night I had admitted to myself that I wanted an actual career, where I could be responsible for more than a recalcitrant printer and in charge of more than a Land Rover full of smelly cages. I wished I could go out and confidently talk myself into a job where I had a degree of control and could make decisions, something where I could have real results, other than a couple more badgers alive in the wild and an owl removed from danger. They were good things, obviously. But transient. Impermanent. Some of the badgers were being 'saved' on an almost nightly basis. A tiny, deeply buried part of my soul wanted to shout about what we did, educate people, change behaviour. But it was only sometimes. I knew I wouldn't be any good in jobs like that. I was born to quietly rescue animals, to keep my head down. Why risk what I had, when what I had was enough? Besides, those jobs I sometimes saw advertised, with pressure and management responsibilities, never had any element of wildlife care in them. They were made of paperwork and forms and telling people what to do and, while I would gladly lose the scraping and shovelling element of my job, the animals were what kept me going.

I gave myself a small shake. It was the fever talking, that was all, making me feel weak and maudlin. I wasn't cut out for moving and shaking, I was one of nature's backroom girls, quietly and confidently saving nature, one irritable hedgehog at a time. I only needed to get my temperature down and I could go back to serving animal-kind and I'd lose this small, itchy feeling in the back of my head that I *could be doing more.*

This feebleness was the only reason that I could possibly find for having gone along with Ivo's 'let's do some detective work'. He'd got me at a vulnerable moment, I thought, sliding the squirrel's cage out of the back of the Land Rover, and I really ought to know better. My main focus here was getting this squirrel back to where he belonged, wherever that might be.

In my hand the cage rocked again as the squirrel swung from the top by needle-clawed paws, and I held the cage up to eye level and squinted inside. A button-bright eye, tilted at an angle from a furry body suspended from the roof, looked back. A tufted ear twitched and then a scuffle of paws sent the squirrel dancing back across the cage to peer at me from the wire door.

It wasn't afraid. In fact, it seemed to rather like my company, thrusting a little nose towards the bars as though in search of a treat. Cautiously I raised a finger. When the squirrel didn't cower back into the dark of the straw bed, I stroked the tip of the furry nose and watched the huge cape of a tail curl up and flick in pleasure.

'You've been hand-reared, haven't you?' I asked it, pointlessly.

The shiny brown conker of an eye raked me for any hint of a snack, found me wanting, and the squirrel bounced back to begin another swinging session around the rest of the cage.

The little creature was restless, lively and in excellent health. It was hard to imagine it remaining quiet and docile for long enough to be handled, let alone put in a pocket. And yet, very obviously, that was exactly what the man had done, although, of course, he couldn't have anticipated ending up dead, even though, dressed as he had been, it had always been a possibility. The local mountain rescue had fetched people down off the hills many a time, occasionally as corpses, when they'd misread the soft swell of the heather-covered hills as benign, a sunny day as steady weather and flip flops and shorts as excellent wear for a day's walking across exposed moorland. A broken leg, a night in sub-zero temperatures, and a sad end was almost inevitable.

But for all its tame and human-friendly behaviour, this little creature wouldn't have hung around for long without a cage. And how did you even *get* it in a pocket in the first place? I mentally ran through the agitations of trying to get this quicksilver-fast creature in a position to thrust it into the depths of fabric without having it shoot up your arm or run downwards.

I mean, maybe if the dead guy had been a magician? Making a squirrel appear? And the squirrel was trained?

No. That was Ivo rubbing off on me again. I half-smiled to myself at how horrified he would be if he knew the effect he sometimes had on me, shook my head and opened the shed, which was currently empty. Normally there was at least one hedgehog and a pigeon in there, handed over to me by members of the public, often when the creatures had been going about their perfectly lawful business. 'He was in the road, miss', 'I reckon it's got a broken wing, love', and I'd keep them until they'd eaten and drunk something and the person who'd given them to me was a safe distance away, and then just let them go in the garden, whereupon the pigeon would fly off and the hedgehog would burble its way into the undergrowth with, no doubt, muttered imprecations in hedgehog-ese about bloody humans.

I put the squirrel, cage and all, into one of the big rodent cages. It had a proper covered section for sleeping and a water bottle, and I scattered a handful of pine nuts across the floor, then opened the door to the travel cage to let the squirrel bounce out and immediately swing up onto the side to stare at me again.

'Who *are* you?' I asked.

'Name's Frank, ma'am,' came an exaggeratedly American drawl from over my shoulder. And then, in more normal, and far more Yorkshire tones, 'What on Earth are you doing with that?'

'Hi, Lil,' I said, without turning round. 'I thought you'd gone to work.'

'Popped home to pick up my sandwiches and check on you.'
She swung on the shed door for a second, suspended by fingertips and reminding me slightly of the squirrel, only less cute and
wearing overalls. 'You were so quiet when we got up, we thought
you'd died.'

'I had a call out.' I pointed to the squirrel, spasmodically flit-
ting around the bigger cage.

'I see that.' She came in closer and peered. The squirrel
paused in its frenzied examination to peer back. 'Never seen one
like that before. Tufty ears and all.'

'It's a red squirrel.'

'Oh, aye.' She continued to squint.

'They aren't local.' I couldn't help myself. 'Nearest colony is
on the border with Cumbria, as far as I know, or Scotland. Oh,
and there are some way down south too.'

'So what's this little chap doing here?' She made a chirruping
noise and the squirrel cocked its head. 'Cute. Seems quite tame.'

'Could be an infill population.' I kept my eye on Lilith. While
not malicious, she had a very rural Yorkshire approach to some
wildlife and couldn't see why some sections might need rescuing,
as opposed to shooting. With squirrels she could go either way,
depending on whether she'd been out tree planting recently.

'Of one?' She turned big eyes on me and her torn dungaree
pocket flapped.

I looked at the squirrel again. It seemed relaxed and unafraid,
but somewhere a colony was missing one of their number.
Another squirrel may be missing a mate. I needed to get him
home, wherever that may be. 'There may be others out there.'

'The cold seems better.' Lil lost interest in the animal and
exited the shed to stand in the sunlight. 'You're not sniffing as
much.'

'Just have to make sure it doesn't turn into a chest infection,' I replied, almost automatically, whereupon she raised her eyebrows at me and headed off to where her bike was leaning against the back wall.

'I'll go and report to Dix that you're not lying cold and stiff in your room then, shall I?' She waved the retrieved sandwiches in my direction, slotted a foot into a pedal and, without a backwards look, pushed off down the alleyway out to the road beyond.

I tidied up, cleaned out and disinfected the travel cage and hung it up to dry, thinking that, while it might be nice to have the house to myself, really it was quite nice to have people checking up on me and making sure that I hadn't died in the night. And, although meeting Dix in the kitchen in the small hours could be slightly disconcerting, it was often pleasant to have someone to talk to as you made a cup of tea when you'd returned from a badger-rescuing mission.

Buying the cottage, from an unexpected inheritance from a grandmother that I had never met – although of course I'd known of her existence, I knew my mother had *had* a mother at some point, she hadn't burst onto the world in a ray of miraculous light – had been sensible. A tiny part of me had wanted to use the money to travel and have adventures, but that part had been wrestled to the ground by the matter-of-fact part. I needed a roof over my head that wasn't subject to the whims of a landlord. I couldn't afford rising rents on a fixed salary. So I bought a two-bedroomed terraced cottage and rented the spare room to Lilith, and Dix. The pair of them were chaotic, noisy, wretchedly unpunctual and random in their habits, but they paid regularly and weren't above sharing a takeaway with me.

What with the satisfactory decanting of the squirrel, the sunlight, the fact that Lilith had thought to come and check up on me and being already up, dressed, plus the residual buzz from being needed by Ivo, I decided not to go straight back to bed.

Instead, I went indoors and tidied up the kitchen, loaded the dishwasher and was just contemplating putting my sheets into the washing machine when a figure appeared outside the back door, vibrating with excitement in a shirt in a particularly violent shade of electric blue.

'You're up! Good.'

Ivo swung through the door and into the kitchen, all loose limbs and blithe good nature as though he simply couldn't contemplate anyone telling him to go away.

'You weren't wearing that this morning,' I observed mildly, stopping mid-cleaning to watch him scan the kitchen for anything edible that someone may unwisely have left lying around. The man was as lean as a python, but would eat absolutely anything that hadn't been licked by someone else. Sometimes he would eat things that *had* been licked by someone else.

'Need to look smart,' he replied, hurling himself onto a chair when there was clearly nothing to eat anywhere. 'We're off to chat to B&B owners, remember?'

'What, *now*?' I was halfway through wiping down the worktop, and stopped, hands on hips like an accusatory mother-in-law. 'Ivo...'

He looked at me steadily. 'Dead bodies don't wait, Cress.'

'Yes, yes they do! Of course they do, what else are they going to do, run away? The clue is in the word *dead*!'

'I mean' – he hunched himself forward over his elbows – 'the mystery of the dead body won't wait. I want to steal a march on the police, basically. To them, this is just an accident in the dark and they'll check the details in case anyone's reported a missing person and do his fingerprints when... well, when they get round to it, but they aren't going to *investigate*. Their only goal is to inform next of kin and get the bloke decently buried.' Now he turned his face up to meet my eye.

'Don't you want to know? For the sake of the squirrel, if nothing else?' he finished, triumphantly, as though putting down the final card in a poker hand that he knew was going to sweep the board. 'You can't let that squirrel stay a mystery, can you, Cress?' His eyes glittered; he knew he had me on the animal welfare thing. '*Can* you?'

I stared at him and felt that familiar twinge in my chest. *How could he look at me and not know?* Then the equally familiar rebound of relief that he didn't and couldn't know how I felt about him. He was my friend. That was fine. 'You're serious?'

'Yep. Deadly, if you pardon the pun.' He reached out and caught my hand. His fingers were warm, his gaze was steady and – well, it was *Ivo*. 'Come with me, Cress. Help me.'

We stayed there for a second, locked in a scene from a 1950s kitchen sink drama, this beautiful man with his eclectic clothing choices, his monied background and his ambition, and me, whose only similarity with him was my slightly odd trousers.

'Don't you want to *know*, Cress?' he almost breathed, the words subsumed under the birdsong from the garden.

This was unfair. If I had ever suspected Ivo of duplicity, I would have thought he was using me; that he knew about the self-inflicted tearing of my feelings when I was around him and was manipulating me for his own ends. Whenever I wondered about him, on dark, lonely nights, I'd sometimes remember that crystal edge of danger that came with thoughts of Ivo, the feeling that he teetered on a knife blade of – something. I would push away the memory I had of once catching him palming tablets. He'd smiled his most charming smile and whirled along with the rest of us to the exam halls, and I'd buried the whole thing under better memories. But, every so often, when he sparkled and glamoured and entertained, I wondered.

'Oh, all right,' I said, finally. 'As long as it's nothing illegal.'

Then, with the desire to test that memory, I added softly, 'I know you, Ivo, remember?'

'That was years ago,' he said airily. 'Besides, I got off with a warning.'

I turned my back on him and finished wiping down the work-top. He'd shown no guilt, no hint that there might be something to hide. His memory had gone to an incident of confused mistaken identity and youthful desire to please from our first student year. *You got off,* I thought, narrowing my eyes in a look that ought to have scorched any germs off the wood grain, *because your mum is a high-court judge and your dad is a journalist for the* Guardian. But I didn't say it, of course. Ivo accepted his back-ground just as he accepted the background of all his friends, as something that couldn't be helped, like an elderly spaniel or a leaky roof, and if you never spoke about it, things would be all right.

'So,' he carried on, stretching out his legs and putting his feet up on one of the other chairs, 'I've got a list of all the B&Bs in Helmsley and a quick sketch of the poor dead bloke in question. It shouldn't take us that long.'

'What makes you think he was staying in Helmsley?' I asked. I couldn't help myself. I was getting involved, even though I didn't want to be.

'No car. At least, no car the police could find. None of the local taxis did a run up out onto the moor last night. I asked them.' Ivo raised his chin. It made the sun shadow his cheek-bones. 'So he walked. And in those shoes he didn't walk far, not at that time of night.'

'He was wearing trainers,' I observed mildly.

'*Cheap* trainers,' Ivo corrected me. 'I had chance for a proper look while the police were faffing about getting the body tent up. Cheap trainers with worn soles and a hole in. He wasn't hiking in from Thirsk in trainers like that. Besides, he wasn't dressed for walking, jeans and a plastic jacket thing, he wasn't meaning to go far. And he'd checked out of wherever he was staying, so how was he going to get anywhere in the middle of the night?'

'You looked at the body? Ivo...'

'Of *course* I looked at the body! I'm a journalist! The police knew I'd look at the body or they wouldn't have left me there with it – I think they subconsciously *want* me to investigate because then they won't have to bother.' He folded his arms at me. 'They've got bigger things on their plate,' he said. 'Ru's been on overtime for weeks. Drugs, you know, the usual.'

He didn't even flicker as he said it. Not so much as a raised eyebrow gave away any feelings about drugs, their inadvisability or the problems that could arise. I shoved that memory of those tablets back down again. I could have been mistaken; it could have been paracetamol.

Couldn't it?

He stood up now, scuffing the chair noisily back on the stone floor that was the kitchen's best feature. 'So, if we want to find out who he was and what he was doing up there with your squirrel in his pocket, it's going to be down to us. Was he meeting someone who was going to drive him somewhere? If so, why haven't *they* turned up? Or was he going to walk back to Helmsley and get the first bus out in the morning, and why would anyone sit about all night waiting for a bus with a squirrel in their pocket?'

I put a hand to my forehead. My head had begun to ache. 'All right, all right. I'll come with you round Helmsley, if only to stop you tormenting the local hoteliers with your endless list of questions,' I said. 'Someone has to keep you out of mischief. Besides, if we find out where he came from we can get the squirrel home, the poor little thing.'

He rounded the table and gave me a sudden hug. 'That's my

Cress,' he said, joyfully. 'I *knew* you wouldn't let me do this on my own! Justice for squirrels! Come on, I've got the car outside.'

As I locked up the house I felt the memory of that hug all along my body. The smooth coolness of that dreadful shirt and the snaggy pull of the velvet trousers, the brief pressure of his arms as he'd embraced me.

Everything in me wanted to lock myself *inside* the house. Apart from the fact that we were probably going to interfere with the police investigations, that I felt dreadful, that I'd rung in sick from work and therefore shouldn't be doing more than a little light shopping – this was *Ivo*.

My friend. That was enough.

3

Ivo handed me the scrap of paper bearing the pencil sketch of the dead man and we headed off to Helmsley.

'Where did you get this from?'

He barely even looked away from the glimmering grey road. 'Well, *I* did it, of course.'

'But it's *good*! At least,' I amended, hurriedly, 'I never saw the man, not properly, only his shoes, so I'm assuming this is accurate.' The sketch was, strangely, very lifelike. The face of a man stared out at me, wide-eyed and worn; his chin was stubbled and his hair raggedly cut. 'I didn't know you could draw, properly.'

I did know that Ivo painted, in his spare time, huge canvases, covered in swirling shapes. He used bright, primary colours and his pictures were meant to represent emotions or dreamscapes, nebulous things. They all looked a little bit like pictures Arthur Rackham might have painted as a four-year-old with a raging temperature.

'Of course I can draw,' Ivo said, casually, as though *anyone* could afford the time and frames to produce things that were bigger than my entire living room. 'I had the upbringing of an

eighteenth-century miss. I can sing and perform country dancing, paint, sketch – I could probably play the spinet if I knew
what one was. I'm practically the missing Brontë sister.'

I thought of my school days. The memory came with the
smell of damp, shouting and overcrowded classrooms with boys
who threw chairs. Country dancing had *not* featured. But at least
I knew what a spinet was.

'Right.' He swung the car into the last available parking space
– because of *course* there would be parking when Ivo needed it –
and looked at me. 'Let's do this thing. I'll talk, you hold the sketch
and look winsome. You do winsome *so* well and I've never really
got the hang. Come on.'

I sighed and reminded myself that I was here to ensure that
Ivo kept his feet on the ground and the rest of him on the right
side of the law. 'All right. But I'm too bunged up for winsome. Can
I do world-weary instead?'

'If you must.' He locked the car and we started down the road.
'You can be the Lewis to my Morse. B&Bs first. We can try the
campsites afterwards if we have to.'

'Not the hotels?' I looked longingly at the exclusive hotel in
front of us. It had a pool and a steam room and the menu
hanging outside covered nearly all of one window. It looked like
the sort of place that would serve wonderful coffee with those
little crisp biscuits, and have plump armchairs, and I already
wanted to sit down.

'They don't print out receipts on little bits of paper, they
email them to you,' Ivo said, vaguely. 'Besides, £75 for one night?
That is *not* hotel prices, at least, not around here.' Then he rang
the bell of the crooked little house overlooking the stream, which
had a 'Vacancies' sign in the window.

The lady who ran the B&B didn't recognise the sketch and
hadn't had anyone check out the previous day. Neither had the

next three places we tried, but in a back street, with a view of nothing more than the vet's surgery and an old coal yard, we found someone who did.

'Mr Williams, that looks like,' the slightly grubby gentleman said, adjusting his trousers. 'He left us yesterday. Why?' He peered at us through smeary spectacles. 'What's he done?'

The smell of sausages was wafting down the hallway to greet us like an enthusiastic spaniel.

'Nothing,' I leaped in before Ivo could say, 'He died.' This man looked as though he may try to charge extra for pre-decease. 'We just need to find out who he is. When did he arrive?'

'Day before. Only booked for one night. Told him he was lucky to get in, this time of year. We're usually full.' The man looked over his shoulder at the hallway of the guest house, as though the immense quantity of clients was about to come seeping after him.

'So it was a short-notice booking?' Ivo's eyes were gleaming. I had to elbow him before he ruined our professional air by jiggling from foot to foot.

The man scratched his chin. 'Yep. Last week.'

'Did he – did he bring any pets with him?' I asked.

'Pets? Oh no, we won't be having animals in here. They mess the place up,' said the grubby man, as though his establishment was scoured on a daily basis, a belief that was belied by the grimy windows and worn hall carpet.

I had a sudden vision of that little squirrel, currently bouncing around in my shed, but previously travelling in a pocket. It would have been noticeable in a B&B bedroom, surely? Bits on the carpet, chewed curtains, strange noises.

'You're sure? No pets at all?'

The bleary face of the B&B owner came close as he peered at me again. 'Told you,' he said, giving off a whiff of fried food and old cigarettes. 'No pets. Not much luggage neither, just a bag thing and his jacket. He said he'd come on the bus and couldn't carry much. We don't allow pets; the wife don't hold with the cleaning. Besides, she's got a cat, big fluffy thing it is, and it has the run of the place so we can't be having dogs and things. He might get scared, apparently, don't know why, thing'd bloody terrify an Alsatian.'

'Thanks, Mr Thixendale.' Ivo was practically on tiptoes now with eagerness. 'This Mr Williams. Did he check in properly? Show you ID and everything?'

The man laughed a raspy laugh that's smoked since it was ten. 'Yep, driving licence. We does things by the board here, cos we gets inspected. And he checked out proper, like I said. Had to, we had a booking for the room from lunchtime today.'

Ivo glanced at me. 'Do you know where he came from? You took his address?'

'Course I did.' A sudden bout of coughing broke the man's face into a portrait of wrinkle, stubble and grey eyebrows. 'There's rules y'know. Came from somewhere southern, made me think of fists, can't remember now. Not allowed to tell you, in any case. Data protection,' he finished, looking satisfied, as though he feared we may have been sent to check up on GDPR breaches, even though Ivo had shown his NUJ card as our introduction. 'Anyway, got to get the dinner on and make sure that bloody cat isn't in the pantry again.' And he closed the door.

Ivo turned to me with a grin so wide his cheeks were under his ears. 'Told you,' he said. 'Williams. Okay, now we've got something to go on.'

I frowned. 'Odd, though. Sounds like he didn't have the squirrel with him here?'

'No pets,' Ivo said, complacently.

'It has to have come from *somewhere*.' I wiped my nose, which had started running again. 'He *must* have brought it with him. But if he'd had it in his room here, it would have left, well, a bit of a mess. They don't exactly lie in their basket on command.'

'Maybe it did.' Ivo nodded towards the now closed door that separated us from the seedy hallway and smell of sausages. 'D'you think he would have noticed?'

'He said the room was re-let almost immediately. If there'd been a mess left, I reckon Mr Thixendale wouldn't be above trying to make us liable for a bill for extra cleaning.' I bit the side of a nail. 'No. He can't have had the squirrel while he was here.'

'He had a bag. And a jacket. Could the squirrel have been in one of those? Or, maybe he was up on the moor to *get* the squirrel?' Ivo was clearly stuck in 'question' mode. 'Is there a national squirrel-smuggling racket going down?'

'Squirrels' teeth go through anything; you can't just put them in a bag.' I chewed the nail a bit more and stared at the peeling paint of Mr Thixendale's front window. 'I presume that the police haven't found his bag, because they don't have his driving licence, otherwise they'd know who he was.' I chewed a bit more until Ivo gently pushed my hand away from my mouth and took hold of it to lead me along the road. 'And there's no such thing as squirrel smuggling; what would be the point? Oh!' I remembered something, the course that Ivo had mentioned that I'd been sent on a couple of summers ago. 'But there *is* an exchange programme.'

Ivo stopped walking, but kept hold of my hand. Behind us, the church bell tolled the hour, long and plaintive into the summer sky, sending a cloud of rooks wheeling and cawing above us. In other circumstances I would have enjoyed this moment. 'What, like a student transfer? We send ours over there and they come back able to swear fluently in a different language and leaving a trail of broken foreign hearts in their wake?'

I stared at him.

'What? My school used to send us to the Dordogne for six weeks every summer. It's where I learned to dance, eat *escargot* properly and say "bof" in a suitably insouciant manner.'

Now I rolled my eyes. 'I don't think there's much call for squirrels gaining fluency in another language and an ability to eat snails without recoiling,' I said, acidly.

'Well, what then?' Ivo had raised an eyebrow. I hadn't seen him this fascinated in ages. The case of the squirrel had clearly engaged him completely and I hated to admit it but it was very nice to see his brain doing something other than working out how many times he could mention garden shed security in one week's online column. The ghastly blue shirt twinkled in the sunlight in a distracting way.

'Isolated animal communities can become inbred if they don't have access to new bloodlines,' I said, trying to remember the lectures. It hadn't been particularly relevant to me then, and during the course I'd got involved with Danny, the guy leading it, who'd turned out to like porn more than real women and squirrels more than either, so I hadn't been in the best frame of mind to concentrate. 'So places with lots of squirrels do an exchange.'

He grabbed me suddenly, letting go of my fingers to put his hands on my shoulders. 'Cress! You mean, there's an illegal squirrel swap going on? Our man was smuggling squirrels?'

Even though the sun was warm, Ivo's hands were warmer. I felt the weight of his touch in every bone and bit my lip. 'No point. There's loads of perfectly legal squirrel movements every year. Where would the benefit be?'

As though he wasn't thinking about anything other than fluffy rodents, Ivo pulled me in closer so he could look into my face. 'Cherchez la profit,' he said, quietly.

'All that time on the Dordogne wasn't wasted then,' I said, quietly but slightly tartly. 'You're still fluent.'

'Very funny.' Another squeeze and he released me so we could walk. 'So. No money in squirrels, is that what you're saying?'

'Nope. None at all.' It was just Ivo, I told myself sternly. This was how he behaved with *everyone*; a casual physical touch here and there, as though he suspected that the rest of the world wasn't real, and needed to reassure himself of its existence. I sneezed violently.

'You're really not well, are you?' Suddenly concerned, Ivo was bending to look into my face, which probably wasn't wise given the velocity of my sneezes.

'No,' I agreed sadly.

'Look, why not come back to my place for a couple of days? I can tuck you up on the sofa there, with... blankets and things, and you'll be handy when I need to throw theories at you. I'd give you the spare room but it's still full of piano – I really *must* get rid of that enormous bugger but it's Dad's and he does play every now and then, but I can't unfold the futon with it there. I've got *loads* of whisky and lemon to pour down you, if that helps.'

I thought of my bed. The sheets needed changing and it was in the front bedroom, noisily placed on a busy street where having the windows open filled the room with traffic fumes and the tinny rattle of shopping trolleys. Then I thought of Ivo's care-less affection, the light in his eyes at the thought that this may turn into a 'real case'. Also, just a little, of his house, which was a gatehouse cottage in the grounds of a large stately home that had belonged to a relative before death duties and the National Trust had come calling. The cottage had its own gardens, which meant it was largely silent, unless someone rode along the track that led through the middle of it, when it echoed to the unseen hooves, like a haunting. The thought of being looked after, even if by Ivo, for a day or so, was immensely tempting too. It shouldn't be. He was my *friend* and I didn't dare admit to anything else for fear of ruining this wonderful, casual acceptance of one another that we had. I liked Ivo more than he liked me, that was all there was to it, and it was my problem, not his.

'I'll need to pack a bag,' I said. 'And leave a note for Lilith and Dix, so they don't think I've been carted off into sex slavery.'

'Tell them you're with me. They'll know you're safe.' We'd reached the car now and he unlocked it and began to slide into the driving seat.

I hesitated for a moment. Was this *really* such a good idea? 'I'd need to bring the squirrel. I can't leave him to Lilith to look after, you know she's a bit scatterbrained when it comes to remembering to feed animals.'

'Fine. It's Exhibit A anyway, I'd like to keep an eye on it.'

'Why? What do you think he's going to do, write a confession note?'

'Just... might be better to have it with us. In case. It can go in the stable, all the horses are out for the summer.'

'Okay,' I said weakly, still, after all this time of knowing him, stunned by the casual way he came out with things like this.

'We can stock up on all your medicines while we're at your place. Apart from whisky I'm not sure I've got much in the cupboard.'

I settled myself in the passenger seat and tried not to look sideways at him as we pulled away. Did my uncertainty show? We'd never spoken about those tablets; I wasn't even sure if he knew that I'd seen him and I didn't want to mention it – I hated to even think *because I was afraid of what he might tell me*. He purported to hate drugs of any kind, but there was a sparkling energy about him at times and a randomness that made me wonder if he might protest a little too vociferously. His scattered focus could narrow under the microscope of his interest at the speed of thought and absorb him as though the rest of the world had ceased to exist. It made him fun, lively, haphazard and arbitrary. Added to that was the fact that family money meant he could afford to be careless and carefree. The sum total was Ivo, an alluring companion with the potential of a tonne of unexploded gelignite.

I looked at him as he drove. His handsome profile was what had originally caught my attention and then we'd become friends and I'd stopped holding my breath every time I saw him, unless it was to worry about him falling over railings or dropping something priceless. But sometimes I'd catch sight of him out of the corner of my eye and wonder. How could someone so good looking, trailing disconsolate, soggy-tissued ex-girlfriends, still be single? He had the astonishing cheekbones of his aristocratic forebears and the intelligence of his somewhat more modern antecedents. He was, basically, God's gift to women, if a slightly scatty one. I didn't know what he thought of me.

Then I wondered again if it really was such a good idea to go and stay with him. But I'd agreed, and it did beat lying alone in my room listening to the world coming and going in the street beyond. And, I hated to admit it, I was beginning to be a little intrigued by the squirrel affair.

4

———

In the end I didn't get to lie about on Ivo's sofa. I hadn't really expected that I would, appealing though the image may have been. By the time we'd settled the squirrel –

'I think we should call him Fred.'

'*Fred*? Oh, all right, we can't keep calling him "the squirrel" I suppose.'

– into his cage in the stables, I felt much better anyway and less liable to languishing. Besides, Ivo's enthusiasm was infectious, and he spread out his sketch of the mysterious 'Mr Williams' on the kitchen table with the air of one unfurling a treasure map.

'I wonder where he travelled from,' he said thoughtfully. 'Our man at the B&B said he was southern. Do you think he looks southern, Cress?'

I was busy sorting out my herbal teas and cold revival kit on the worktop and glanced over my shoulder. 'How exactly does one look "southern"? He looks like any other bloke to me. Just deader.'

'You are cold and heartless, Cressida Tarbet, and lack any

form of imagination.' Ivo traced the sketch with a finger. 'I just think he does.'

'Not enough whippet and surly machismo to be northern, you mean?'

'But how can we find out *where* in the South?' He was frowning now, resting his chin in his hand and staring at the face looking up at us from the table. His expression was so concentrated that it looked as though he wished he could pull those lines from the sketch and directly into his brain. 'Williams. He showed his ID so I guess we can assume that's his real name.' A sudden shake of the blond head and he was up and restlessly pacing. 'Someone must be missing him. And he came from somewhere that reminded our man of a fist? Do they fight a lot, typically, down south?'

'Why this, Ivo?' I asked. 'You've been involved with police stuff before; there were those farm break-ins last summer and the organised fly tipping – why do you feel you've got to start poking around in this case? Tell the police who he is, let them do their job, and we can just assist where needed, surely.'

Ivo stopped pacing, his back to the Aga. 'I don't know. There's just *something*... plus, you know, he had a *squirrel in his pocket*.' He caught my eye and waggled his eyebrows, which made his piercing struggle for purchase again. 'So now I've got you to help too, and that's never going to be a bad thing.'

Unless you are me, I thought. 'I'm only here so we can get our squirrel home where he belongs. He's tame, someone must be missing him.'

'We really need to find out where he came from.'

'Squirrel or man?' I asked, tidying a pile of damp tea towels away into the washing machine.

'I thought man might be easier, unless you can interrogate

the squirrel. See if he talks with a cockney accent, knows about jellied eels, that kind of thing.'

'No red squirrels in London—oh!' I slammed the washing machine door and stood up, struck with a sudden thought. 'But we just might be able to do better than that.'

I pulled my phone from my pocket. 'You have a secret squirrel identifier on your phone?' Ivo sounded perplexed. 'This is getting away from me now.'

'Don't be daft. What I *do* have is a friend in a lab.'

'Bobbing around in a jar of formaldehyde, knowing you,' Ivo muttered. 'Where does this lab friend come in?'

I was scrolling through my contacts list hoping that he'd remember me. Danny had been the guy I'd met on the squirrel course. While I had been sent as the only person from our centre available for travel, he'd been there as a specialist and we'd spent a wonderful weekend in Brighton before deciding that we'd never work as a couple. 'I'm not sure. But it's worth asking, because if he can't help, he might know someone who can. I told you before, squirrel groups can become isolated and inbred so the bloodline is strengthened by bringing in breeding stock from distant groups?'

'You did.'

'Well, someone has to check squirrel origins. For that, Danny is your man. So there must be a DNA database somewhere. We just might be able to ask Danny to persuade someone to find out where Fred originates from, which would at least give us a starting point for finding out how to get him home.'

Ivo stared at me for a moment and then whirled me into a frenzied waltz that swept all loose material from the surfaces and included it in our cyclone of movement. Magazines flipped and flew, bits of paper typhooned to the floor, a pair of socks that had been hanging on the Aga rail spiralled to the tiles and even a chair was forced to slide out of our way.

'Cress, you're a frigging *genius*!' Ivo sang as we Strictly'd our way around the kitchen. 'Find out where the squirrel came from, and we're practically home and dry!'

Enjoyable though it might be, I had to stop him when my hip slammed against the table and I groaned. 'It might not tell us anything,' I said, pulling him to a standstill. 'It may not even be relevant. But it would be something. I need to talk to Danny.'

'Boyfriend?'

'Long ago.' I went back to scrolling and found Danny's contact details.

'Likely to rekindle?' Ivo had let me go now my hands were full of phone again.

'No.' I pressed the button to dial. 'He's rather fonder of virtual sex than the real thing, unfortunately. Plus, he lives about two hundred miles away. Nice guy, not for me.' *He's not you.* I sat hard on the words to stop them blurting out. My masochistic tendencies to stick around a man who had no interest in me other than as a friend was my own problem. At the other end, the phone started to ring. 'But I'm hoping he's still got fond enough memories of me to—oh, hi, Danny? It's Cressida...'

While I spoke to Danny, who did remember me, which I wasn't sure whether to be flattered about or not, Ivo paced and listened. He always behaved as though he couldn't listen efficiently if he wasn't on the move, and gave the impression that he'd be walking away during any conversation, if the people he was conversing with couldn't keep up. He seemed worried; there were tense frown lines creasing his forehead and those blue eyes were scrunched up as if he were trying to see his own eyelashes.

When I hung up on Danny, Ivo leaped in front of me. 'Sounds like he knows a man.'

'Well, he's going to text me the details of someone we could send a sample to. Someone at the University of York who owes him a "favour" apparently. I'd have more faith if he didn't keep saying it like a gangster who'd kneecap anyone who didn't do as he said. But,' I sighed, 'that's Danny. Wants to be Danny Dyer, in real life is more Danny de Vito.'

'You really have to "know people" in the squirrel world?' Ivo stared.

'It's more the scientific world. We want results fast, which means pulling strings.'

'Ah. *Puppet* squirrel world,' Ivo said, and grinned.

I had no idea how everyone he knew hadn't already slapped him.

'I'm going to make sure Fred is all right out there in the stables,' I said, giving Ivo side-eye, which didn't discourage him at all. 'That poor creature has been through a lot in the last day or so, he could be in shock.'

Fred did not appear to be in any kind of shock. He heard us coming and clung to the bars at the front of the cage for a second before whisking away to bounce off the rest of the walls. He and Ivo had a lot in common, I thought, holding out a hazelnut and having it swept from my fingers by a tiny clawed hand. Intelligent bright eyes scanned my face for a second, then, with a press of fur, Fred was gone again, to eat his prize in the dark depths of the housing section, from where I could see his tail curled up over his back. A contained package of energy, like an elastic band wound up and waiting for a single touch to unleash potential. Or snap and take your eye out, in Ivo's case.

'Is he all right?' I'd made Ivo stand at the door, so as not to upset the squirrel any more than was necessary. 'Confessed to the vile killing of Mr Williams, strangled with his tail or something?'

I turned. Ivo was silhouetted in the doorway to the old building, where a wide door led to the cobbled passageway that linked all the loose boxes. Everything was panelled in mahogany, the rails that gave the horses a view from their stables were polished brass, and the floors were immaculately swept. The National Trust ownership only covered the house and grounds, but this place was still kept as though the general public might pop round for a look. Hell, it was kept as though the *king* might be round any moment.

'Who does all the stable work?' I asked idly, ignoring his wilful whimsy. 'I'm guessing you don't get up at six to muck out.'

Even though we'd known each other for so long, had been in and out of one another's houses since we'd become friends and had spent far too many university nights drunk together at various parties, I didn't know that much about Ivo's life. He had a way of talking for hours and sounding as though he was giving you the secrets of his universe, until you woke up and realised that you still had no real idea what he thought about anything, or, indeed, if he thought at all.

I had, during some of my darker, most lonely, moments, wondered whether he was keeping things hidden on purpose.

'There are – girls.' He waved a hand. 'Lovely, lovely girls. Oh, and some lovely boys too. But mostly girls. Nothing to do with me, it's all parental, I just live here. The aged Ps are usually in town, they've got a little place over there' – another wave – 'for holidays.'

'Town' must be London. I really couldn't see Ivo's parents, whom I'd met once or twice, as people who'd be happy with a small North Yorkshire market town where asking for daikon would get you narrowed eye looks of deep suspicion and possibly followed home by people throwing stones.

Fred swung back to the front of the cage and tipped his head to one side to look at me again out of those shining brown eyes.

His fur was red silk in the sun that came through the barred windows and his tail twitched interrogatively.

'No, no more nuts, sorry,' I said, putting my finger to the bars and hoping he wasn't a biter. But then, would a man have put a squirrel with a biting habit in his trouser pocket? Seriously?

A narrow head, rounder than that of a grey squirrel, rubbed against my fingertip for a second, as though to reassure himself. Then, with another tilted-head look, he was gone, tail whisking a dismissive farewell, back to the nest box.

'He's really, really tame,' I said, going back to Ivo, who was still picturesquely outlined in the doorway. 'I mean, ridiculously. I still think he was hand-reared.'

'And that's illegal, you said?' Ivo moved to let me pass him out into the stable yard. Everywhere smelled of horses and saddle soap.

'Yep, unless you're properly licensed. Those guys' – I jerked my thumb over my shoulder to indicate Fred and his ilk – 'they're protected up the wazoo. We're probably breaking umpteen laws by having him here, except that I've got exemption because of being wildlife rescue and everything.'

I sounded slightly smug and I knew it. Wildlife rescue was important. It was a real thing. I just had to keep telling myself that.

'You' – Ivo coiled an arm around my shoulders – 'are a valuable person to know, Cress.'

I leaned, for one second, into the embrace. 'I have... certain skills,' I said.

'So why do you have a degree in History, from Cambridge no less, but your skill set is British wildlife and its protection?'

Ivo was looking at me carefully now. I wasn't used to such intensity from him. Well, certainly not outside his areas of particular interest, and I wasn't sure how I felt about being one of those.

'Can I gently point out that your degree, a very, very good one too, is Philosophy, Politics and Economics? And that you work on a local newspaper covering stories about stolen bikes and criminal damage?'

With a twitch of a shrug Ivo was away again, twisting out into the sunshine like a trapped gale. 'I like to confound explanation,' he said. 'Besides, PPE is a great degree to have if you want to go into politics.'

The thought of Ivo being a politician clanged in my head. Two things further apart I found it hard to imagine and I simply couldn't reconcile the image of politics, with a lot of sitting down and big dinners, and Ivo and his perpetual motion and compressed energy. I laughed.

To my relief, he laughed too, and didn't question me any further about my degree. It was odd, I thought, as we walked back down to the little gatehouse that was his home now, that we'd known each other for so long and this was the first time that questions like this were being asked. Almost as though we'd been happily friendly on a superficial level before, but something about this squirrel business was making other, deeper issues surface.

Maybe we were just growing up, I mused, following Ivo into the shadowed coolness of the house. It was situated on, or more exactly, *over*, a track that led up to the big house and had once been part of the carriageway, now disused. There hadn't been much call for sweeping up to the gates in a coach drawn by sweating horses in the last hundred years or so, and the gatehouse now only heard the passage of local riders off for a canter in the parkland. The cottage arched over the track with two rooms on either side, necessitating either a marathon run up one staircase, across a landing and down the other or a quick, chilly trip outside when you wanted to go from the living room to the study. Ivo got around this by only using half the house on a daily basis. His bedroom lay in the room that straddled the gateway. He liked the echoes, apparently, but I couldn't comment. I'd never been in there.

'So, what's next?' I asked, then sneezed again. The cold medicine must be wearing off, but I wasn't due another dose for a couple of hours. Bugger.

He looked at me appraisingly. 'First, I make good on my promise to tuck you up on the sofa,' he said, a wide-flung hand indicating the furniture in question. 'Then, I'm probably going to think. I may throw questions your way though, so be prepared. Tea?'

I nodded and sat down on the blue velvet sofa. Despite its apparent modernity and trendiness of fabric, it was over a hundred years old. Ivo treated antiques as useful things rather than as ornaments, in an offhand way that made me feel simultaneously comfortable and slightly edgy. It was great that these things were being utilised rather than kept behind glass and admired, otherwise, what was the point of them? But, conversely, it was horrific to drop and break something to be casually then told that it was two hundred years old, or rather, it *had* been.

It made me very, very careful around things in Ivo's place.

I blew my nose, copiously and saw him wince as he carried through two steaming mugs. 'I've made you nettle tea,' he said, handing me mine. 'It's good for colds.'

I pulled a face. 'Can I not have good strong Yorkshire tea instead?'

'Can you taste it anyway?'

'No, but...'

'Then you may as well have something that's doing you good

instead,' he said, sternly for Ivo. 'Since you could be drinking anything. Get that down you while I think.'

I sipped. He was right, basically all I could taste was 'hot' with a hint of sweetness from the spoonful of honey he'd stirred in. Apart from the fact that the tea was a pale greenish colour, I could have been drinking bathwater. Then I rested my head against the high sofa back and watched Ivo.

Ivo didn't do anything sitting still. His brain only seemed to work when he was in motion. 'How long for the DNA test to be done?' he asked, then looked at me. 'No, don't answer, I'm not asking, I'm just thinking. DNA test, find out where – Fred, is it? Find out where he comes from. Might give us something to go on, because it's all we've got.'

He twisted his lip and frowned, pacing between the large French windows that opened out onto the garden at the side of the house, and the sofa where I was languishing like a Victorian in the latter stages of consumption.

'We know our dead man is called Williams,' I threw in. 'So there's that.'

'Yes. Gives the poor bloke a name at least, so we don't keep calling him "the body", which is just distasteful.' Ivo finished another circuit of the living room and stopped, staring out into the garden with his back to me. Outside, a rose that was growing up and over the window in an almost unbearably attractive way blew in a breeze and tapped pink heads against the glass in a soft kiss of petals. Ivo sighed. 'University of York, you said? Maybe we could get our squirrel sample over there today for them to start work on? What do you have to do, swab his cheeks? And I'm going to check with Rufus, in case they know more about our Mystery Man.' He rattled the catch to the window as though checking it was still closed and the rose couldn't get in and savage us. 'He's not allowed to tell me anything, obviously.' He spun round now and his grin was wickedly manic. 'But as we already have a name, he won't have to keep it secret, and I might get something out of him.'

I sighed. It really was very pleasant being here. The sun filtering in through the roses, the polished and cared for antiques, the smell of the nettle tea that came and went as my nasal passages cleared – it was all contributing to relaxing some of the tension I found myself permanently holding. My shoulders began to slump and my uniform jumper snagged and caught against the velvet of the sofa back.

'Are you all right, Cress?' Ivo surprised me with the question. I'd probably been drifting off to sleep.

'Mmm? Yes, why?'

Now it was Ivo's turn to look surprised. 'I just wondered. You don't – I mean, obviously, we haven't got that kind of relationship or anything and for all I know you're... but I don't know.'

'Finish a sentence mate, please,' I said tiredly. His habit of talking as though the other half of the conversation was being filled in 'off-screen' could be wearing when you weren't feeling your sparkly best, and weren't psychic.

He sat down beside me, moving a set of cushions aside and heaping them onto his lap in order to have room. 'I've never said this before and I don't know why, but you always seem a bit...' He waggled a hand. 'Worried when you're with me. As though you're looking over your shoulder all the time. So, *are* you all right? It's not going to cause – problems for you, if you're over here helping me find out about our friend Fred out there?'

He jerked a hand up, towards the stables, which were visible through the shimmering summer air as an eighteenth-century block on the horizon.

Define 'problem', I thought. Torturing myself with thoughts of what I wanted, but couldn't have, and which teetered on the edge of not knowing whether I really *did* want, or whether it was the allure of Ivo, wasn't a problem as such. More a psychological condition. 'No. I'm officially off sick for a week,' I said. 'I told you that.'

'Nobody else going to give you hell if you're with me?'

'No.' I frowned. 'Who else *would* worry?'

Ivo was up again, cushions bouncing to the floor as he moved across to one of the bookcases built in to the gatehouse wall. 'I don't know, do I? That's why I'm asking.' He tipped a couple of volumes, stared at their spines.

'Only Lilith and Dix and I left them a note.'

'Oh. All right. If you're sure.' He moved across to the small table, which looked as though it formed a receptacle for all the post that had ever come through the door, envelopes and brochures and leaflets tottered in an uneven pile across its highly polished surface. He left the books out of alignment on the shelf and I itched to go and push them back in, but this was his house. If he wanted to live as though he'd been burgled and was waiting for a police visit, that was up to him.

'Ivo, are you asking if I've got a boyfriend who will object to me being here?' It struck me suddenly, in a heart-pounding moment, that this could be the case. *Seriously?* Why the hell would Ivo be worried about that? Did he think I'd got a burly seven-footer lurking in the shrubbery to leap out and yell 'Aha, I have you now!' and pound Ivo into the sandy soil of the bridle-way? He needn't have been so concerned. The number of men willing to hang around waiting for me to be available between variable working hours and random wildlife call outs was currently nil. It would, perhaps, have been easier if there had been someone. I could have used their concern over my absence as an excuse for the nervous, edgy feeling that I had when alone with Ivo. If he even *suspected* how I felt... I felt my face heat up with advance embarrassment. 'If you are, the answer is no. You already know my track record isn't exactly stellar, and I am currently single, thank you very much for reminding me yet again about my general failure with the opposite sex.'

He wasn't looking at me. The table stood in a patch of shadow that made his luminescent shirt look a more normal colour, took the shine from his hair and made the curve of his shoulders look depressed. 'Sorry,' he muttered.

'It's fine. Ivo, I wouldn't have come if I thought it would cause anything other than Lilith taking over my half of the fridge and possibly using some of the special coffee I've got hidden away behind the mugs.' I picked the cushions up off the floor and noticed the rug was some intricate weave and probably worth more than my house.

He bounced back. Ivo always did. 'Just checking. Didn't want our peregrinations to cause you problems.' Even from the dark corner, where he was sifting through the postal pile like a man panning for gold, I could see the twinkle back in his eye. 'That's good. That's good,' he repeated, seizing the entire heap of envelopes, coloured leaflets and bits of card and sweeping the lot into a handy bin. 'Really need to tidy up in here.'

'Might be an idea.' I eyed those askew books meaningfully and he shuffled over to push them back into line.

'Danusha comes twice a week,' he said, apologetically. 'To stop everything descending into chaos. Mother insists,' he added, mutinously. 'They own the place after all, so they're entitled to not have it fall into ruins around me because I can't... focus. Apparently.'

'I'm here so we can find out about Fred, and what he was doing in a dead man's pocket,' I reminded him. 'Not buying the place.'

'Yes. Yes!' Ivo leaped into animated life again, as though his thoughts had come back from whatever family-related journey they'd been on and were being forced to the matter at hand. 'I was going to give Rufus a bell, wasn't I?'

He groped through the various pockets in his clothes. The shirt had big, gappy pockets and the trousers looked as though they'd been created for a seventies music revivalist to trek through the Badlands. They had pockets everywhere. At last he produced his phone and I left him to it.

I went back out to the stables, and stood and watched Fred fling himself at the front of his enclosure in the hope of some more nuts for a moment.

Practicality helped, having something else to think about other than the terror of revealing more than I wanted to to Ivo. 'What the hell are you doing here?' I asked him, although why I thought interrogating a squirrel was a good idea, I wasn't sure. 'You must be missing your people, or whoever reared you. Or your squirrel friends. You've not been out in the wild, have you? You're way too tame.'

Fred, of course, gave nothing away, other than a desire for more hazelnuts and a possible yearning to be stroked. He was as flickery and fast as a speeded-up film, constantly in motion, apart from moments of brief, intense attention, and reminded me of Ivo.

I had to stop this. I blew my nose sturdily and shook my shoulders, and reminded myself yet again that Ivo had the concentration span of a goldfish, the general temperament of a slightly worried reptile and the flightiness of the average kestrel. In short, he was not a man you had a relationship with, except possibly a very short and incredibly tempestuous one. He was likeable, yes, he was attractive too, but could anyone really want a man whose brain seemed to resemble a flicker book?

I shook my head again. No. Ivo was fun, and my friend, and I had to *stop* this. I was dangerously close to becoming obsessed.

Then he wandered back into the stable yard, all tousled hair and weird clothing like a slightly less confused David Bowie without the make-up, and I had to give myself another stern inner talking to.

'The man's name was Williams,' Ivo saying into his phone. 'He was staying at Bay View B&B, so you might want to pop round there and take a squizz at the register for an address... Oh. Okay.' He looked across at me and made a comedy 'resigned' face. 'Well, that's... no. No, of course, you never told me that. Never a word of insider information has passed your lips. Okay, well, later then.' He pulled the phone away from his ear, disconnected the call and performed a series of ballet leaps across the cobbled yard, which brought him up against me.

'They've what appears to be two rival drug gangs kicking off and our man has had to take a back seat,' he said, slightly out of breath. 'They're rushed off their feet so Ru was very interested that we'd already got a name.' He grinned at me, smugly. 'I told him where to go to check for an address, always assuming that Mr Williams didn't give a fake one to our fragrantly lovely Mr Thixendale.'

'But why would he give a fake address?' I leaned against the warm stone of the wall. The smell of horse had seeped into the mortar and the sun was squeezing it back out, so the whole place smelled as though a troop of phantom cavalry had just ridden through.

Ivo sighed. 'Ah, no reason. No reason at all. A night in a seedy B&B is hardly something you need to hide from your relatives, so the police will be able to head to Fist City and find his next of kin. They owe us, big time.'

'They didn't know where to st
found that receipt for the B&B.'

The smug grin was getting out of
genius.'

'You're a something, certainly,' I mut

Ivo jiggled on the spot. 'So, our ma
sounds like a fist can be safely left to the
informing relatives thing. You and I are let   question mark of a squirrel and how to return   to his proper
home. Right?'

'Pretty much, Hercule. I'm guessing the police won't tell us
the address to give us a heads-up on poor Fred's point of origin.'
The warmth and certainty of the stone behind me was comfort-
ingly solid in comparison to Ivo's constant movement. 'Though I
suppose that depends on whether Fred was actually his, or
whether he stole him from someone who reared him.' I sighed.
This was too complicated when all I really wanted to do was
stand here, washed by the sun's warmth, and admire Ivo from a
distance. Quite a large distance, if he was going to keep jittering
like that.

A breeze ran through the rose bushes and arrived with us,
smelling delicious. For some reason it made me shiver.

'I suppose so,' Ivo said slowly. 'Are we dealing with squirrel
smuggling or squirrel theft? Although, I am reaching the conclu-
sion, heavily influenced by my need to get this story up online,
that there's not a lot of difference when it comes to it – the
squirrel is illegal.'

I shrugged.

'But *why*?' He was almost wailing now. 'The market for
second-hand squirrels must be infinitely small and not really a
crime that ought to be committed by someone who wears really

a jacket, which, I have to say, was committing
in its own right.'

I don't know, do I? I work for a wildlife rescue unit, not
pol. My exposure to crime is almost entirely through
episodes of *Midsomer Murders* and Agatha Christie. You're the
crime guy.'

Ivo stood still for a second, waiting for his brain to catch up,
and then he was pacing again, small circles. He started talking
too, a continuous stream of consciousness that I had to work
hard to keep up with. 'Ok. Okay, maybe... maybe our man was
here to hand over the squirrel to someone... they... there was an
accident, our man fell and hit his head before they could meet
up. There's no signs of a fight, no injuries on our man apart from
the obvious one and besides, once he was dead what was to stop
someone just taking the squirrel off him? Small, largely harmless
rodent, what's it going to do, karate chop them to the ground?
Unless... unless they didn't know the squirrel was there, in which
case why the hell *was* the squirrel there? And in his pocket?' He
suddenly stopped, turned and looked at me with ferocious eyes.
'Secret squirrel?'

'Shut up.'

'No trade in squirrel smuggling... ok, maybe forget the squirrel. Meeting someone to... to... but what? Exchange something?
Get information? But in that case, *why the hell take a squirrel*?'

'I think you might need to calm down, Ivo,' I said, now a little
worried by the frenzied thought processes.

'The police don't seem particularly bothered about the
squirrel angle.' Ivo came and stood right in front of me again. I
imagined I could smell hot velvet and combusting brain cells.

'Sounds as though they're busy with other things though.' I
nodded at his phone, which was causing his shirt pocket to gape.
'It's just an accident.'

'We could be ahead of the curve here.' He sounded worryingly calm now. When Ivo was calm, you waited for the explosion; he was the human version of Yellowstone – there was an awful lot of activity under the surface and sooner or later it would break through and ruin your holiday. 'While the police are tearing about the county in their big boots on drug raids, we could solve this. We could break this case, Cress.' His expression had become radiant; there was practically a religious experience going on under that loose shirt. 'We really *could*,' he whispered. 'I could get a job on *The Times*.'

I opened my mouth to say that, surely, he could ask his dad for an 'in' with the *Guardian*, where his father had been a lead journalist on the political pages for so long that he now got TV slots and was recognisable everywhere from *BBC Breakfast* news shows to *Have I Got News for You*.

But no. That wasn't Ivo. He didn't want to succeed simply through parentage, I knew that much from our many drunken talks in kitchens. He wanted to achieve on his own merit, which was laudable. It seemed rather cruel to point out that this Great Case that we were blowing wide open was hardly going to put him in line for a Pulitzer.

'Tomorrow I can take a sample to our contact at the university,' I said, to bring him back from his imaginary forays into the world of Proper Journalism. 'Danny's squaring it for us.'

Ivo was suddenly concentrating again. 'And remind me again how we get this "sample"? Do we have to persuade the squirrel to spit in a tube or pull out his teeth or something?'

For someone with a very good degree, Ivo could be surprisingly obtuse sometimes. 'No,' I said, patiently. 'A hair will do. I have to pull one out so it's got a root, that's all.'

As one, we looked at the stable again where Fred was bouncing off the bars with a pinging noise.

'Do not ask me to hold him down.' Ivo shuddered. 'That squirrel makes me look laid back and relaxed.'

This was the first time I could remember Ivo raising his own energetic and twitchy nature, and I wanted so much to comment. To ask something, to get some clarity about what it was that made hanging around with him feel a little like sitting on something unexploded and ticking. But, by the time I'd organised my thought processes, he'd already headed off out of the yard again.

I gave Fred a stern stare. 'Just be glad I haven't got any tweezers on me,' I said.

Fred bounced a bit more, unbothered. 'Test away,' he seemed to say. 'I'm 98 per cent rubber ball and 2 per cent elastic, good luck.'

Possibly I hadn't thought through the DNA testing mechanics. Ivo could have a point, I thought, and followed him into the house.

5

The weather broke overnight. I woke from my position on the very comfortable sofa to hear Ivo in the kitchen and rain gurgling from the gargoyled downspouts. The rose beyond the window now hung soggily, with dejected petals occasionally pattering against the glass like soaked fairies.

I'd actually had a decent night's sleep for the first time in a while, and my head felt clearer. Clear enough at least for me to wonder what the hell I was doing, encouraging Ivo in this current journalistic endeavour.

'Tea? Toast?' He bounced into the room and twitched the duvet aside so he could sit at my feet, thrusting a plate and mug in my direction. 'I hope you didn't mind the sofa? My spare room is full of all the things I needed when I moved in and then discovered I didn't need at all. And that piano. Anyone staying over sleeps on the sofa. Really ought to do something about that.' He sighed.

'Thank you. I – what on *Earth* is that?'

'Smoking jacket. I *think* Mum said it used to belong to Oscar Wilde. Or Noël Coward. One of those guys anyway. She's related, well, distantly. Not to both, only to one of them, but I can't remember which.' Ivo's wiry frame was resplendent in a crimson velvet... *thing* that hung to his knees, knees that jutted out decked in far more prosaic cotton pyjama trousers. 'I use it as a dressing gown.'

'Of course you do,' I said weakly. Outside, the rain blew and the windows rattled. Ivo was quiet for so long that I eventually looked away from my tea. 'What?'

He shook his head. His hair swept the collar and I wondered how the velvet of the jacket and the velvet of the sofa didn't bond together in some kind of huge Velcro mass and stop him moving. 'Do you have issues with the way I live?' he asked eventually, and, for him, quietly.

I frowned. 'No. It's just, all the antiques and lovely old furniture and everything. The way you treat history like it's utilitarian.'

Ivo stretched his legs out and stroked the scarlet jacket as though it were a pet. 'What is it for?' he asked. 'If not to be useful? You can only put so much stuff in museums. And things like, well, this jacket, the glassware, the books – they were made to be used, not kept in a cupboard somewhere and only looked at.' Then bird-bright eyes tilted my way, his head angled so he could look at me from under his hair. 'Or is it because I can afford to replace them?'

After yesterday's interrogation about my relationship status, this was another of those in-depth questions that I wasn't used to from Ivo. We'd always taken one another's lives pretty much for granted. He didn't comment on the smallness of my cottage or my limited wardrobe and I didn't goggle at the fact he had fresh flowers in vases on every antique surface and used crockery older than my house. Anyway, now I knew the flowers were probably down to parental influence and the incredible 'Danusha', which took some of the shine off.

My answer *should* have been: 'No, Ivo. It's nothing to do with your lifestyle. It's because I like you so terribly, so horribly, and I fear that you may be as careless with your relationships as you are with your things; that nothing is precious or worth caring for because it's all so disposable and easily replaced. I couldn't *bear* to be that disposable thing that's nice to have in your life for a while and then discarded.' That's how I felt and what I thought. But we didn't have that kind of relationship, and he would have laughed at my reasoning, brushed it away with a casual keep-nothing-for-best attitude and I would find myself spiralling down into love with this beautiful, random man.

Right now, it was only distance that kept me safe.

'It just annoys me,' I said. 'To see such valuable things being treated as though they came from IKEA. I know what you're like.'

Then I hunched my knees up to give him more sofa room and we ate toast and drank tea while the wind curled its way up the outside of the gatehouse like ivy, and tapped stems against the windows. The breeze howled down the track and boomed against the underside of the archway as though a thousand ghostly carriages were hurtling their way to the house, but in here it was domestic and comfortable and addictive.

'Right,' I said, drinking down the last of my tea and happily appreciating the fact that I'd been able to taste the toast. 'Shall we head to the university then? To get our Fred tested?'

Ivo didn't, as I'd expected, leap to his feet. He sat thoughtfully, chewing a sourdough crust and staring at a point in the middle of the room.

'Ivo?' I prompted.

He shook his head for a second. I didn't know whether he was dismissing me or his thoughts, but then a beaming smile lit his face and he grinned at me. 'Of course. Um, Cress...'

'What?' I asked cautiously, in case he was going to follow this up with something dreadful. With Ivo, you could never be *quite* certain of his conversational twists and turns.

'If Fred – well, if he turns out to be from somewhere else, not around here I mean, somewhere geographically, would you want to take him back? And, if so, will you let me come with you?'

There was a small crease between his eyes, I noticed. The sort of crease normally seen in people who habitually wear glasses but have forgotten them; the kind of crease caused by squinting or frowning really hard. Ivo was worried. And Ivo was almost never worried, not on a micro scale. He worried on a planetary basis – about global warming, bee deaths, pollution of the seas and single-use plastics, but seeing him worried about something as small as a squirrel was certainly a first.

'Of course I'll take him back,' I said. 'Someone must be missing him if he's been hand-reared. I suppose our Mr Williams could have been the one who reared him, but in any case there must be somewhere to take him back *to*, because he most certainly didn't bring Fred up in his trouser pocket.'

'And you'll let me come?'

I sighed. 'Yes, Ivo, if it's that important to you. Why do you want to come anyway? A sudden urge to check out squirrel breeding programmes?'

Ivo jumped up, toast crumbs spraying across the rug. 'Excellent! No, really brilliant, Cress. Fabulous. Road trip.'

'He might turn out to have come from somewhere twenty miles down the road. Not much of a trip, more of a bus ride.'

'I just *feel*...' Ivo rubbed his hands up and down his jacketed arms and I winced for the aged velvet, hoping he didn't still have butter or jam on his fingers. 'Fred is central to all this.'

'What's "all this"?' The duvet fell away as I stood up and revealed my nightshirt covered in a tiny puppy print. 'We don't even know if there's anything dodgy going on.'

He didn't answer. 'Do you want a shower? You can use my bathroom, upstairs on the right. There are towels and... stuff.'

'Soap, Ivo. It's not an exotic concept.'

But he didn't answer this either, just waved a hand at the hallway, from which the stairs wound their Georgian way up to the first floor, and curiosity got the better of me. I didn't *really* need a shower but I did want a look at the rest of Ivo's house and this was a great excuse. All my previous visits had been hasty, just-passing-through ones, never giving me enough time to do more than use the loo, let alone to examine the architecture.

A window on the landing arched like a quizzical eyebrow letting in some rainy grey light down the left-hand stairway and giving a view of the stables, and also illuminating a mural painted along the landing wall. There were cherubs and pots and it looked like a picture of an orangery in a nudist colony. Very Restoration, with topless women hanging out of windows and saucy men gazing up at them from behind the topiary. Why Ivo's family couldn't just have wallpaper like us plebs I had no idea.

On the right-hand side was the mirror-image arched window, allowing in a greenish light, filtered through ivy growth, because the place was hot on symmetry but not so good on actually letting in daylight. The rooms on that side of the gatehouse were really only used when Ivo threw a party, the study, which contained the piano too large for the space and a tiled-and-panelled utility-cum-boot room. From comments made by many of our university friends, up for the shooting and general Yorkshire summers, it wasn't that unusual to only live in half your house. If I only lived in half of mine, I wouldn't have been able to lie down or cook dinner.

I locked myself in the exotically decorated bathroom filled with wall paintings of foliage and nymphs and indulged in the rainforest downpour from the walk-in shower. It was wonderful and I felt far more human when I came out, back in my work uniform again, as though the wildlife rescue jumper gave me legitimacy. If anyone asked what I was doing with a red squirrel, I could at least point to the badge on my chest and not feel as though I were committing some dreadful wildlife crime. Little puffs of Ivo's really expensive shower gel filtered through the scratchy wool of my top; I hadn't stinted myself in there.

His bedroom was at the top of the opposite flight of stairs. It would have been very bad form to have peered in through the door to check it out, so I only looked sideways at the bits visible from the landing. A huge and rumpled bed, a large window seat cushioned in the ever-present velvet and bearing a book that lay crumpled-paged, face down with its spine bent like an accident victim, blazing its title in lurid purple print and an almost unreadable font, into the air.

The book was *Committing the Perfect Crime.*

Despite the heat of my recent shower, my body went cold under my thick work jumper. Not a physical cold, but a creeping internal chill that pulled at my spine and made the hair on my neck prickle. I had to lean against the doorframe for a moment to take the weight off my legs while my brain processed.

No. Not Ivo. Never Ivo.

I thought of the speed with which he'd been at the scene and his glee at having something to 'investigate'. It would be just like Ivo to have read something, somewhere that set him off. While I didn't think... no, I really *didn't* think that Ivo had anything to do with the man's death; his bedtime reading could simply have encouraged him to build a mystery out of circumstance and unconnected events.

Ivo would never hurt anyone. Then a little voice, deep down inside my head, whispered, *He'd be certain he'd get away with it.*

He's clever and his mother is a high-court judge. Maybe he'd put his faith in the family to sweep any case against him away?

But what crime had actually even *been* committed? Unless Ivo had scared our Mr Williams into falling over and cracking his head, and he'd planted the squirrel in his pocket... I shook my head. The ferocious temperature I'd been running alongside this cold was giving me stupid, feverish ideas.

Slowly, slowly, I made my way down the impressive staircase with my joints almost creaking, to find Ivo bouncing around in the living room, fully dressed. He didn't *look* guilty. In fact, he seemed only too keen to get to York and get Fred tested, and that would only get us closer to finding out what really had happened up on that moor in the middle of the night. If he really *were* guilty, surely he'd be trying to put it off, throw me off the scent?

Not Ivo. Not my Ivo.

Unless... I watched him looping around the room, supposedly tidying up but actually causing more chaos – unless he suspected how I felt? Did Ivo know that I was halfway in love with him? Did he think I would cover for him, keep secrets, blur lines? Was that how he saw me?

Oh, for goodness' sake! This was getting beyond cold-medicine hallucinations and into actual brain-fever territory now. Ivo could be odd, yes. But I liked his cheerful random branch of weirdness. It made him fun. Made him unpredictable, a whirlwind of ideas, activity and quotations. Made him adorably Ivo, a continent away from my stolid, unimaginative workmates. Although, they were steady, reliable, always turned up when they said they would and didn't feel the need to go and look up a Tennyson poem in the middle of pulling electric fence off a fox, so there was that.

I didn't really think Ivo was involved in anything nefarious. It just wasn't the sort of thing he would do.

But he did sometimes get *ideas*. That book... it might have given him a nudge. A hint of 'would it be so bad if...?' that he couldn't resist following through to the end?

Behind me, Ivo dropped a cushion that he'd been half-heartedly rearranging. It caught the side of a vase, which tipped, and water and flowers cascaded over the floor in a mirror image of what was happening in the weather outside. 'Oh, bugger,' said Ivo, mildly, watching the water drip from the edge of the table into the puddle, and beginning to pick up the flowers.

'I'll get a cloth,' I said. 'Mop the water up first, before it does any damage, then worry about the flowers.'

He gave me a rueful grin and I went off into the kitchen to search out a cloth, feeling my shoulders drop a little. Nobody *that* disorganised could be part of a crime, however persuasive his bedtime reading might be.

I was rooting about under the sink when the thought struck me, that Ivo might have got me to help him investigate as an alibi, and I didn't dare let myself wonder whether, if it came to it, I would lie for him.

I mopped up the water while Ivo fiddled about, picking up the vase, putting it down to gather the dropped stems, then trying to pick it up again with his arms full of wet foliage, which tipped it over and more water dribbled onto the carpet. I took the vase, mopped again, and stood the vase upright, somewhere out of Ivo's random flailing reach.

'So.' He took the soggy cloth from me and threw it into the sink, scraped the dropped flowers off his shirt and flung them in on top. 'How are we doing this? Do you need me to get our Fred in a headlock so you can pluck him? Won't it hurt?' Then, with a slightly worried frown, he added, 'And will he bite?'

I thought of the book, crumpled and careless on the window seat by Ivo's bed. 'I think it's best if we take him to the lab to get the hair,' I said. My mind was running ahead of me now. If we took Fred into the university lab, they'd know about him. More people would have seen him. Just in *case* Ivo had been up to something, my brain was whispering, the more people who knew I was with him and we had the squirrel, the better. 'If we take the hair sample there, there's less chance of cocking up and contaminating or losing it.'

'Good idea.'

That reassured me. Ivo didn't want to keep the squirrel a secret. I watched him pulling on his boots, which looked as though they'd come from an army surplus store. He sat on the bench in the small porch, where riding crops stood in an old umbrella stand. Everything was spun with cobwebs, and an ancient, tatty side-saddle shed its stuffing on the floor. 'Do you use any of this?' I asked.

Ivo glanced up and suddenly seemed to notice all the equestrianism around him. 'No, not really. I should clear it all out, shouldn't I? Make a bit more room?'

'Not if you don't want to.'

But he'd started collecting armfuls of whips from the stand. Dust billowed; they didn't seem to have been touched for years, and Ivo's loose jacket was decorated with strands of horse hair whose owners had probably been contemporaneous with Marengo. Then he stood, uncertain.

'We need to get to York, Ivo.' I took a wobbling schooling whip from the pile under his arm. 'These can wait.'

He turned in a circle, the crops scraping the wall. 'But you're right. It should all go, there would be more room. We could put a little table there instead.' He pointed, and half the whips fell to the floor, like spillikins.

'It needs a coat of paint and a good dusting.' I looked up. Probably ancient beams were festooned with cobwebs, into which straw and hay was woven like some huge pagan symbol. 'But anyway. York.'

'Yes!' He dropped the bundle still under his arm onto the bench. More dust issued into the air and the little porch was now full of it. Ivo didn't seem to care, but that was Ivo all over. Impetuous and careless. My heart gave an uncomfortable thump under the sturdy wool of my work jumper. 'Let's take Fred on his day out to the big city.'

'I'll put him in my carry cage. We can't lug the big one around the labs.'

Ivo shrugged. I had to admit that I was watching him more closely now. Looking for signs of guilt? Or just admiring the way he was dressed in the close-fitting sandy trousers and the shirt with lace foaming around the neck in a way that would have made Byron take notes, and, possibly, a couple of line drawings?

'What?' Ivo caught me looking at him. I must have had a thoughtful expression on my face, rather than this just being the way my eyes were pointing, because he looked almost smug.

'Wondering about your costume choices. You've always been about the velvet and the suede and everything, haven't you? Even back at university you wore clothes that looked as though you wanted to be stroked.'

His smugness increased a notch and he grinned. 'I get dressed in the dark a lot,' he said. 'It helps.'

I smiled and shook my head. Nobody this winsome could be guilty of anything more than, maybe, dodging a parking fine. Surely.

We drove to York through a random scatter of showers. Most of the other traffic was optimistically heading in the direction of the coast, and the open stretches of road seemed slightly unnatural at this time of year. The minster stood on its bubble of hill, highlighted by the sun, which picked it out like a spotlight on a superstar, and the river ran alongside the road, a silver artery following our progress as we circumvented the city.

We turned off the main road and approached the university, all modern and ergonomic amid the history. The buildings looked oddly misplaced, as though someone had beamed a modernist architectural sample book into Rome and then put a pond in to blur the join. At least there was plenty of parking and we found ourselves a spot outside the university labs. I carried Fred in his cage up the stairs, following the directions that Danny had texted me, and with Ivo trailing me anxiously.

'It won't hurt him, will it?' He caught me up on a landing and peered in at Fred, who cocked his head and peered back.

'No. Just a pulled bit of fur. Like getting his tail caught on a twig or something.'

'Oh. Good.' He ran a couple of steps ahead and then stopped to turn back. 'You're sure? It's not like that time at the vet when my dad told me they were only going to give poor Tosca an X-ray and she came back three days later looking like Dr Frankenstein had had a go at her?'

'No! Why would I lie to you?' I wondered who or what Tosca had been.

'Dunno. Why did Dad lie?'

'Maybe he genuinely thought she only needed an X-ray. Perhaps it came as much of a shock to him.'

Ivo stopped dead, hand on the stair rail, feet arrested in action, so he looked like a freeze-frame. 'I never thought of that. Look. Floor four. This is us, isn't it?'

Danny's 'mate in the labs' turned out to be Ginny, a pretty girl with purple hair, who'd been briefed on our request and who turned out to be a dab hand at squirrel wrestling. We extracted the required hair, complete with root bulb, to Fred's distinct chagrin, while Ivo bounced about keeping up a running commentary.

'Is he always like this?' Ginny asked me quietly, tipping her head in Ivo's direction while she secured the hair sample in a tube with a stopper and wrote my name on it.

'I'm afraid so.'

'Wow. He makes the squirrel look restful.' She looked in at Fred again. He was grooming his tail and peered out from beneath it at us with one narrowed eye, keeping his paws on his fur. I hoped he didn't think I was going to make a habit of extracting it. 'Cute, though.'

I wasn't sure if she meant Fred or Ivo and didn't want to commit either way, so I just grunted and moved the cage from the desktop where it had been resting while we'd accosted the squirrel.

'How long before you know anything?' Ivo bounced happily alongside us. Fred side-eyed him, but as Ivo hadn't been part of the tail-pulling horror, he was clearly excused suspicion. The squirrel flung himself at the mesh and flashed his white-streaked underparts, in case there were treats.

'Tomorrow, or maybe this afternoon.' Ginny turned the tube holding the gathered hairs. 'Luckily, this comes under my PhD, so I'll get a go on the machines next time round. I'll just need to extract his DNA and cross match against the profiles, which should tell us where he's from.'

She squeaked between her lips, which brought Fred back to the bars again, and Ivo cocked his head. 'He's very responsive.'

I was going to choose to assume she meant the squirrel. 'I think he was hand-reared,' I said. 'Someone will be missing him.'

The now-reappeared sun slanted through the blinds that were drawn in a pathetic attempt to shade the lab from its onslaught, and fell in hot shreds around the room. Fred gleamed liked burned ginger where its rays hit his fur and his eye reflected us in a saucer-shaped alternate universe. Ginny squeaked again and tufted ears wriggled, triangulating the sound.

'It's very quiet.' Ivo leaned against a desk. 'No students?'

'Not many.' Ginny jerked her attention back to the other centre of attraction. 'They've all left. We've just got summer schools and some of us beleaguered post grads, which is why I've got time for your squirrel.' She tilted her head, but he didn't pick up the hint. 'Lots of spare time,' she threw in. 'I'm sometimes quite bored, really.'

'Uh huh.' He slouched off back around the small lab, looking at wall posters of flower parts and fiddling with a pile of microscopes on a table.

I smiled. Ginny slumped with disappointment, and we left her to carry out her tests, the squirrel cage tucked under my arm with Fred pinging around the bars again.

'She was angling for you to ask her out, you know,' I said, as we reached floor three, our footsteps echoing up the empty staircase, accompanied by the metallic sounds of our caged friend.

'*Was* she?' Ivo looked stunned. He draped himself over the rail, bending backwards so he could look up the narrow stairwell, back where we'd come from. 'Seriously?'

'Oh, come *on*,' I said, exasperated. 'You've had girlfriends, Ivo, I know you have! So this *ingénue*, "what, little ol' me?" act must work on some people.'

We clattered down the remaining stairs and out of the main doors into the steel-bright sunlight. Fred tucked himself away at the back of the cage.

'I don't...' Ivo started, then shook his head briefly and stared out over the water that made this part of the university look like a nature reserve. 'I don't always pick up on things like that. It's not an act, Cress.'

His voice was quiet, almost serious now, which, from Ivo, was always surprising. It made me – what, nervous? I busied myself with tucking the cage into the back of Ivo's car and not looking at him. There were shades of things in his tone, things unsaid, things he wanted to say but needed the right time for, and, if any of those things were going to be an admission of inclusion in the crime that had brought us here – well, I didn't know how I would feel about that.

I turned my face towards him, closing the boot carefully so as not to alarm Fred. 'Hopefully Ginny should have a result in the next day or so.'

It was a pointless sentence, just a rehash of what she had said herself only a few minutes before, but it broke his mood and stopped the look that had crossed his face.

'Yeah, then we can get Fred where he belongs and find out a bit more about what our Mr Williams was doing up on that moor!'

'We may never know that, though.' I leaned against the door while Ivo fiddled about, getting in. 'If it really *was* just a bloke taking his pet for a night walk and hitting his head on a rock in the dark.' *And,* I thought quietly, *you're using his name like you know him – where is this driving licence that the police could have used to identify him? Was all that going around the B&Bs just a ruse to throw me off the scent? Did you already know who he was?*

I watched Ivo carefully. Surely, if there was anything he needed to tell me, any involvement he had in any of this, now was the time?

'I know.' His thoughtful expression didn't change. He sighed. 'I know, Cress. I can't help hoping though, that this will be the big one. The story that I can follow through on, that leaves everyone talking.'

'The case that makes your career? Does that still happen, given social media and online news pages and all that?'

I had to avert my eyes now and stare at the bonnet of the car, where the heat was making the air shimmer in a haze of unreality. This whole *thing* felt unreal. Yesterday I'd been lying in my sick bed with no worries apart from running out of tissues – come to think of it, the cold was a lot better today, maybe the nettle tea had helped – and today, here I was wondering what the hell was really going on. I worked in a wildlife rescue centre, for goodness' sake, not Agatha Christie Land.

Whatever depression had made Ivo look cast-down and thoughtful had clearly passed, because he gave me a big grin and bounced on his toes for a moment. 'I dunno,' he said. 'Worth a shot though, isn't it?'

'Look, poor Fred's frying in there.' I pointed at the back of the car. 'Let's go home and wait for Ginny to get us the results. Then we can return Fred to his people, that's the really important thing, and – well, you can take it from there, can't you?'

Ivo opened the car windows, but didn't start the engine. The thoughtfulness was back. 'Shall I cook dinner tonight, then?' he asked, as though we'd been discussing food for the previous ten minutes. 'I can check in the freezer, there's probably some duck or something.'

The conversational ground had shifted so fast that, even knowing Ivo as I did, I found it hard to rebalance myself. 'Er,' I said, adjusting from thinking about the future of Fred to thinking about meals. 'That sounds nice, thank you.'

'Well, you are staying. I only really cook when I have guests.' He started the car and we circumnavigated the geese, who were wandering across the tarmac, with caution.

'Do your parents fly in food parcels the rest of the time?' I sounded a little more acerbic than I'd meant to, and saw Ivo flick me a look.

'I eat a lot of sandwiches,' he said, almost apologetic. 'Cooking for one, well, seems a bit of a waste of time. D'you find that? Or do you cook for your housemates as well?'

'No, I... look, can we go back a couple of conversational steps, please, Ivo? Fred. We return him, and then what are you going to do?'

'Ask questions. Mr Williams either took Fred with or without permission, and either of those possibilities will mean something. And if Fred was actually *his*, which, given his pocket location is a distinct probability, then maybe someone can tell us what on Earth he was doing in Yorkshire.' Ivo negotiated the roundabout and we slid down onto the bypass in a haze of conversational acceleration.

'What if it turns out that Mr Williams was a hermit, with no friends, no colleagues, who bred red squirrels in his shed in his spare time, what then? What if there's no one to ask?'

'You said you have to be licensed to keep them? The squirrels?'

'Yes, but he might not have *had* a licence. It's possible Mr Williams got hold of one some other way, for some reason. Red squirrels are hardly up there with Golden Retrievers as suitable pets.'

There was a pause. I didn't want to see disappointment on Ivo's face so I kept my eyes averted, looking out of the window at the clouding landscape, where another savage band of rain was heading in to sweep holidaymakers into town from the beaches. He seemed so set on this being a mystery that would be easy to solve, like a TV programme. All the clues, neatly laid out for us to track back to the point of origin, where a moustache-twirling bad guy would tell us all his plans just before the fortuitously called police swept in to arrest them and tell us how great we were. Perhaps *that* was what his bedtime reading had prompted him to think – that life had a narrative. He didn't seem to have considered the general messiness of life, or the random behaviour of humans.

I just wanted to get Fred home.

A thought struck me. 'Oh God. What if he really *was* an illegal squirrel breeder, working on his own out of his garden shed? What if there's a whole shed full of squirrels somewhere, and he's dead and nobody is looking after them?'

'Is that likely? Someone would have to know, surely? An entire shed of squeak and rattle, the neighbours are going to wonder.' Ivo put his foot down and the car overtook a Kia full of disappointed shrimping nets, sending road spray over the windows.

'It's illegal. He's hardly going to ask people round to admire his pets, is he?' I had horrible visions of a bunch of red squirrels, unfed and unwatered in the heat of a smelly locked shed and it made me fidget in my seat, and gave me a burning feeling of urgency deep in my chest.

'So we have to identify Fred's place of origin and get there before they realise that nobody is around to feed them?' He gave me a quick, almost amused, look. 'Good. I'm glad you're fully on board, even if it does mean you're going to be worrying about the poor fluffy creatures.'

I stared out again at the acres of hillside, fields of ripening barley bending soggily under the weight of the rain. 'Yes. But then, he *must* have had other people who knew what he was up to. What would he tell everyone he was doing in his shed for hours? And if he's been supplying squirrels to other people – I mean, *who*?' I shook my head. 'None of this makes any sense at all, to be honest, Ivo.'

'Probably not.' Ivo overtook another car. The Volvo buzzed along, windows dappled with raindrops and, in any other circumstances, I would have enjoyed the journey, having Ivo to myself in the cosy confines of the car. 'But there's just *something*,' he said. 'I can feel it. Even if we bring in a ring of illegal squirrel breeders, hey, that would be a result, wouldn't it?'

I couldn't think of a reply that wouldn't puncture his *Scooby-Doo*-esque good nature. Nor did I really want to. Although I didn't, for one second, believe that a dead man with a squirrel was the ringleader of an international racket of any kind, I couldn't bring myself to wipe that expression of anticipatory glee from Ivo's face.

He was happy. He was investigating, which, he seemed to believe, was his job. There were many, many faults in this line of thinking, which I could have pointed out. But to utter any of them would be to take the shine off Ivo's day; it would remove his focus and leave him flapping around, adrenaline-fuelled but no longer with any point. And I really didn't want to do that. Okay, I may have to inconvenience myself for a few days, following him about so we could track 'clues', but this investigation would run its course and peter to an end of shrugging and, perhaps, a shed full of illegal squirrels. Ivo would count anything a result, and all I had to do was hang onto him to make sure he didn't enthuse himself to death or get so carried away that he'd be arrested for interfering with a police investigation.

Yes. That was why I was here, sitting in the front of the Volvo, with Fred scraping the bars of his cage behind me like a prisoner intent on attention, watching the grey band of rain sweeping across from the hills to envelope the vale in squally splatters. To keep Ivo out of trouble.

Not at all because I was enjoying, in a somewhat masochistic way, having Ivo to myself.

'So, yes, duck,' Ivo said suddenly, as though that conversation hadn't been roundly supplanted. 'I do a very good plum sauce, you know. Unless you'd rather get a takeaway?'

Conversational ballet, that's what it was. There may be many intricate moves, but the dancer always returns to the resting position, and clearly, tonight's dinner was Ivo's 'resting position' for now.

'No, duck sounds great. I'll give you a hand and you can show me how you make your plum sauce.'

There was a moment's silence. The car began to swish as the rain settled on the road surface.

'Actually, I feel I may rather have talked up the sauce,' Ivo said at last. 'It's basically jam with a splash of balsamic.' He flashed me a grin, one eyebrow raised. 'And there goes my secret recipe. I may have to kill you now.'

'Don't.' The image of the body lying, feet protruding from under the flimsy police cover, was still with me. A glimmer of an image of Ivo standing above it wielding a weapon flickered in the back of my brain for an instant, then degraded and fluttered off with other unworthy thoughts. 'This week's already had too much "dead" in it. And anyway, you wouldn't,' I said, half to myself.

He was looking at me, I could tell, even though I was still keeping my eyes on the view beyond the windscreen, where rain hissed as though a pantomime villain had just come on stage. 'No,' he said softly. 'No, I wouldn't.'

Did he suspect any of the things that had gone through my mind? I turned to look at him, but he was staring out at the road in front, his expression neutral. A few stray hairs caught wispily in his almost invisible blond stubble and dragged along his cheek. Long eyelashes, very visible at this angle, shaded his eyes.

He was almost impossibly beautiful, and almost impossible at everything else.

'You're an absolute bugger, Ivo,' I said, equally softly. 'Completely impossible.'

'Yes, yes I am, aren't I?' he replied, pushing his hair away from his face with a wrist, and grinning happily. 'Shockingly dreadful. Don't know why anyone puts up with me.' Another quick, sideways look. 'Don't know why *you* put up with me.'

'Because you're doing the driving; this is all your idea. And you've promised me duck in plum sauce.'

'Oh yes. Suppose I have. Glad you have designs on my culinary abilities.' Another cheery grin. 'Because I haven't got any others.'

'Apart from the drawing, the French speaking and the country dancing,' I said, without thinking.

'Ah. You remembered that.'

'Of course I did. You were busily comparing your achievements to Regency ladies, I think, and that somewhat sticks in the memory.'

'I lied about the country dancing.'

'I'm sure Jane Austen will get over the disappointment.' I met his eye and suddenly we were both laughing at the ridiculousness of the conversation. Ivo didn't *do* ordinary conversation. I'd never really heard him small-talking his way around a room; he would normally insert a chat-jemmy into any discussions about the weather or house prices by asking if anyone knew the best way to split willow to make hurdles or something equally random. You didn't chat with Ivo, you embarked on a convoluted word-rollercoaster and you hung on to see how much made sense.

If you got off at the end with your hat still in place, you counted it a success.

6

Back at the gatehouse, I decanted Fred from his travelling cage. He swung his way out and into the larger one, pausing only to hang briefly on the front bars and eyeball me with a stare like a newly uncased conker. His ears twitched so that the tufts of hair that sprouted from the top of each one waggled and he seemed most perplexed.

'Were you hoping we were taking you home?' I asked softly to the intense gaze. 'Sorry. We will, as soon as we find out where you're from.'

Another moment of reflected light and then the little squirrel bounced away again, flashing his white stomach in the glimmer of sunshine that saw fit to creep through the barred glass of the stable windows. I sighed and went to head back indoors, walking past Ivo's car parked neatly on its grassy spot alongside the bridleway, when I had a thought.

Ivo had found that hotel receipt up on the path where the man had died. But he wouldn't have had the time or opportunity to search for anything else. He said that the litter pickers had been there the day before, so, as he'd proved, anything left there was a result of that lone walker coming along in the dead of night. Did I really believe that?

I stopped dead, one hand on the still-warm car bonnet. Yes. I believed Ivo had found the receipt, of course I did. But he hadn't found the driving licence, which might still be up there, somewhere, hidden amongst bracken and fern. Or in Ivo's pocket, being kept from the police for his own reasons?

The kitchen window had been thrown open, and from inside I could hear Ivo singing along with the radio and the sounds of cupboards opening and closing as he, presumably, gathered the ingredients for his plum sauce. He seemed happy and relaxed, or as relaxed as Ivo ever was, and his relaxation would have put fully wound elastic bands to shame.

Did I *really* think Ivo had anything to do with the death of a man on a lonely footpath in the dark?

Then I thought of the path as I knew it. Rarely travelled, except by the horse riders and gamekeepers, and the occasional walker. Maybe that driving licence was still up there? If it was – it would put my mind at rest that this was nothing to do with Ivo, and maybe *I* could find it. I was, after all, far more used to combing through undergrowth than most people. An injured small creature will burrow itself in to feel safe, and there's nothing like a fingertip search through vegetation on the hunt for an injured fox cub – all the while waiting to have those very fingertips bitten off by a fear-crazed creature – for teaching you how it's done.

I tried to keep away the thoughts that Ivo might have already found that licence. He couldn't. He wouldn't. After all, why would he have kept it, rather than handing it over to the police now we already knew the man's identity? It was only his utter, unwavering focus on there being something to investigate that made me think otherwise, after all.

Plus, there was that book beside his bed.

'Ivo?' I shouted in through the open window. 'Can I borrow the car for a bit?'

The singing stopped, although the radio continued to play, echoing off the high ceiling so that it appeared Harry Styles was serenading from inside a bucket. 'The car? Yeah, course you can.'

'Where are the keys?'

There was a moment of frantic-sounding activity, lots of movement of stuff and the clatter of bowls, then a fistful of keys appeared on the window ledge. 'Don't be too long, Cress, I need serious sous-chef-ing in here if I'm not going to go mad and produce sweet-and-sour doorhandles.'

'I won't. I've just got to... pick up a few bits.'

Ivo's face appeared behind the keys, hair dishevelled and his frothy collar jutting at odd angles. 'Have fun.' He grinned and then bobbed back to whatever he was doing.

I picked up the keys. It was so typical of Ivo not to say 'be careful with the car', or anything else that indicated he cared at all about his belongings. He'd always had an open-handed attitude to his things, as though he didn't care; it was part of the 'antiques are to be used' frame of mind. Although I had once seen him upset, when another friend had 'borrowed' some books and then lent them on in a chain, which meant Ivo never got to the bottom of who actually had possession, and had to relinquish them to the great unknown. He'd been quietly disappointed, a view of Ivo that had made him even more attractive to me. He hadn't got angry, he hadn't gone storming round to the first borrower demanding to know what right they thought they had to lend on things that weren't theirs. He'd just sat on the edge of his bed, head in hands, staring at the gap on his bookshelf, saying 'my grandfather gave me those books' as though he couldn't comprehend where they had gone.

That was Ivo. Thoughtlessly generous. Impulsive. Hopelessly attractive.

I drove the car up to where I'd parked yesterday, and walked out along the trackway. There were marks of booted feet in the new mud; the police had been back since it had rained, but the little tent was gone and there were no other signs to show that someone had met a sudden end amid the heather and boulders, until I stood right where the body had lain. There the under-growth was crushed and trampled, but any blood had washed away in the rain showers and the sheer force of nature was returning the place to its innocence.

I lifted my head and looked outwards. The view was wonder-ful, the sky stretched like a canvas with far hills printed flatly upon it; one way the heaped rise of the Yorkshire Wolds looked green and smooth, the other way, the more wooded Howardian Hills, rugged and determined. Behind me, the woods sloped down to meet the rise of the moors. And in front of all, the blue-grey of the moorland in a foreground of sprouting heather bells and the green upthrusts of bog-myrtle and sedge. The track formed a peaty outline, curving across the moor, with the woods that edged it dropping away down the steep hillside. Nothing to see here, apart from a glorious view. Not something you would come to appreciate in the middle of the night. Even the wildlife would mostly be invisible, apart from a few owls and the odd stoat. Definitely no red squirrels.

I walked a little further down the path, avoiding the muddier spots, where puddles lurked dark and hidden under the roots of the bracken that grew alongside. Far off to my left, away towards where I knew Beverley and Hull lay beyond the swollen rise and fall of hills, clouds massed and a gauze of rain dragged along the edge of the view, coming this way.

I lowered my eyes, looking for that driving licence. Or – well,

I didn't know what. Anything. Anything odd, anything extra. The beaten down nature of the undergrowth did not exactly enthuse me with possibilities; it looked as though the police, despite my reservations, had given the area a pretty thorough check for anything dropped or discarded. There was nothing to see apart from peat that gave up its water-loading in a boot-squelch when stepped on, fingers of rock, a lot of view and even more sky. No small, plastic oblongs bearing a helpful picture, name and date of birth, no carefully typed confessions. Not so much as a bit of blown tissue bowling along over the hoof-marks.

Had Ivo *really* found that receipt just lying in the mud? And nothing else? It hadn't, perhaps, been in the 'bag' we'd heard about from Mr Thixendale, and surreptitiously removed by Ivo to create a mystery, just for him to solve?

I tucked my hands in my pockets and shrugged my shoulders up against the bustling wind, which came in smelling of the distant sea. Rain was fringing its edges and the far hills were no longer visible behind an approaching shower, so I moved back, off the track and into the shelter of the overhanging trees. Tiny deer paths streaked through the wood, marking where the animals headed through cover and down the hillside, and I took one of these, treading carefully amid the upthrust roots and bramble snares until I was well under the branches of some spindly birches that cuddled up against conifer cover.

The rain had come in earnest now; it whispered and gossiped its way among the leaves down to earth, plashing and spattering onto the track but mostly missing me, huddled under my umbrella of branches. I leaned back against the trunk of a birch, rough with lichen and wind-scoured bark and pushed my hands further into my pockets. The occasional drop hit my head as the wind shoved body-sized gusts between the growth at me, and I moved further back to use the trunk for more cover.

Nothing here but wet. No evidence, no signs that anything had happened here, other than a casual passing of tourists and view-seekers, and I began to realise how stupid I felt. Almost as though I had to find *something* to give legitimacy to my coming up here in the first place. What on Earth had made me think that Ivo could have had anything to do with what had happened here, apart from his bedtime reading material?

I smacked my hand against the tree, wanting to punish myself for the thoughts. Why did I do this to myself? Why couldn't I get caught up in the enthusiasm that he had for this case without looking for some hidden darkness? After all, here I was, spending time punishing myself in an enjoyable way with a man I had fallen for practically on the first day of university. He wanted me around. And yet, here was me, being the 'yes, but...' girl, when I should let go, enjoy the moment, and stop trying to find ulterior motives in everything.

I knew Ivo. Knew how his flyaway attention span could so easily get caught up in things that were less than savoury and how hard it was for him to extricate himself. Ivo was the kind of person who would take something offered at a party to avoid giving offence and then find himself trying to hide stolen goods in his house while the police battered the door down and big men with dogs and minders climbed out of the upstairs windows.

But, as he said, it had only been the once and he'd got off with a warning. Ivo's general ineptitude and his ability to dig himself a very big hole armed only with good nature and a desperation to be liked had been visible to the judge. Having an incredibly fortunate background and parents in the public eye had, admittedly, pushed it further into their line of sight, of course.

Water dripped dismally off the overhanging leaves and I gave myself a talking to. I was flailing and I knew it. Caution was practically my middle name, a dislike for not knowing what came next, a desire to have every eventuality mapped out and accounted for. Spontaneity was just a collection of vowels as far as I was concerned – I didn't understand it. Which put Ivo at the opposite end of the behaviour see-saw to me, and I didn't understand him either.

I didn't truly think he was hiding Mr Williams' driving licence. On the one hand, it just wasn't *Ivo*, but on the other hand, what *was* Ivo? He was my friend, but that was where any certainties ended.

I was trying as hard as I could not to think what I really felt. *Just because I really like him doesn't stop him being a bad guy, it just stops me seeing that he might be. Just because I want him to be more to me than a friend doesn't mean he wants the same or is doing anything other than using me as cover. I could get really, really hurt and yet, here I am.*

The feeling made me colder than the rain, which had percolated down through the trees now and was dropping occasional icy fingers down my collar. To distract myself, I started walking along between the trees, parallel to the trackway, dodging whippy branches and hitting my hand against scabby trunks. *Don't think, act.*

I'd walked back to where the body had been found now, and peered out at the site from between the trees. Rain spiralled the surfaces of the puddles. It was getting harder and more persistent, so I huddled back into the woods again, coiling back deeper into cover and catching my foot on something that crunched slightly as I went.

I bent down to see what it was, scrabbling with my fingers until fragments of wire and wood came to light, covered with a blown scatter of last autumn's leaves, which were scudding around in the wind. It was nothing much, a splintering of plywood and metal; it could have been an old piece of fencing, discarded when the new one was replaced. But there was something about the angle of the wood, the gauzy metal sheet, that was familiar. I stirred my hand through the leaves and came up with more bits, flat panels torn where the screws had given way, metal catches flapping uselessly with nothing to attach to.

I knew what this was. We used them ourselves at the wildlife unit, for transporting sick or injured animals to the vet or from the place they were captured to our holding pens. I had one right now, back in the stable entranceway. It was a small-animal transport cage. Smashed and ruined, but, presumably, how Fred had been moved from place to place. Mr Williams could have had him in this in the B&B and nobody would have known. If he'd thrown his jacket over the box it would have looked like a bag or any other luggage; all the sides were solid wood with only the front having a tight metal panel, and even that had the mesh so closely woven that first sight wouldn't have shown a squirrel.

This was a *clue*! Suddenly as overjoyed as though I'd solved an entire murder mystery, I scrabbled about until I had collected as many of the pieces of cage as I could find. The top, with its handle, was intact but the rest was smashed and broken. All the bits were mostly in the same place, with a few pieces swept against tree trunks or concealed by leaves, and I cuddled the splintered wood and loose hinges to me under my jacket against the rain, then headed back to the car.

If this really was something to do with why Fred was here, then Ivo couldn't have had anything to do with it. The thought made my heart lift. Because if he *had*, he would have removed this. My hands shook slightly on the steering wheel and I had a moment of knowing what Ivo had meant when he said he just *knew* things were important. Somehow I just *knew* this cage was important, it meant that Fred hadn't been trouser-transported around the place, and *that* meant he'd been brought here on purpose. It meant that Mr Thixendale had mistaken it for a bag – its size and narrow dimensions could have been mistaken for a small satchel, particularly if it were covered. Which meant no bag that Ivo could have furtively searched.

My hands were still shaking. *Ivo couldn't have anything to do with this.* For the first time in two days, my breath came more easily, and it wasn't because the cold was finally leaving my respiratory system, it was a weight lifting from my chest and heart.

That cage was broken and casually slung into the woods. The litter pickers would have found it if it had been there all along, nobody would leave a scatter of metal just off the path, where animals could be injured by it. I found it, so it all made it more likely that Ivo had found the receipt, on this otherwise immaculately litter-free bridleway. He may even have seen the cage, but mistaken it, as I had at first, for bits of fencing. Only because I'd known what I was looking at had I picked it up. The weight lifted further, freed my neck and then my head, and I found I was sitting up straighter, breathing more deeply and handling the car like a Formula 1 ace along the narrow lanes back to the gatehouse.

Not Ivo. He was just caught up in this, the same as I was.

I pulled the car into its usual space and got out, clutching the wooden splinters and protruding screws to my chest, ignoring the scratches and snags in the same way as I would ignore the nips and claws of a small animal. Ivo was still in the kitchen; I'd not been gone as long as I thought. All that skulking about in the woods and second-guessing Ivo had made time slow down uncomfortably, but here in the real world it was still music and cooking smells and an unreasonable amount of blue smoke.

'Is something meant to be burning?' I asked, coming through the door into the living room, where Ivo was piling old newspapers up on the floor.

'Burning?' He looked up at me and I felt that flash in my heart for a second. I was halfway in love with this man. 'Oh, shit!'

He abandoned the newspaper pile, which promptly toppled, and ran into the kitchen, where he swore in a continuous stream of consciousness while, from the sound of it, running water into a pan that had become far too hot and was spitting and letting steam join the smoke.

An alarm went off in the porch, and Ivo ran through, grabbed a newspaper and began flapping it in the direction of the shrill noise, while water ran in the kitchen and splattered from the sink onto the floor.

I couldn't help but grin and continue clasping the bolts and splinters. Ivo was back to being my lanky, blond-haired friend. That shadow of suspicion had faded, although it was rapidly being replaced by a degree of unexpected annoyance at his inability to concentrate on cooking to the extent of burning a pan.

'What happened?' I asked, when he finally stopped flapping, sorted out the spilled water, and came to sit down, ignoring the re-scattered papers on the carpet.

'I was heating the sauce, then I thought about what you said about clearing out the porch, so I moved some of these papers out from the bench. Then I started reading as I was tidying and' – he spread his hands in apology – 'I forgot the sauce.'

'Is it ruined?'

'I can make more. Why on Earth are you sitting as though you're expecting your appendix to burst?'

I frowned, then realised that I was leaning over my knees, still embracing the tatty pile of screws and broken wood. 'I found this. Up in the wood near where the body was, just off the track.'

His eyes flickered from my lumpy bundle to my face, and then back again. He didn't speak.

'It's an animal transport cage, one of the small ones. It means that Fred was carried up there, then something happened, I don't know, maybe our man dropped the cage and it broke and Fred got out and he had to get him back again and he slipped and fell?' I rattled to the end of my conclusions. Ivo was still looking at me. His continued stillness made me nervous. Wasn't I *meant* to find this? All the doubts came flooding back and I felt them settle on the back of my neck.

'You went up there just now?' His voice was toneless. Very level. 'Without saying?'

Oh God, was he about to confess something? 'I was just... wondering,' I said, slightly pathetically. 'If there was anything that might have been... missed.'

'But we could have gone together.' He sounded flat. 'Scoped the place out and looked for things. You didn't tell me you thought there might be something else.'

'I didn't *know*.' A sharp edge dug into my stomach. I wriggled and a screw fell to the floor, its silver brightness shining like a fallen sun amid the newsprint and dust. 'I only went on the off chance. Looking for stuff.'

Ivo's gaze fell away from my face and he sat on the floor by the newspaper pile. 'But without me.' His eyes seemed to move over ancient headlines. 'You didn't tell me where you were going, and you went for another look – without me.' His mouth twisted. 'You thought this case might be something to do with me?' He reached out and began folding the edge of the nearest paper, pleating it into a fan of print. 'You don't trust me and so you went up there without saying in case there was something incriminating.'

A flat statement. And honestly, nothing I could deny, so I sat, silent, with several of the sharper pieces of wood digging into my ribs. My heart was digging into them from the inside too, seeing the closed-off expression on his face.

He bent forwards, rubbing his hands over his face. 'Oh, Cressida,' was all he said, as his cheeks moved and reshaped under his fingers. 'Were you going to destroy it, or confront me with it?'

I still didn't speak.

Ivo took a deep breath and held out a hand. 'Can I see?' he asked, his voice still strange, even and lacking his usual exuberance. 'The cage?'

I unbundled my front and let the random collection fall to the floor in a shower of pieces. 'That's all I could find.' My voice didn't sound normal either. It was much smaller than usual, which wasn't surprising because I'd had to force the words out down a throat that felt as though I'd swallowed a mousetrap. 'I was really looking for the driving licence.'

Ivo looked down at the ramshackle bits and pieces. I saw his eyes flicker, taking in the catch, the screws, the bolts and the smashed wood, but he didn't really seem to be processing any of it. It was almost as though he was using the time to think of something to say. My heart began to beat faster, until I could feel it in my ears.

Please don't have anything to do with this. Please.

Eventually, and still looking at the floor, he spoke. 'Cress, do you trust me?'

I had no idea what to say to that. Part of me wanted to scream, 'I'd trust you to the end of the Earth, you mad, unpredictable fool!' but that would make me sound like the female lead in a 1950s film. Another part of me wanted to say, 'I like you a lot, but your behaviour is sometimes that of a person whose moral compass seems to have been assembled in a magnet factory.' But the hurt in his voice meant I had to say *something*.

'You were so sure there was something going on,' I said in a tiny voice, keeping my eyes on him. 'The driving licence that nobody has found, where *is* it? And you're sometimes just so...' I whirled one hand in a wordless indication. 'There's that book I saw beside your bed, about committing the perfect crime. You could be mixed up in all sorts. I wouldn't know.'

He stood up suddenly and walked over to the window. The rose knocked to come in again as another violent squall blew through. The windows boomed and rattled in the rapid gale and, for a moment, they were the only noise in here, apart from my heartbeat, which was trying to drown out the wind.

'You thought I'd searched the body and taken the driving licence, what, and the receipt?'

My silence must have indicated that this was precisely what I *had* thought.

'And you went up there to try to find it, so that I would be exonerated? Or to prove something to yourself?' Ivo sighed. 'Oh, *Cressida*. Do you really think I'd involve you if I were caught up in something shady?' Ivo asked at last. 'I mean, *seriously*?'

I didn't say anything again. It was beginning to dawn on me that, if Ivo really *had* got himself involved in anything illegal, then the last thing he'd want to do would be to bring someone else in. He could have pretended to investigate by himself and he wouldn't have had any inconvenient questions to answer, or someone berating him for burning the plum sauce. He could have sat in here, in his gentleman's smoking club of a living room, in his Dorian Grey outfits, and nobody would be any the wiser.

'I had to know,' I said finally, when it became obvious that he wasn't going to speak again until I did. 'You're odd, Ivo. You say it yourself. You could have *anything* going on in your head and I'm not sure that even a professional mind-reader could have any idea what it was.'

He turned around. The light of the window behind him made

it difficult to judge his expression because most of him was in shadow, with the rose banging frantically just behind his left shoulder as though the ghost of Gertrude Jekyll wanted a word. 'I don't have the driving licence, and I never touched the body. The book is a novel,' he said. 'It's rubbish, by the way. And I have ADHD. I thought you knew.'

'I thought that was for kids,' I said, feeling my brain expanding with the possibilities.

'You don't get better.' Ivo still sounded strange. 'I was diagnosed at eight, spent most of my adolescence medicated. Now I dip in and out of the tablets, depending on whether I need to be – normal, for want of a better word. I thought with you...' He stopped again.

ADHD. Attention deficit hyperactivity disorder. Of course. *Of course.* My mind felt like a giant Jenga as the thoughts, memories and probabilities slotted in. The randomness, the scattered behaviour. The occasional intensity. I should have seen it before – only I'd been too busy putting it down to drugs and a highly indulged upbringing. Those tablets I'd seen him take, the ones we'd never spoken about – not something illegal, to keep him awake or to sharpen his wits, but actual medication. *Of course.* The relief was so total it almost felt solid.

'Oh, Ivo,' I said, and I stood up now too. 'I am so sorry.'

'It's not something to be sorry about. It's just a thing about me. Like having blue eyes and a patch under my nose where I just can't grow a moustache.' He was still speaking as though he were disappointed in the world. 'I thought, with you, I didn't need to pretend.' He carried on talking, his face still shadowed by the outdoors. 'I thought you didn't care about the... about my eccentricities, shall we say? I really thought you liked me as I am.'

'I do.' I took a step towards him. 'I really, really do.' Oh no. No, Cressida, stop now before you... 'I liked you from the first time I saw you, pulling that stupid suitcase on wheels into our student flat, doing your Sebastian Flyte thing with that rubber duck of yours.'

Ivo coughed. 'You remember Donny the Duck? Wow.'

'Of course I do. I remember just about everything you've ever done, every expression that's ever crossed your stupid face, every daft comment and every weird outfit.' Too late now to start pulling punches. Everything was coming out and I couldn't stop if I wanted to. 'And I kept hoping you'd ask me out or want to hang out with me as more than part of the group, but you always went out with girls who were seven feet tall and looked like they should be on the cover of Vogue, and whose parents had the chalet in Switzerland next to where you skied.' I took a deep breath and tried to regain some composure. 'Or something like that.'

Too much, Cressida. But at least I managed to keep it all in the past tense, when every atom has been screaming to get into the present. This doesn't make me so vulnerable; there's nothing to fear in the past tense.

'But they were only...' He shook his head and the collar of today's absurd shirt flopped. 'No. No they weren't. And you could have asked *me* out, you know. Twenty-first-century, female-centric society, finger on the pulse of the zeitgeist and all that. Ah, well. We missed our chance there, didn't we? Those *tempus* have well and truly *fugit*. But I've been wondering about that driver's licence myself – where *is* it?'

There was a sensation in the middle of my spine, as though I were melting. The slow drip, drip of the loss of the tension that I carried in my shoulders whenever I was with Ivo; the horrible feeling that he might, at any time, explode into song lyrics or start clearing out a drawer while we were supposed to be revising, or helping with something, or that he might shut himself into his flat for a week and only emerge when tempted out with treats, like a rescue dog in a new home. It *wasn't* drugs and I *hadn't* imagined it. Ivo was just – well, being Ivo. But he was right. We'd missed our chance. Our time had been back then, when we were young and life could be stitched together from casual sex, late-night parties and frantic weekend revision sessions. Now we were grown-ups – no more Donny Duck, no more spontaneous relationships. That was then and this was… *safer*.

'I'm sorry,' I said again, with a little more emotion. 'I really never even thought.'

'Bet you thought it was cocaine. You did, didn't you? Coke, or some other substance that keeps me on my feet when everyone else is dropping; revising all night then leading a guided tour all day and dancing alone when everyone else has gone?' He sat, suddenly, in the armchair and a small puff of dust wafted up around him. 'This is my *brain*, Cress, and sometimes it just won't turn off. Of course, other times it won't fire up and I get over-faced by things that most people wouldn't even notice, but, hey.'

He looked at me. Tousle-haired, one side of his collar jutting up under his ear, the other side lying like a hound's tongue across his throat. 'This is me, Cressida, and I'm tired of pretending. I'm glad you're my friend. And please notice that those are two separate sentences and I'm not trying to get rid of you.'

There were blue shadows under his eyes, I noticed now. Things about Ivo that I'd carefully not seen because I thought they were symptoms of drug use, like the fact that he didn't always shave and he often looked – not tired exactly, but as though he had been living on fumes and excitement for days. I'd overlooked these things because of the general beauty of him, but now I looked properly and without the tiny, suspicious lenses of fear, he seemed ragged and tense.

I wanted to hug him. But I didn't dare. 'You are impossible, Ivo,' I said softly. But it meant something different now.

Into all this, my phone rang. Ivo jumped, I swiped at my pocket and knocked the phone to the floor, where it continued to buzz, raising more dust from the rug.

'Hey!' It was Ginny. 'Can I speak to Ivo, please?'

I looked at him, perched on the edge of his own chair with his eyes wide. 'Maybe better to talk to me,' I said gently, hoping that this was going to be news about Fred and not an offer of gig tickets. Being the third wheel in a relationship was kind of my default setting, with Lilith and Dix, and Ivo and whoever his latest gorgeous companion was, and I wasn't about to start it with her as well.

'Oh, okay. I've run Fred's test.'

'Wow, that was quick.'

Over on the chair, Ivo perked up. 'She's got a result? That's amazing, those machines must be really efficient.'

I shook my head at him sadly. Ginny had clearly given him priority treatment in an attempt to impress. Poor girl.

'We brought up all the current results and we got a match straight away, luckily your little guy is from an established colony.'

Established colony. That meant he *had* been brought in from somewhere else. 'Whereabouts?' I asked, trying to beat Ivo away from the phone as he attempted to listen in. I could have put it on loudspeaker, but didn't want to listen to more chat-up lines while Ginny flirted and Ivo... did whatever Ivo did.

'Isle of Wight,' she said, surprising me, because I'd been thinking of somewhere much closer, Cumbria, perhaps, or the Scottish borders. 'Your lad is genetically from there.'

'That's fabulous. Thank you so much.' My mind was whirling.

'And Ivo's not there?' Ginny's voice was dropping with disappointment. 'I wanted to ask him... something.'

Ivo made a 'ker-ching' gesture, listening over my shoulder, then shook his head when I looked at him questioningly and my heart rose. We'd both so nearly admitted to something, I didn't want real life to blow it apart, not just yet.

'Sorry, no. But thanks again.' I disconnected the call. 'We owe that woman a large bottle of something. Or, in your case, a date.'

Ivo raised an eyebrow and straightened his collar. His piercing fell out again. 'Can't go on a date,' he said cheerfully. 'I've got company, it would be rude.'

'Have you?'

'Well, kind of. You're here and I am attempting to feed you my duck in plum sauce, that's all the distraction I can cope with right now. Besides, she's got purple hair and that's a touch too try-hard for me.'

I shrugged. 'I'm only here because you felt sorry for me and my acres of snot.'

He laughed then and grabbed at my hand, whisked me into a 'waltzing' position and cantered the pair of us around the floor. I felt every finger pressed into the small of my back and the cool clutch of his palm against mine as though my body were made of Plasticine. Each touch would remain embossed into my skin forever.

'I do, and I did, and this is marvellous!' He half-sang the words. 'And Fred is from – oh, of course! Fist! Of course!' He laughed and I began to fear that our recent conversation had turned his brain.

'Back two steps, Ivo, and I don't mean dance-wise.' I was a bit breathless and it came out as panting.

'Fist! Mr Williams! I bet you a glorious date in a London eatery of your choice that he came from Andover! Andover Fist!'

Another turn around the furniture, as though the tiny living room had turned into the *Strictly* set.

'Oh, what? No, that's dreadful.'

'I'm not responsible for it, blame our B&B man with the sausage smell.' We whisked to a standstill beneath the window and Ivo bent me over backwards in the traditional 'final flourish'. 'He didn't really look as though he were up to quipping *bon mots* in Latin, did he? We, my dear Cressida, are off to the Isle of Wight to find out what our Fred was doing being carted all the way up here!'

He held me for a moment too long and our eyes met. His contained that wicked anticipatory look that I knew only too well. Ivo was plotting and planning, three moves ahead and several bits of paperwork behind and any regrets for the lost chance of emotional entanglement would have to wait.

'Are we?' It was all I could think of to say.

'You want to get Fred home, don't you?'

'We'll need to book the ferry,' I said, the voice of reason to his flight of fancy. 'And somewhere to stay, it's a long way and we won't get there and back in a day.'

'Oh, Ru has some friends with a holiday home there,' he said as carelessly as though this went without saying. 'Cowes week isn't until July; I'm sure they won't be down yet and we'll be able to borrow the place.'

'Stop it,' I said, but I was grinning. 'That's just ridiculously coincidental.'

Ivo gently released his hold on me, one finger at a time, so I didn't fall. I collected myself and my dignity and sat on the sofa, having to move another pile of newsprint to do so. 'No, no,' he said airily. 'Ru sails, or he did, before he joined the police. He may still do, not sure, I've got no interest in boats. But loads of his sailing friends have places on the island, for the yacht racing and all that, and I'm *pretty* sure I can blag us a couple of nights for business purposes.' He smiled. 'Sometimes being posh has its uses.'

'You are impossible.' I seemed to say this a lot lately. The smell of dust and burned sauce was getting through to my cold-thickened sinuses, so I went over to open the window, watching him watch me.

'I am. It's been said by many, many people. Pretty much every previous girlfriend, most of my teachers, two private tutors and my parents.' He sat on the arm of the sofa while I breathed in the welcome fresh air and peeled splattered rose petals from the glass panes. 'It's what I am though, Cress. Not *who* I am.' His voice was a lot softer now. 'And it's not always a bad thing. I think fast, I make connections other people don't; I *see* things other people don't because my brain is going a million miles a minute. If I'm really, really into something, then I can focus like nothing you've ever seen. To the exclusion of all else, actually, which, now I come to think of it, can be a bit of a bugger.'

I heard him get up and walk behind me and, even though he didn't touch me, I could feel him between my shoulder blades. 'But that's me, Cress. Like Alice, six impossible things before breakfast. I can't help it.'

I turned around and almost collided with him, he was so close. The lace from the ruffles on his shirt scraped against my cheek, it was like playing Sardines with Gabriel Rosetti. He smelled of burned jam and hot upholstery, but it was the most alluring perfume I'd ever smelled, and I was so tempted to reach up and touch his face, with those huge blue eyes boring down into mine, and cup my fingers over his carved cheekbones.

But I didn't. Instead, I took a small step back and a deep breath. 'I know you can't, Ivo. A lot of things make sense now,' I said gently.

'I've never made sense in my life.'

I let out a silent thank you to any gods that may be listening that he couldn't tell how very desperately I wanted to say, 'You do, to me.' Every inch of him exerted an almost magnetic pull, and for ten pence and a filthy duster I would have thrown myself into his arms.

But this was Ivo who wasn't like other men. I'd seen him careless with other people's feelings – not exactly "love 'em and leave 'em", he was more exquisitely mannered than that – and I couldn't have borne it if I'd reached up to touch his face only to have him back off in a state of well-bred horror amid stammered apologies. Nothing would ever have been the same again, and I'd rather have as much of Ivo as I currently had, than none at all.

'Ah, you're not that bad.' I had to smile then. He looked like a Labrador who'd heard his supper dish rattle. 'You might talk gibberish, but some of the actual words are kind of comprehensible. I'm sorry if being ADHD has made you feel that people look at you differently though.'

I got another grin but it was one that came with a self-deprecating swing of the shoulder. 'I cope. I survive. I just wanted you to know, that's all.'

'Thank you for telling me,' I said. 'But, look. We've got this whole business of Fred going on and we need to concentrate on that. I understand now why you're fixated on getting to the bottom of all this, I really do, but we need to make getting Fred home a priority.'

I watched Ivo's face as I spoke. I could see his acceptance of the facts in the way he ruefully raised his eyebrows and his mouth wandered about as though words were queueing up inside it. Finally he said, 'I am the king of inadequate multi-tasking. But you are right, I suppose. We need to get Fred home and I need to stop obsessing about finding out who Mr Williams was and why he was there. It doesn't, in the hugely enormous scheme of things, matter quite so much.' But there was a twitch to his lips that made me think he wasn't being entirely serious.

'We need to send something to Ginny to thank her for rushing Fred's results through. She must have put her own research on hold to...' I so nearly said, 'to impress you', but Ivo already knew that Ginny fancied him. I didn't want to push my luck by reminding him. 'To get them to us so fast.'

'Hmm.' Ivo scraped at one of the side tables with a fingernail. 'I hope you're not trying to talk me into taking her on a date. As I said, purple hair.'

I took a deep breath. I was his friend. That was all. 'You could have a quick dalliance,' I said. 'You've not been out with anyone for ages, and she seems nice.'

'I quite like the idea of being a dalliance.' Ivo had moved away now; he was back with the pile of newspapers. 'Makes me sound rather dashingly romantic, don't you think?'

'The phrase "dashingly romantic" just makes me think of premature ejaculation,' I said and gave him a severe look. 'And she may not even want to go out with someone who can't cook.'

'Oh, no problem there,' he said cheerfully.

'You burned the sauce!'

'I meant the premature ejaculation,' Ivo said, in a 'hurt' tone. 'But you're right. I'll send her something. Flowers?' He looked around the room. There was still a damp patch on the carpet from the last flower-related incident. 'Maybe not. I know, there's a gala dinner thing the police are holding, in aid of something or other, I'll send her a couple of tickets. I'm sure Ru's got some spare.'

'You don't think two tickets might send her the wrong message?'

He frowned, looked thoughtful, put a finger up to where his

piercing had previously precariously lodged, and then bent down to scan the carpet for it. 'Bugger. That keeps happening. Don't know why I bother with it. What message?'

'Message?' I'd got left behind again.

'What message might it send to the lovely Ginny if I were to donate her a couple of, very expensive, I may add, tickets to a policeman's ball? Ah, there it is.' He picked up the fallen eyebrow ring, stared at it for a second and then put it on the table. 'The pictures will go into *Country Life*. Or *Tatler*. She might like that.'

'Don't be obtuse, Ivo.' I gave him a stern look. 'She'll think you want to go with her.'

'I can't send her *one* ticket though, can I? That's like saying, "Hey, I know you're Belinda No-Mates, here, go to this party entirely on your own. You might meet a burly chief inspector to marry and have a load of little sergeants with."'

'You have a point.'

'Can I be absolutely clear here?' Now he sounded exactly like he did when he'd been making one of his speeches at the debating club at uni. Ivo was going to be a gift to politics one day, but whether it would be to his own side or the opposition I wasn't really prepared to say. 'You're saying that I can't send two tickets because she will assume that it's an invitation to a date. But I can't send her one ticket, because *that* would be an implication of utter loneliness and desperation. How many tickets would you consider to be optimal in this situation?' He gave me a smile of such charm that I could feel a spontaneous smile breaking out on my face. 'Bearing in mind that they're about a hundred and fifty quid a pop and I really can't afford to send her and an entire friendship squad?'

'Um,' was all I could say.

'Perhaps just the flowers then.'

'You,' I said, 'and I know I am repeating myself here, are

utterly impossible, Ivo.' My voice rasped a little with relief that he was dismissing, out of hand, the idea of taking Ginny on a date. Several of his previous girlfriends had had hair that had been far more startling than Ginny's purple.

'Well that's decided, excellent.' He swept out into the kitchen and I could hear him opening cupboards and clattering dishes and pans. 'Excellent!' he said again, jauntily.

I let my heart settle and my composure return before I went after him, to oversee the sauce.

7

The duck had been, as I knew it would be, excellent, as had the sauce. Ivo may have given the impression of having a butterfly mind, but when something got his attention, he could focus to the exclusion of all else and it made him a terrific cook. He also arranged for us to borrow his brother's friend's house, while I booked a ferry crossing, although I didn't mention the squirrel. If he'd been illegally removed, the paperwork to return him could have held us up for weeks, particularly if there was even the chance of any diseases among his compatriots. I really didn't think I could cope with weeks of Ivo's speculation while Fred languished in quarantine.

Bright and early the next morning, we packed up the car. Well, Ivo was bright. I'd had a somewhat disturbed and over-heated night on the sofa. Although Ivo had offered me his bed, I didn't think I would have slept any better there. In fact, it would probably have been worse, with the haunting thoughts of past lovers in every book and painting. So I'd stretched out on the long velvet couch and sweated into the perfumed air of the warm night, meanwhile overhead Ivo clattered about packing things and birds tap-danced on the guttering.

As a result, at 5 a.m. I was gritty-eyed and the remnants of the cold were making themselves felt in a headache and raspy cough.

'More nettle tea?' Ivo asked, in a sympathetic tone as I swept my meagre belongings into my holdall and wished I could look wistful and ethereal in my leggings and T-shirt, rather than like someone whose much needed yoga class has been evacuated.

'No, thanks. I'm fine, it's just a bit early.' I put my wildlife rescue jumper around my shoulders. I may need it, if anyone questioned me about Fred. 'I'm going to have to fetch a tetchy squirrel now. If I'm not back in ten minutes, he may have eaten me.'

'Deliciously edible as you are,' Ivo replied, pertly.

'Stop it. You sound more camp than that Noël Coward jacket of yours.' It was a quick rejoinder, to cover my ridiculous blush at his words. I didn't think there was anything personal in it, but a stupid tiny bit of my pride wanted to pretend that there might be.

'Well, it *might* have been Oscar Wilde, I'm still not really clear on that point.' Ivo pinged the car open and leaned against it, toning wonderfully with the morning in his scarlet block-print trousers and emerald green shirt.

'Neither of them was a bastion of alpha maleness though, were they?'

'I suppose not. But then, I've never been an alpha male. Nor, I suspect, a beta. I'm somewhere around the middle of the alphabet; if a lambda male is a thing, then I'm it. I can change a light-bulb and wrangle moths, but I cry at *Titanic* and hug everyone. What's that, in your Man Alphabet?'

I shook my head, 'I think it's just *you*, Ivo,' I said, leaving him looking smug while I went to crate up Fred for his long journey home.

'If this were a film,' I said to the cocked ears and bright eyes that met me when I went into the stable, 'you'd be getting together with a troupe of your squirrel friends to find your own way home.' I held the travel cage against the door. 'I suspect you'd be building tiny rafts and drawing maps on acorns or something.'

Fred tipped his head the other way and pinged around the cage.

'And the grey squirrels would be the enemy,' I carried on, lost in my world of cute cartoon animals. 'You'd have an unlikely ally; maybe a fox or something. Or an owl.'

Fred scuttled into the travel box and I closed the door. 'I have a horrible feeling that Ivo might be catching,' I said. 'The entirety of that previous whimsical statement is definitely more of an Ivo thing than a Cressida thing.'

Ivo had loaded our bags into the car, programmed the sat nav and left a corner so that we could wedge Fred into the boot. Now he was perched in the driver's seat with his legs sticking out of the car, watching me. 'Five hours, the sat nav says.' He leaned back and fiddled with the dashboard.

'We're on the three o'clock ferry. Plenty of time and we can share the drive.' I closed the boot, aware of Fred's little furry face peering at me through his bars. He was probably sick of being carted around the countryside like a difficult suitcase. 'You're going home, Fred.'

Fred passed no opinion on this. I strapped myself in, took a deep breath and said, 'Right Batman, let's high tail it for the hills.'

Ivo started the car. 'Am I Batman? I thought you were Batman.'

'Who are you then? You're definitely not Robin. Catwoman, maybe?'

He looked sideways at me. 'No. I'm the Joker,' he said and

there was a weight of meaning in his tone that made me think again of that book I'd seen beside his bed. *Committing the Perfect Crime.* Had he put it there on purpose, for me to see and misunderstand? But then I thought of the hurt on his face when he'd thought I didn't trust him, when I'd possibly suspected him of keeping information from the police.

'Ivo...'

'I've never told anyone about the ADHD thing, you know.' His voice was more normal now.

I didn't know what to say to that. 'None of the girlfriends?' I asked in the end.

He shook his head and he accelerated the car out onto the main road. 'No one. Some people may have guessed but nobody has been crass enough to ask. So I hope you feel special.'

I chanced a quick look at him but he was keeping his eyes on the road. 'I don't know what to say,' I said, truthfully. 'Thank you doesn't seem appropriate.'

'I just wanted you to know. None of it is deliberate. None of it. I don't do things to be annoying, and I don't forget stuff because I don't care. My executive functioning skills are non-existent, and I operate purely through the means of writing everything important down.' Another sideways look. 'I wanted you to know. Now, shall we have some music? What do you fancy? My playlist might be a little heavy on the pop side, so if you want to indulge your taste for thrash metal, now is not the time.'

We squabbled lightly about music until I fell into a doze, half-dreaming. His recent mentioning of the ADHD had puzzled me – was I really the first person he'd told outright about it? Or was he trying to make me feel special, for some reason? But then, the way he dropped it in then wheeled away, like someone throwing a huge rock into a still pond and being afraid of the ripples – that wasn't the mark of someone used to airing it regularly. He almost seemed ashamed, or afraid, when he mentioned ADHD, and I didn't know why. But then, my exposure to it was mostly limited to workmates talking about their own children or nieces and nephews and making it sound as though ADHD mainly caused a lot of noisy gardens and a need for help with schoolwork. Ivo had been brilliant at uni, and was restrained, often to the point of reticence.

We reached Southampton, with a couple of driver-swaps and opportunities to open the car up to let Fred have some fresh air, while we sat charging the car, and ate ice cream and debated the merits of London Grammar of whom Ivo, it seemed, was irrationally fond.

The ferry crossing was smooth, punctuated by boats that flew around us, all sail and elegance, like water-bound birds, and then we landed and drove off the ferry into what felt like 1950. Narrow lanes held cyclists and horse riders and we headed up a hill where little cottages hung over the road, all white paint and half-timbering. I half expected the Famous Five to wander into view amid the lacy wash of cow parsley and buttercups that ornamented the roadsides. It was improbably quaint and brought me out in a longing for fresh lemonade and gingham. As we climbed, the sunlight winked and reflected off the sea and seemed to illuminate the countryside in bright, sharp colours, as though the scenery had been painted in shades of acid.

'I thought we were staying in Cowes?' I asked, bewildered.

'*Sort* of Cowes.' Ivo was watching the sat nav. 'But a bit higher up.'

'A bit higher up' turned out to be a lap boarded building set amid treetops and looking out over the water, all carefully decorated and having more than a little of the 'curated' about it. The wooden roof arched overhead like a sail, the floors were boarded like a deck and self-consciously rounded windows like portholes peppered every wall. I wasn't sure if I was supposed to sleep here or take it out for a trip around the bay.

'Your brother's friends have a "thing" about boats, don't they?' I put my bag down in the hallway, a little afraid to walk any further in, just in case we cast off.

'Huh.' Ivo carried Fred inside and put his cage on the floor. 'At least it's available for us and we don't have to explain the squirrel.' He put the key back in the keysafe on the wall very carefully. 'There. Now we both know where it is.' Then, off my look. 'I lose keys a lot. Put them down and can't remember where or they fall out of my pockets or, I dunno, maybe the universe swallows them. Living with my brain feels a bit like that, you know. As though the universe is swallowing me up.'

He wandered through, down the wood-framed hall and into a large living room that jutted out above the trees to give the impression now that we were in a hot air balloon, floating towards the water. 'Nice enough, I'll give them that.'

'Not enough clutter.' I followed him. In contrast to Ivo's place, with the heaped bookcases, velvet sofas and general air of well-used antiquity, this house looked as though it was automatically scrubbed every morning. All linen and wood and clean lines – it must be like living in Sweden.

'They let it to film companies, when they're not down for the sailing,' Ivo said, picking up a little model of a yacht that sat on a wide window ledge. He said this as though it were the most natural thing in the world. 'I think it was once a major part of a Netflix series.' The boat went down and he stared out of the window. 'I take it this isn't your kind of place then, Cress?'

'It's very – well, it's a bit clinical, isn't it?' I looked at the neutral colours, the stonewashed rugs. 'Looks like you could do an appendectomy on the table.' I waved a hand at the adjustable light fittings that hung, hooked, on the beams above the table in question. 'I think I may have got used to pots of riding whips and enough old newspaper to housetrain several litters of puppies.'

'Good,' he said, 'far healthier way to live. Right. What now? Do we tout Fred about the streets stopping passers-by to ask if he looks familiar, or what?'

'"Do you know this squirrel" sort of thing?' I sat experimentally on one of the sofas. 'No. I've made contact with the local Squirrel People – they're the ones who look after the local population and who co-ordinate squirrel swaps. They're most likely to know Fred, or where he may have come from.'

'Oh Lord, the Squirrel People.' Ivo looked at Fred, who was perched outside the sleeping box with his tail curled up over his back. 'I think they may have featured in one of my more gin-sodden nightmares. So, when do we meet them? Do we have to wait for them to come down from the trees, or what?'

'Stop it.' I made room for him to sit next to me. It felt surprisingly natural to have him here, squashed against me by the bolster-like cushions on the sofa, as though we both sat on a cloud. 'No. I made an appointment for us to go over to their headquarters tomorrow morning and they're going to run their records, check Fred for a microchip, all that, for us.'

Ivo stared at Fred, who stared back with his tiny hand-like paws clasping the wire grill at the front of his cage. 'They microchip them?'

'If they're kept in captivity, yes.'

'Wow. I've only ever had dogs. Well, the family had a spaniel when I was young. And the horses, but they don't really count as pets.'

Ivo and Fred continued to eyeball one another, like a prisoner who knows they will be out any day now watching a guard who's been giving them a hard time.

'We have to be able to identify them,' I said reasonably. 'If they're breeding in captivity.'

Ivo stretched his legs out and arched his back, his shoulder moving against me. He'd done the majority of the driving while I'd slept and I felt a momentary guilt that I'd let him. 'I thought, maybe a page of mug-shots? Like a sort of squirrel *Crimewatch*.'

'Are you tired? Should we – have an early night or something?' I didn't edge away from having him so close. It felt as though the sofa was cuddling us together, and I was enjoying the sensation.

'Any reply I might make to that would sound sleazy and unworthy of me.' He jumped up again. 'No. Let's go out and have something to eat.'

I looked out of the window, across the treetops, which concealed the roofs of what looked like very expensive houses towards a town that had seemed, on our brief drive through, to consist of a load of Michelin stars, nailed together. 'Er,' I said. 'I'm not sure.'

'My treat.' He didn't look at me now, he swivelled his eyes back to Fred. 'I know the best places, after all.' Ivo held out a hand to me. 'Come on. There's a great little seafood shack tucked away off the beaten track; you'll love it. All fresh stuff, plaice and... and... well, they have fish.' He'd clearly exhausted his piscine knowledge, but I *was* hungry. 'And after that, maybe we could do a drive by of the Squirrel People's headquarters, suss out the lay of the land, all that.'

I took his outstretched hand. He was just so full of movement and enthusiasm that turning him down wasn't an option. I had a brief flash of what it would be like to be in a relationship with Ivo. A butterfly mind and a careless attitude to things – could I really ever want that? For this man, whose hand closed carefully around mine, who anticipated my reticence to spend money and knocked it away with his generosity; this man with his hair currently pointing in more directions than three dimensions could encompass, slightly stubbled and wearing a paisley shirt that gave fractals a bad name?

And I answered myself, silently. *Hell, yes.*

But he'd talked about wanting to date me purely in the past tense. I'd had my chance, apparently, although I hadn't known it at the time. My fear of getting involved with his flightiness and reckless disregard for things like deadlines had made me keep Ivo at arm's length when I could have been getting involved. And now? Now he was my friend, and knowing the reason for his shocking timekeeping and desperate week-long revision sessions had come too late. Half a decade ago I could have cast caution to the wind, although, I suspected that, in the case of dating Ivo, half of it would have blown back and hit me in the face.

That was then. This was now. And dinner – was dinner.

8

We ate in a tiny building up a sandy track, overlooking a bay where trees ran down to the sea like a playgroup day out and the rest of the coastline stretched itself out into the distant setting sun. A stack of rocks that could have been a ruin or just a geographical feature formed the back wall of the restaurant, and we ate fresh fish and debated whether the owner had insurance in case a landslide flattened his entire kitchen. It was the kind of conversation that Ivo was best at. He was never going to be a 'stand quietly and look at the sunset' person. At least, not for very long. By the time we'd finished, the sun had fallen into the ink-black sea and night had crept over the sky. It was too dark to hunt down what he insisted on calling the Squirrel People, who were really the local squirrel trust, so we went back to the boat house in the sky, fed Fred, and went to bed in rooms so widely apart that it felt as though we were making a point.

I slept in a tiny single bedroom up in the eaves, with Fred huffily clumping around his cage for most of the night. Ivo took one of the bigger bedrooms, which looked as though the captain of an eighteenth-century schooner had felt homesick and recreated his natural environment on land. It only needed a harpoon and some ropes and you could have keelhauled whales in there, or whatever it was you did to whales when at sea – my knowledge of cetaceans was limited to some lectures on dolphin rescue.

I lay awake for a while, listening to the unfamiliar calling of gulls on the roof and the distant swoosh and sway of treetops caught in a sea breeze. A few days ago I'd been wallowing in my sick bed, and now I was on the south coast of England with a man I was half in love with and an orphan squirrel. In a house that looked straight from a Sunday supplement advert, having eaten at possibly the most picturesque restaurant ever.

A brief memory from childhood flashed into my brain. My mother, in an uncharacteristically chatty moment, had pointed to a house we were passing as the bus droned up yet another hill on its way into town. 'I grew up there, you know,' she'd said.

The house had been, to my young eyes, huge. Old and detached in an orchard of, as I always remembered it, flowering fruit trees, with a scramble of outbuildings half concealed behind clematis and jasmine and a long driveway down to the road. I'd wanted to ask her then about her family, whether she'd had the brothers and sisters I felt the lack of so acutely, and what it had been like to be at the boarding school she'd occasionally dropped mention of. But when I'd looked at her face, reflected in the window of the bus's top deck, it had had such a sad, closed expression that I hadn't dared. She'd blown her nose and changed the subject, but every time I'd taken that journey subsequently, I had looked out for the honey-stone building amid the trees and wondered.

Much of the story had come out later, of course, but too late for me to be understanding during a childhood of coupon-clipping, penny-saving and charity shop clothing. Was that one of the reasons I found Ivo so attractive? Knowing that his upbringing had been very similar to the one I'd been denied? Was it less sex-appeal and more a second-hand jealousy that drew me to his carefree ways and careless generosity?

Grumpy gulls stamped on the roof with the noise of men in boots, gargling their cries to one another, and I pulled the pillow over my ears and went to sleep.

The next morning we drove out into the countryside and found the Isle of Wight Red Squirrel Protection Society, while Ivo complained about the lack of available vowels to turn them into a proper acronym.

'You just can't *say* IWRSPS,' he said. 'It's ridiculous. Sounds like some kind of visual impairment, where you see hornets all the time. They should think about their branding.'

The HQ was a Portakabin down a forestry track. Even the Volvo struggled with the pits and ridges of winter storms and large vehicles, and we ended up parking next to a big black van, which was evidently the Squirrel People's transport and no more able to cope with the churned-up surface than the Volvo.

'What do we tell them? Do we say where we found him? And what happened?' I asked, as we picked our way over the mountainous terrain of mud.

Ivo hesitated. For a moment his eyes flickered as though he were reading an internal list of instructions. 'Let's not,' he said.

'Why not, though? Surely, just asking if they've got an exchange programme going on isn't really a job for MI5, is it?' I tried, unsuccessfully, to tiptoe over the top of two ridges, the depths of which contained some unpleasantly greasy-looking water.

'Well, no. But it doesn't look like a straightforward job, does it? Midnight, moors, all that, it just has *clandestine* written all over it. So, they may not want to be admitting to anything, and might, in fact, lie to us. Let's keep it easy. We're finding out where he came from and who took him to Yorkshire, and then we can take it from there. Let's have it that you had the squirrel handed in to you and you're just returning him, shall we? See what they say to that. Hard to see that the world of illegal squirrel movement has stretched its hand out as far as Yorkshire, or even *why*, but, well, you never know.' He grinned at me. 'Come on.'

I stopped walking for a moment and Fred's cage swung perilously in my hand. 'Are you trying to make this mysterious again, Ivo?'

His smile was nine-tenths Puckish now. 'Maybe. Little bit.'

I 'tch'd' and then we pitched and tossed our way over the final bit of track and up the steps to the door, which opened to reveal an office full of hot electrical equipment and a desk. Behind the desk was a red head in a green jumper very similar to mine, except for the logo. She was hitting the side of a printer very hard and swearing. Fred instantly went into his sleeping quarters and hid. I wished I could join him.

She looked up when she saw us come in, her face tight and full of frustration. Then she saw the cage, my wildlife rescue jumper and put two and two together, although Ivo's eye-bending shirt was probably causing her to come up with the answer of fifteen.

'Ah! You're the Yorkshire people, yes? With a squirrel?'

Ivo gave her one of his 'set to stun' smiles and introduced us. I stayed quiet and watched his charm at work. 'We are, and we'd just like to know if you recognise him and where he may have come from,' Ivo said. 'Bit of a mystery, him turning up in Yorkshire.'

The girl, whose name label proclaimed her to be 'Sally', gave me a glance that seemed to have some suspicion built in. 'I'll scan him as soon as I can find the scan gun,' she said, her local accent as soft and rolling as the waves. 'No idea what one of ours would be doing away from home, though.'

'No exchange programmes or anything?' I asked.

She hesitated, momentarily, and I wondered whether she suspected us of stealing Fred and was waiting for us to ask for money to return him, but her pause was seemingly only occasioned by the need to give the printer another battering. 'Not as far as I know, but they don't always tell me. In fact, they frequently don't tell me if we're moving offices or firing people, I'm meant to find out through osmosis. Ah, here it is.' Sally moved a pile of printer paper and gestured to me to put Fred's cage down. I saw her glance sideways at Ivo and frown again. She definitely thought we were up to something, although she might just have been stunned by Ivo's sex-appeal.

Expertly, Sally opened the cage and grabbed Fred in a fist. His little head protruded, looking hugely indignant, but he stayed still while she ran the microchip detector around the back of his neck and stared at the readout. She frowned again and bit her lip.

'Well, he's definitely one of ours,' she said slowly. A moment of clattering on a keyboard and she stood back, looking a little worried. 'Yep. He's 13721. Two-year-old male, found as a newborn in Borthwood copse and raised in our unit here where we keep the squirrels that we hand rear for one reason or another and that can't be released.'

She was still speaking slowly, as though trying to come to terms with Fred's sudden appearance.

'Wow, 13721? We've been calling him Fred.' Ivo looked at the little squirrel, still being held by Sally, but now looking resigned to his fate, like a prisoner of war who's tunnelled out and made it to the border, only to be recaptured.

'Fred. Yeah, that's a good name.' Sally looked at us again.

'How did you get hold of him?' The suspicion was leaking out in her voice now.

I opened my mouth, but Ivo leaped in. '*Bit* of a long story, he was – removed from someone and given to our Cress here, who works for a wildlife unit.'

'Removed? What, like surgically?'

'Someone found him, that was all. He was loose up on the moor.'

Sally smiled now and it made her slightly pale face become animated and lovely. Ivo smiled back. He also looked animated and lovely and I felt like an Ugly Sister, but I smiled too, just in case anyone was looking at me. Ivo was being so economical with the truth that it would probably last for a week. I wondered why, then reasoned that it was his reporter's instinct at work. Either that or he'd watched too many *Miss Marple* episodes and was keeping back information for his own reasons.

'Oh.' Sally looked at Fred again. 'I wonder how he got there? That's very strange, as far as we knew he was still out in our unit.' Her words sounded a little forced, as though her brain was busy and I saw her glance, just once, quickly at the window beyond which the shadowy figure of a man came and went. 'But then we don't exactly count heads. And I suppose there's a chance one of the others here might have agreed a movement, and I've just not seen the paperwork. But if he was being moved properly he should have been in a transporter case; how come he was loose?'

'We think the case must have got broken or otherwise disposed of,' I said. 'And Fred escaped.'

'No sign of it?'

I was about to tell her that I'd found it, smashed, but Ivo interrupted. 'Oh, and by the way.' He pulled a piece of paper from his pocket. 'Any idea who this might be? We think he might have had something to do with Fred being in Yorkshire.'

It was the drawing he'd done of the deceased Mr Williams. Sally took it and I saw a quick flash of surprise cross her face. 'Weeeelll,' she said slowly, 'I'm not completely sure, but it does look a bit like a guy I've seen hanging round with Tony.' She looked up into Ivo's face. 'When you say "might have had something to do with Fred being in Yorkshire", do you mean that there's something fishy going on?'

Ivo laughed his best carefree laugh. It was very convincing and I wondered how many times it had taken me in. 'No, nothing like that. Nothing suspicious. Just someone said they saw a man who looked like this who possibly had something to do with squirrels, and we're – well. We're just nosy, aren't we, Cress?'

A printer beeped on the other side of the room and threw out about fifteen sheets of paper, then two red lights came on and it stopped.

'Tony. Is he man or squirrel?' Ivo went on and Sally laughed. I adjusted my position in the corner and tried not to feel like a third wheel.

'Tony. He works here. In fact, I think he's round the back in the unit. But he can be a bit...' She waggled her hand. It was still enclosing Fred, who waggled with it and looked even more resigned. 'Strange. I sometimes wonder...' She tailed off, stretching out a leg and giving the newly jammed printer a hefty work-boot to the side. 'Bloody cheap equipment!'

'We have the same,' I sympathised. 'Told to print out a hundred and fifty leaflets advertising a fundraiser, but it's not that easy when the printer jams every five copies.'

She nodded and I was worthy of a smile now. 'I sometimes think it would be quicker to sit down with a pack of crayons and just do them myself. How are we supposed to raise money when we can't even print out the begging letters?'

'Right, well, if you two have finished bonding over rubbish

electronics, can we let Fred in with his fellow squirrels?' Ivo asked, with a nod to the still enfisted Fred. 'He's probably had more than enough of being portable. We'd love to see him return home, especially Cress, who's been looking after him.'

As he spoke, he gave me a sidelong look with a hint of something in the depths of his eyes, behind the otherwise bland appeal of his gaze. I wasn't quite sure what it was, but it looked like he wanted my agreement.

'Yes, I'm going to miss him horribly,' I said. It was true, to a degree. Without Fred, without all this tiptoeing about trying to detect things, I'd have no reason to stay at Ivo's and torture myself with thoughts of what might have been. But I would miss the squirrel.

'Oh.' Sally looked out of the Portakabin window behind her. Looking properly, I could see a large fenced enclosure out there, and a man who now seemed to be sweeping in a sullen fashion. 'I'm... I'm not sure. Tony doesn't really like strangers very much.' She lowered her voice, although Tony could only have listened in if he'd had the hearing abilities of a bat. 'He has some mental health problems, you see,' Sally said, confidentially. 'Can be a bit prone to – well, irrational acts, if you see what I mean. Nice as pie one minute and the next...' She mimed an explosion. In her fist, Fred corkscrewed through the air wearing a deeply pissed off expression.

'We'll be very circumspect,' Ivo pressed the point. 'Truly.'

I stared again at the figure outside, a shaded outline beyond the grubby windows, and hesitated. I really did not want to have to come face to face with someone who might start swinging at us with any work equipment he had to hand.

Out of Sally's line of sight, Ivo trod deliberately and slowly on my foot. 'It would mean a lot,' I said, somewhat tightly. 'I'm going to miss having Fred about the place.' The weight of Ivo on my instep added a tiny bit of emotional wobble to my voice and I saw him give me the smallest of nods.

'Well, all right. I'll come and introduce you. He's a little volatile and I don't want to risk him storming off.' Sally seemed to remember she still had the squirrel in her hand then, and diverted via her desk to poke him into his travel cage. Fred shook himself and started to groom his fur. 'He's really keen on the job, and it's hard to find people who stick around once they realise it's mostly photocopying and fundraising.'

'Oh it is, isn't it!' I burst out. This was one of the banes of my life, along with Dix's inability to hold a tune in the shower and having Ivo as a friend. 'So many people think it's all nursing wounded animals back to health and grateful looks as we release them back into the wild. Lots of cuddling fox kits and badger cubs.'

Sally threw me a look of understanding. 'People underestimate the sheer amount of shovelling, don't they?'

'Nobody ever wants to muck out. Or get up in the middle of the night because someone has reported a goose struck by a car on the A170 that you know is going to be gone before you get there.'

'And the biting! So much of the job is getting bitten!'

We grinned at each other. Any enmity I'd felt towards Sally, which had mostly been occasioned by her admiration of Ivo admittedly, evaporated in our mutual admission of the sheer drudgery and physical pain that working with animals incurred.

'Right, lovely bonding moment,' Ivo said. 'Now, are we going to let Fred go, because I want to show Cress some of the beaches while we're here.'

'You're here on holiday?' Sally was a little perkier now we'd stopped talking about the frustrations of small-animal management.

'Oh yes. Just for a couple of days. Heading back tomorrow. I've been before, but Cress has never visited, so we're going to have some nice meals, do some sightseeing, that sort of thing.' Ivo bounced.

'Good idea!' Sally's whole demeanour had changed. Her face had relaxed from its tightly worried expression and she looked far more animated as she picked up the cage and began a monologue of the best beaches on this bit of the Isle, throwing in advice to visit a ruined castle and a brewery too.

I frowned to myself. Ivo hadn't mentioned beaches to me. Was this another example of his butterfly mind coming out with the first idea to occur to it? Or had he said that for a purpose?

We went out of the Portakabin by a back door, which brought us, via another set of muddied stairs, to the front of a large wire-mesh pen. In fact, it wasn't just large, it was huge. Inside it, I could see the man who'd been visible through the window armed now with a set of clippers, trimming back some undergrowth. His head was bent and he wasn't wearing gloves; his hands were a mass of scratches and beads of blood.

'Tony!' Sally called across. 'These guys have a returned squirrel! Number 13721, apparently found up in Yorkshire, which is a bit of a mystery.'

Tony looked up. He was dark and stubbled and his uniform stretched across wide shoulders. '*Thought* I hadn't seen him about lately,' he said, coming over and rolling back the sleeves of his coat to reveal arms also covered in scratches. 'He's a devil for making me worry. I was wondering if he'd gone into one of the nests and – well – died. I was going to start looking for him when I'd finished this.'

Reassured by his not immediately assaulting us with the broom, I gave Tony a small smile, but worried a tiny bit about him going to look for a deceased squirrel. What was he going to do with it if he found it?

'No need now.' Sally handed me Fred's cage. 'He's back.'

I opened the front of the cage, which now had a Fred stuck to it. He swivelled out into the open air, eyeballed me, and then flung himself into the nearest bush, from where he scurried up to a branch and sat, looking down on us. 'Bye, Fred,' I said, slightly sadly.

'Oh, you called him Fred? I call him Swoop because he's a devil for suddenly dropping down right by you and making you jump!' Tony said, watching the little squirrel with happy interest.

'Do you give them *all* names?' Sally asked, almost impatiently. 'I mean, how can you even tell them apart?'

Tony shrugged. 'Like people. They've all got different faces y'know, Sal. You just have to look at them properly. Take your time, and all that.'

'Nice if you can,' she retorted, sharply. 'I have to do the paper-work. It's all right for you being able to be out here, faffing and fiddling and being "at one with nature", some of us have to deal with keeping the place running.'

'Oh, ah,' Tony said, in a tone of such resigned agreement that I knew this argument was perpetual. I was mildly reassured that Sally didn't seem to feel that he was so volatile that she had to soothe his feelings at all times, and I felt a knot of tension in my stomach begin to relax. I'd been preparing myself to hide inside the Portakabin if Tony had reacted badly.

I thought that Ivo might whip out the picture of Mr Williams for Tony at this point, but he didn't. Perhaps, like me, he was unwilling to risk an outburst when we were shut in a metal cage with no form of protection but some spindly trees and an unseen audience of squirrels. Sally didn't stomp off back to her printers either despite the fact that we could hear something whirring and clicking uselessly inside the Portakabin. Overhead, Fred clung to his branch for a second longer, peering down at us between the hazel leaves, which, highlighted by the sun shafting between the trees, shone like emerald chips. Then he stretched and yawned, giving us a glimpse of incredibly large teeth for such a tiny mouth, and bolted upwards to vanish in a haze of green and gold.

'Could we... could we come back and say goodbye?' Ivo asked tentatively. 'Before we leave?'

I, who had been thinking we'd head for home today, and who would be more than glad not to have to spend another night amid lime-washed wood and taut linen, frowned. 'Shouldn't we let Fred settle? He's been disturbed enough, what with – well, being deserted on a moor.'

Ivo gave me a sideways look that was unreadable. 'But you'll miss him, won't you, Cress?' He leaned against my shoulder. 'Just pop in to say goodbye before we head home; we'll never see him again, remember.'

I wanted to point out that, should I have felt the need to say goodbye to every animal that I rescued before either it, or I, left, I would never get anything else done, and that the animals wouldn't care and would most likely be relieved if they never saw me again. But I didn't. Ivo's weight against my shoulder seemed to render me dumb.

Sally looked at us thoughtfully. Tony picked up his clippers again and began snipping away, adding to the trailing tangle of offcuts at his booted feet. 'I suppose it wouldn't unsettle the squirrel too much,' she said slowly. 'If you just wanted to say goodbye before you left.'

'They don't mind.' Tony forced himself further into the bramble thicket, thorns squealing against his sturdy coat. 'As long as you don't bring a brass band. And young Swoop, he likes a bit of human company so he'll probably be around.'

From high in the tree above our head there came a quick kerfuffle of shaken branches and squeaks, as though a high-pitched wind had moved through. Leaves fell and scattered on our shoulders.

'Only, I ought to be here; it's my job to keep an eye on visitors,' Sally added.

'I'll be here,' Tony said comfortably. 'It's fine, Sal.'

Sally, clearly uncomfortable with the thought, bit her lip again. I side-eyed Tony and wondered about the nature of his sudden explosions. He'd not shown any hints of sudden explosive anger since we'd been here, but maybe that *was* the problem? If he could go from the laid-back tidying up persona to irrational and potentially violent fury without warning, then I guessed it could be dangerous.

'I can be around,' she said finally. 'Tomorrow morning.'

'Oh, we won't be leaving late,' Ivo said blithely. 'We've got a long drive and we need to get back.' His ability to extemporise so casually astonished me and I realised that Ivo could be very good at what he did, when he wanted to. He had a swift capability that I'd never seen before and I wondered whether the 'baffled buffoon' that irritated and intrigued me in equal measure was only half the story of the man.

Sally seemed to relax. 'That will be fine, then. I have to be at a school to do an educational visit at twelve, so if you can be here before then, that would be great.'

As she led us to the enclosure gateway, not giving us any further chance to look around at the squirrels, I heard her phone ring in her pocket. She opened the complicated mechanism that kept the wire-mesh door closed, ignoring the unidentifiable tune playing somewhere in her trousers and I looked back over my shoulder to see Tony leaning against a tree and watching us go. Low, diagonal beams of sunlight blurred his edges and the green of his shirt and trousers blended him even further into the background.

Ivo was trotting alongside Sally and engaging her in conversation about the best, and quietest, beaches. He almost seemed to have forgotten I was there.

We trooped back through the Portakabin, knocking the mud from our boots on the top step, and Sally led the way briskly through, between the clicking and flashing machines. Her phone had stopped ringing now, but she took it from her pocket and laid it on the desk without looking at it. I knew what that was like; when you were on duty the phone almost never stopped with reports from the public about random swans, loose cattle (not our problem), adders in the forest and injured deer. It was hard to have a single conversation without being interrupted by pleas for help, and I admired her for being able to not answer. I bet she'd snatch up the phone and return the call as soon as we were out of sight, just in case it was an animal in need of urgent attention – ours was a job it was very hard to put on hold, and the guilt you felt for not permanently being available could be incredible. Sally was clearly very good at what she did.

As we walked through to the main doorway, I noticed an unusual printer, sleek and black, half tucked under a desk. It gleamed a green light amid all the red and orange 'jam warning' and 'out of paper' that illuminated the inside of the office like tiny fairy bulbs. Something clearly *did* work; it looked modern and extremely hi-tech, and I would have asked Sally about it if she hadn't been sweeping us so quickly back through the office to the entrance. It looked like something we ought to have in our workplace, indestructible and efficient, and I made a mental note to ask what it was when we came back the next day.

'I'm really sorry,' Sally said, when she could get a word in edgeways past Ivo's profuse thanks. 'I would have loved to give you a tour of the place, or show you our rescue facility, but' – she waved a hand to indicate the Portakabin, from whose windows reflected warning lights were throwing tiny flickers onto the fresh leaves of the overhanging trees – 'there's just so much to do and only me and Tony to do it, and I have to get the resources prepped for the school visit and none of the machines are playing ball.'

'I would have loved to have seen everything,' I said, genuinely. 'But it's fine. We'll pop back tomorrow to check that Fred has settled back in and then we'll head back to Yorkshire, but I hope we can stay in touch.'

'Of course!' She seemed more effusive now; perhaps my obvious enthusiasm and disappointment in missing out on seeing any more of her projects had endeared me to her. Or perhaps it was the possibility of staying in touch with Ivo, as she was clearly very taken by him, with his excellent bone structure and classy accent.

'And you ought to return that phone call,' I said, nodding back through the office to where the phone sat on her desk.

'Oh! Yes,' Sally spoke slowly now. 'Yes, I suppose I ought.' She eyed me thoughtfully again. 'It might be something that needs urgent attention.'

'It usually is, isn't it?' I wondered why she seemed to think I may be responsible for this, then realised that she would be holding me responsible for being here and thus preventing her from answering in the first place.

Sally waved us off, watching as Ivo turned the Volvo in the narrow muddy space at the top of the lane and raising a final hand in farewell as we shot off back to the proper grip of tarmac.

'You didn't show Tony the picture.' I turned in my seat to face Ivo.

'Didn't want the chance that he might go off on one, not with you there in the firing line,' he said. 'That's why I want to come back tomorrow, I can do it then, if you distract Sally and stand somewhere a really long way away. Oh, thanks for agreeing to stay the extra day, by the way.' He gave me half a smile and a wink. 'There's a few things I'd like to check out before we go back, and I really do think you could do with a holiday.'

The competence that I'd seen in him was fading now, as though he found it an effort to maintain. It seemed to be breaking down into the usual good-natured bafflement that was my Ivo.

'Me? Why would I need a holiday?'

'You've been unwell. You need to recuperate.'

'Which is precisely why I took the week off work, and yet I've been dragged to the far ends of the Earth in search of a squirrel-smuggling racket that has yet to be resolved,' I said, smartly. I didn't want our killing time on the Isle of Wight to somehow become my fault. 'I ought to be lounging around in the sun, eating vitamin-C tablets and drinking orange juice, not spending my time in some millionaire's playpark.'

Ivo said nothing for a moment. He drove carefully down the narrow lane, overhung with fresh green and surrounded by banks woven with pink campion and ragged robin, overtopped by the umbrellas of cow parsley and hemlock. Grass scraped the Volvo's bonnet, sending cascades of pollen blossoming into the air like tiny escape pods.

Finally he spoke. 'What do you think is going on there?' He sounded as though he really cared about my answer.

Going on? Apart from chronic underfunding, with which I

was only too familiar, I hadn't noticed anything suspicious at all. '*Is* there anything going on?'

Ivo looked at me and it was a look of peculiar intensity, as though his thoughts were off elsewhere doing their own thing but leaving his body here to drive the car. 'I don't know,' he said. 'But I was itching in there. Oh, not *actually* itching, not like an allergy or anything, more... more a kind of itching in the back of my head, do you understand?'

'Can't you just have a spidey sense, like other people?' I asked and he grinned now, ruefully.

'I know, I know, it sounds weird. I *am* weird, I admit it! Not exactly your normal, run-of-the-mill, "the two defendants were found guilty of stealing a motorbike and there's another cow stuck in the river at Malton" local journo, am I? But I really and truly can't help it, Cress; I don't *want* to help it, this is who I am. How I am. Things just sort of prickle away in my brain and I can't let them go until I've processed it all properly and something about this whole squirrel thing is going niggle, niggle, niggle. I need to ask Tony about the bloke in the picture.' A car was approaching down the narrow lane and Ivo slowed the Volvo. The oncoming vehicle was coming faster than was wise.

'You may have missed your chance.' I had no idea how he could do this. On the one hand he was mentally working on the mystery of Fred as though it were something he needed to solve, and on the other – on the other he was being Ivo as I'd always known him. As though two men existed within the same body, fighting for dominance.

'I know. I'll try tomorrow, while you're distracting Sally. I get the feeling that she thinks Tony will actually detonate on impact or something, but I didn't get the feeling that he was that kind of person, did you?'

'No,' I said slowly. 'But then people with anger issues don't exactly have it tattooed on their foreheads, do they? If everyone had their personality problems out there front and centre, it would make life so much easier for everyone.'

'Would it?' He twitched the wheel and the car tilted at an uncomfortable angle, two wheels breasting the grassy edge to the road to allow the SUV to pass us in the lane, heading down towards the forest. It was still going too fast and made no attempt to get out of our way. 'Do you actually think I'd have an easier life if I had "can't concentrate, random focus, unable to order life correctly" where everyone could see? Seriously?'

I had a tiny inkling now of what it must be like to be Ivo. That duality of concentration versus distraction, at war inside his head all the time, must be exhausting. Something warm hit me in the heart as I realised just how many times I'd seen him fight himself to stay in a conversation when I'd thought he was being deliberately awkward. In reality he'd really been struggling. The feeling wasn't pity, it was more like admiration.

'Okay, maybe not.' I closed my eyes. Ivo wasn't my weird friend any more. He was a man who carried demons, demons he'd let me see for the first time. Things were, as Lil would have said, 'getting way complicated'. 'Fred didn't seem that keen to run back to his mates, did he?' I asked, half sleepily, to change the subject, and probably rhetorically since Ivo hadn't really been watching.

'Mmm.'

I opened one eye, but Ivo was concentrating on the road, flipping glances into the mirror to watch the SUV squeezing its way down the inadequate width of the lane behind us. 'Maybe...' I said cautiously, and then stopped.

'Maybe, what?'

So he was listening to me. 'Maybe there really *isn't* any mystery? Maybe Tony's friend "borrowed" a squirrel, just to show off, maybe he has a girlfriend he wanted to seduce by means of a cute furry animal?'

'In *Yorkshire*?' Ivo's incredulity rang around the inside of the car like the singalong pop songs he was so fond of.

'Yorkshire girls are allowed to date out of county,' I pointed out. 'We're not constrained to only mating with our own kind.' This was the Ivo I was used to; it was reassuring to have him asking random questions again.

'I suppose so.' Ivo tapped at the wheel, a tune only he could hear. 'But unless someone comes forward, it's going to be impossible to find out who he was meeting up there. If, indeed, he was meeting anyone and not just going for a particularly ill-advised late-night walk. With a squirrel.'

'In a box,' I added. 'Which, somehow, got broken.'

Tap, tap, tap. Ivo's inner tune stepped up the tempo. 'Could have broken when he fell though.' He flashed me a quick grin.

'And thrown itself off into the bushes beside the track?'

'You sound like me now.' The grin widened. 'I thought you were all about the "just an innocent man taking his pet for a wander"?'

I chewed my lip, thinking. But it was hard to think seriously when Ivo was giving it his best *Columbo*, and just having him sitting beside me was distracting enough. 'If the box broke when the man fell, it could have been trampled and kicked off the path. There are a lot of deer tracks up there, and it would only take a few coming through to smash up one of the transport boxes; they're not exactly reinforced oak planking. I broke one once by stepping on it, so, it could happen.'

'Oh I do love an analytical mind!' Ivo pulled the car over into a gateway and stopped. 'So, the transport boxes aren't particularly strong?'

'They don't have to be. For small animals you want to keep

them safe from the outside, not the other way around, and we sometimes have to carry the boxes quite a long way. So we need them light, easy to carry and as long as they fasten tightly so the animals can't get out – that's the main thing. If the carry box was what Mr Thixendale mistook for a bag, maybe Mr Williams was using it to keep other things in, like his driving licence? So *that* might have got lost somewhere out in the forest too.'

'Oh.' There was a despondent tone in Ivo's voice now. As though I'd told him unicorns weren't real, a kind of reinforcement of a fact that went against a hope he'd held dear. 'Bugger. You make it all sound completely rational. I was thinking something nefarious might have happened to it. That out there now there's someone who's stolen our Mr Williams' identity and is, even now, running up huge debts and hiring helicopters in his name. That, or aliens took it.'

'I'm sorry.'

'No, no, you're perfectly right. I'm getting carried away again, aren't I? It's part of my problem, I get an idea in my head and that's it, fixed, and it won't go away until I can positively prove that I'm wrong. But your idea sounds so... so sensible. No mystery other than why he took the squirrel, and that might have just been because he could.'

He was giving me another insight again. Little by little, I thought, Ivo was opening up, becoming less of the one-dimensional happy-go-lucky friend and more... something else. I had no idea how to deal with that, so I went for matter of fact.

'And why he took it up on the moor in the middle of the night.'

'Yeah.' But he didn't sound any more cheerful. Ivo not cheerful was a difficult concept; anyone who wore blue velvet trousers and a shirt that Adam Ant might have regarded as being a little too 'over the top' practically had cheerful fitted as standard. But now he dropped his head forward until it rested on the steering wheel in an attitude of abject misery that made me ache.

'Why don't you take me to one of these beaches you keep going on about?' I tried. 'You told Sally we were on holiday. You told *me* I *needed* a holiday, but you're acting like a nineteenth-century poet who's just had his daffodils napalmed.'

Ivo tipped his head so that he could see me. 'I'm having a wallow,' he said.

'I can see that. But it occurs to me that wallowing isn't good for you, whereas walking on a beach and possible paddling would be a lot better for your mental health.'

He grunted and turned back to face the dials and buttons of his dashboard. 'Lewis would never have said that to Morse, you know.'

'But Morse was his boss, and you're my...' I caught myself just in time, before I found I was trying to define whatever it was that we had. '...you're the Mitchell to my Webb.'

'I'd have said I was the Stephen Fry to your Hugh Laurie, myself.' As though the change of subject had jerked him out of his misery, Ivo sat up again. 'After all, I've got the Oscar Wilde jacket. Possibly. Or Noël Coward.'

'So, let's go to the beach.'

'Oh, all right.' Another grin, broader and more filled with mischief than the last. 'You're really good for me, Cress, you know that?'

As the car bumped back out onto the narrow lane and the sunlight reached us again from between the high banks and overhanging trees, I wondered to myself how I'd got drawn into all this. I mean, yes, obviously, *Ivo*, but he was, as we'd established, just a friend. He was gorgeous, that went without question, with the most brilliant mind I'd ever met. But was that brilliance at the expense of other people constantly having to buff it up and polish it to keep it shining? With their own mental gloss being overlooked?

Could I, in short, really stay his friend? Could I seriously see myself riding shotgun forever on his more elaborate schemes, while he carried on wooing and winning the girls on the sidelines? It had been fine up until now, but this new version of Ivo, with the confidences and the unwarranted intimacies, could I *seriously* have a friendship with him, without breaking my heart? It already felt as though I was treading too close to a self-drawn line that I hadn't been aware of. I *knew* Ivo now, not the superficial, amicable, almost sibling-like knowledge I'd had before, but seeing him as a real, complex person. Which had only made him more attractive and heartbreak more inevitable.

I'd been stupid. I'd blindly set myself up as the 'good friend'. Ivo had needed someone to talk to – and there I had been. Here I was, pretending that I was here to keep him company when really I had wanted more of Ivo than he could give, and deep down I knew it. I had *always* known it.

And it hurt.

9

We found a beach and spent a happy few hours collecting shells and dabbling our feet in the fabulous blue water. Ivo bought me an ice cream and I bought him a huge whirl of candy floss, uncertain as to whether putting sugar into a system that was already rebounding to levels of energy unequalled by anybody over the age of seven was such a good idea.

I kept all my thoughts to myself. Agonising over my stupidity gave me an almost pleasurable pain, after all, here I was. Beautiful beach, fabulous scenery, and the man I cared about most in the world – I had everything, didn't I? I wanted to bang my head against something for my idiocy, but as Ivo was the only solid thing to hand, I didn't.

Ivo marvelled at the intricate swirls of the shells, at the colour of pebbles and the feel of the dark ridged sand under our feet. It was a little bit like being with an alien who had just beamed down onto the planet, such was his joy and focus on things that I took for granted.

'Don't you have an off switch?' I asked, licking the remainder of my Mr Whippy out of the end of the cone.

He thought for a second, looking down to watch the tide sucking shingly sand around his bare toes. 'You sound like my ex-girlfriend,' he said. 'And the one before that.' His tone was neutral, observational. 'Am I that difficult to be around? Seriously, Cress?'

I frowned. 'It's just that you make me feel...' *Careful, Cress...*

'Tired? Annoyed? Frustrated that you can't get a word in? Irritated because I'm not paying attention?'

'...one dimensional.'

That stopped him. He'd been listing provocations almost resigned, running through them like a litany of faults he'd heard so many times that they'd become defining characteristics. Now he had to think.

'*I* do? Make you feel...'

'One dimensional, yes. As though I'm plodding along on a single path, while you're taking all the interesting diversions, absorbing all the views and then coming back to me a bit sad that I haven't seen what you have.' It was true. Discounting all the *other* ways he made me feel, this feeling that I was slightly inadequate led the way.

'Wow.' Ivo pushed his hands into his pockets, making the sleeves of his shirt roll up and exposing his wrists, long and pale, to the sun. His hair flopped down, hiding his expression as he perused his feet, splayed across the sandy ridges through the bubbles and splashes. 'That makes me sound a bit like a red setter.'

'There are certain points of similarity,' I said, and then smiled when he looked up to meet my eye. 'Aristocratic, long-haired, inability to come when called.'

Now he waded towards me, clonking slightly because of all the shells he had pushed into his pockets. They bulged, making him look as though he'd gained weight in very specific places. 'I always come when called, Cress,' he said, almost inaudibly over the sound of a nearby set of toddlers shrieking into the water armed with buckets. 'Always. I might not be reliable on my own time, but if you need me – I will be there.' He touched my shoulder. 'And thank you.'

'For comparing you to a red setter?' He actually looked a lot more like an Afghan hound right now, with the sun shining on his blondness and bone structure that jutted like a pyramid.

'For making this' – he put both hands alongside his head and wiggled his fingers – 'sound like a positive thing. Sorry, by the way, if I make you feel a bit weird, I truly don't mean to, I can't help thinking along fifty different lines at once and choosing the most interesting one to follow up. It's just the way I'm wired and I do try to keep a handle on it.'

'Could be worse,' I said, trying cheerily to lift his slight mood of sadness. 'After all, it's your following up of the strange squirrel affair that's brought us here, and you were right, I did need a holiday.' I waved a hand, indicating the beach, which was filling rapidly, and the multicoloured cliffs. 'This is lovely.'

This was reassuring. I could keep the 'we're just friends' act going, all light-hearted and cheery. Inwardly I congratulated myself on my acting skills. I'd not had much call to exercise them on the British wildlife, but they were turning out to be a pretty good asset.

'Come on then.' Ivo grabbed my hand. 'If you like this, you'll love this little cove I know. We can pick up a picnic, head over there, sit on the cliffs and watch the sun go down, to round off the day.'

From another man this would have sounded like a romantic proposition. I looked at him sideways. 'That sounds nice. Cheaper than going for dinner, too.' *Friends, friends, we're just friends, tralalala.*

My jaunty tone and evident practicality made him tilt his head. Suddenly I was being scrutinised in a way that felt a little like being under a spotlight. 'We can talk, is what I meant.' He lifted my hand and shook it lightly. 'About... things. About how we think everything could pan out regarding our friend Fred and his mysterious relocation to Yorkshire. About...' He looked down now at my hand, still in his, and ran his thumb over the scars and scratches that always adorned my limbs, because life with small furry animals was, as Sally and I had agreed, more biting than bonding. 'About what it is that you always seem to be shying away from.'

Then he began wading back towards the dry sand, tugging me along with him like a small dinghy in the wake of a liner.

Oh no. Did he know? Had he seen? I could only hope that he had no idea how I felt, or, that if he did, he had good enough manners to honour my self-respect and pretend he hadn't.

'Me?' I protested. His legs were longer than mine so I was having to trot, and consequently spraying seawater up my legs. 'I'm not shying away from anything! You're the one who avoids subjects!'

'Only because they just slip past me,' Ivo said to the now crowded beach, neatly stepping around two small girls splashing one another in the shallow fringe of breakers. 'You do it actively.'

We found our shoes and socks, abandoned in the midst of a family group who were setting up windbreaks and rugs, and put them on. I carefully dusted the sand from my feet, pulled on my socks and began lacing up my boots, only to see Ivo shove his socks into his pocket and pull on his shoes without having once undone the laces. I opened my mouth to ask if he wouldn't be horribly uncomfortable with sandy feet in the walking trainers he'd chosen to wear today, but then bit my lip. Ivo was an adult, and quite capable of making his own decisions, but if he once complained that his shoes were rubbing I'd be justified in giving him a what-did-you-expect look. Besides, I was busy crafting my response to his accusations of my superficiality. I could do it, there were a hundred-and-one reasons why I kept things light and I could bury the reality beneath them. Then we trudged up the beach and into town, to argue lightly over sandwich fillings.

* * *

My phone buzzed with the receipt of a text.

> Hi, it's Sally. Feel bad that I never got to show you our squirrel rescue facility. Come early tomorrow and I'll take you down and maybe we can compare notes! I don't get to meet other people who understand what it's like. Around 8?

I read Ivo the text as we drove. The little cove he had in mind was a fair way from Cowes and I'd lost all sense of direction, so I was glad he knew where he was heading.

'Do you want to?' he asked, stopping at a junction and squinting at a road sign, which made my confidence in him waver somewhat. 'I thought you wanted to head back straight away, soon as we'd said "bye" to Fred?'

I stared down at the text again. There was something in those few words that gave me a warm feeling. Friendship offered, a nice, simple friendship; it would be refreshing in comparison to the one I was currently wading through. 'I think so,' I said. 'I don't meet many people generally in the rescue profession. Apart from my workmates, and when we're sent on courses. There aren't many people who know what it's like being in the middle of a muddy field at three in the morning, trying to untangle a fox from an electric fence.'

Sally wanted to make contact again, wanted to talk. To show me what she did; the successes of animal rescue could be few and far between and it was nice to celebrate them with someone who understood that animals died far more often than they thrived, and that not crying over each failure didn't make you hard, it made you practical.

And also someone who knew that you *did* cry over the failures.

'Yes,' I said, as the car moved off along yet another curving lane through birdsong and branches. 'I think I'd like to see their facilities.'

'Okay then. We can book an evening sailing, drive home overnight. Make the most of our last day down here.' He pulled the car to the left down a very narrow turn that looked more like a gateway than a road. 'But while I'm showing Tony the picture of our Mr Williams I might ask why Sally has seen them knocking about together.'

'Just be careful. If he's prone to outbursts...' I trailed off.

'I can handle myself.' Ivo flexed a bicep at me. 'I can swear in fifteen languages and I'm a black belt in miso.'

'Bean paste?'

'If anyone comes at me in anger, I swap recipes with them until they calm down.' He flicked me a glance. 'Seriously, Cress, I'm a journalist. D'you not think I've been in dodgy situations before?'

I opened my mouth to reply that negotiating with escaped bullocks and interviewing the victims of bike theft wasn't really a preparation for being imprisoned in a Portakabin with an irrationally angry fifteen-stone bloke, but I didn't. He knew. Of course he did. Having the personality of someone running in a speeded-up film didn't mean Ivo was stupid.

'Fine,' I said. 'It could be useful.'

'Of course it could!' Fingers fidgeted on the wheel. 'I'd still like to get to the bottom of the Fred mystery before we go. Poor impulse control could be my friend here. Look, this is the place.'

It was a tiny, chalky-floored car park at the side of the road, empty of any other vehicles, although a worn path in the grass showed where people walked out across the hilltop. Above us the sky spread navy blue, humped with clots of cloud that lay dark along the horizon, threateningly flat-topped as though shaved at the sides.

'Looks like a storm coming in from the sea,' I observed.

'Slow moving. Won't be here before tomorrow,' Ivo said confidently. So confidently, in fact, that I raised my eyebrows at him. 'Weather forecast, before you ask, not my own assumption.' Ivo unloaded the carrier bags of picnic that we'd bought, and a rug from the boot. 'If we walk out along this path a bit, we can see down into the cove Ru and I used to swim in sometimes. It's great, really private, only one little road in and visitors don't know about it.'

'Surely you and Ru were visitors?'

'We didn't drive in, we came on the boat. And don't roll your eyes, it wasn't *our* boat, it belonged to Ru's sailing friends.'

We trudged along the little beaten-grass path. I'd got sand in my socks and a wary eye on the clouds massing on the horizon, so I wasn't as filled with the joys of a country walk as I usually would have been, even with Ivo twinkling glamorously beside me, seizing grass stems and pulling seed heads to scatter across the turf. Cliffs arced around behind us, running sheer to the sea in patches of green and white, where plants were gaining a foothold in chalk. Far beneath, the sea threw itself against boulders, half-hearted in the heat.

'Here,' Ivo said suddenly. 'This is nice.'

The grass sloped here, down to a fence that would prevent us from sliding off the edge of the cliff into the water, and below us a narrow cove was visible, just a crack of an inlet with a small sandy fringe and waves that beat against the encircling cliffside.

With anyone else, it would have been romantic.

'Very pretty,' I said.

'And again, like you mean it.'

I glanced at him. He wasn't looking at me, instead he was staring up across the grassy hillside, eyes focussed on the far away. 'Sorry, Ivo,' I said. 'It really is lovely, thank you for bringing me.'

Now his gaze snapped back to me and his eyes were searching my face as though he thought I might have some ulterior motive. 'We need to have a chat,' he said. 'Sit down. But let me do the blanket first.'

Meticulously he laid the tartan blanket he'd removed from the car boot across the grass, twitching it into place several times until he was satisfied with its smoothness. Then he carefully aligned the picnic-carrying bag on one side, and indicated, with a formal wave of the hand, that it was ready, so I felt like royalty when I finally collapsed onto it.

'What do you want to talk about?' I kept practicality to the fore. I could do this. I really *could*.

Ivo sat down beside me, legs folded in front of him, like a slim and attractive Buddha. 'You're having thoughts,' he said, very matter-of-fact. 'About me. I can tell, believe me. I've seen that look on so many faces over the years.'

I was startled. I'd been hoping for something more general, or even personal to me. This approach took the wind from my sails. 'It's this business with Fred,' I said. 'Not you, specifically.' Lying through my teeth in case it wasn't too late to save myself.

He turned away and began unpacking picnic comestibles. 'Oh, there is *such* an enormous "but" coming along any minute,' he said, without any notable self-pity. 'I can practically hear its engine already.'

I looked around. This rural retreat, backed by the sea and with a soundtrack of gulls and wind-fondled grass, was practically made for blurting out confessions. Love and friendship and longing and fear. 'I don't understand any of it,' I went on. That was honest, at least.

'Chug chug chug chug, woooooo!' Ivo supplied.

'I'm just worried that – no, it's not a worry, that's wrong, it's just this *thing* in the back of my mind, telling me that there's no more to it all than Tony's friend borrowing a squirrel. But you're so certain...' I tailed off. I had hoped I'd shovelled enough words in to distract him, but he was looking at me now with such an expression of kind understanding that I felt I was admitting to some awful infraction. As though I had been found out and dealt with and my admission was surplus to requirements. My heart was beating so hard that I felt sick, and this clifftop wasn't the only thing that felt precariously poised over a long drop.

'You feel as though you're going along with me to keep me happy,' he said.

Ok. Ok, yes. Practicality. Reality versus feelings. I could do this. 'No. Well, yes, a bit.'

There was a small, sad silence. Into it came the soft sound of waves breaking and a far-off car engine, then an ominous roll of distant thunder.

'I don't want to bring you down,' I said quietly. 'I'd love to believe that this is going to be the case that makes you famous, but I can't help thinking that it might all be part of your...' I took a breath. 'That it might be one of your obsessions and you're not seeing clearly because of that getting in the way. I wish I could just roll along with you, but I keep remembering that your parents have someone to clean the house for you and you burned the sauce because you were looking at newspapers.'

I swallowed hard. *Had I done it?* I had the feeling that as long as I could keep the focus on him, on pragmatism and the realities of friendship, I might get out of this with my heart intact. Or, if not intact, at least not shredded into tiny tatters, I'd settle for that.

Ivo tipped his head. One hand combed the soft pile of today's velveteen trousers, restless and looking for input. 'I'm twenty-seven,' he said.

'I know. So am I.'

'No, what I mean is, I haven't killed myself yet. I haven't burned to death in a culinary conflagration or poisoned myself with inadequately refrigerated pork products. I can cope, Cress. Just because my life looks random and unfocussed to you, it doesn't mean that I don't know what I'm doing. Okay, sometimes I'm late to a meeting or I turn up to a black tie do in a 1970s glam rock outfit, but I have workarounds. I have reminders on my phone, a calendar for appointments, Alexa for timings. My brain is' – he did the finger-thing again – 'and it can make me unsystematic, overloaded easily and an absolute *bastard* about anniversaries. But I'm still here. Still standing.' He reached out a hand and laid it on my wrist where I was sprawled on the blanket. 'Is that not enough for you?'

Enough. Enough for friendship? It always had been. Ivo had always been more than enough to be my friend, and it hurt that he thought that his ADHD made him not friendship material. His randomness and his occasional pinpoint focus made him *him.* But this conversation was beginning to feel dangerous. There was a look in Ivo's eye that I wasn't used to seeing, a look of trepidation, as though my answer to his question could hurt him more than he was capable of dealing with. I could take away that look by telling him that my reluctance around him wasn't due to his behaviour it was because I wanted Ivo as so much more than a friend, but... I twisted my tongue in my mouth to stopper my lips. I couldn't do it. Not even to take that look from his face, I couldn't open myself up to him. I couldn't take that leap.

Ivo drew his knees up. It was a childishly defensive gesture and I knew he was trying to shield himself from my words. 'But isn't that friendship, Cress?' he asked softly. 'Everyone has to make allowances for other people. Unless they are identical twins, of course,' he went on, in a more normal tone. 'But even then, they are two different people, so, yes. Nobody is perfect. Friendship should be people caring about each other. Looking after one another.'

'I don't need looking after.' It sounded stiff and as though I'd pre-arranged the words. *Oh Ivo. Friendship. Can't you see me, protecting myself here?*

'No. No, of course you don't.' He'd lost the gentle tone and assumed a practicality. 'What you do need is a few of these amazing sausage rolls, however, and some crisps. There isn't a drama in the world that isn't better with pastry products and Pringles.'

'Ivo...'

He shook his head. 'It's all right, Cress. I'm not pushing anything. Well, anything other than these spectacular rolls. You know how you feel, and, believe me, I'm not a stranger to this situation. I've learned to accept with grace and poise the fact that not every woman wants to hang out with someone who's got a brain like a TK Maxx on sales day.' He grinned at me and passed me a packet. 'Even if he is *utterly* gorgeous and fanatically devoted, when in the field.' Another grin, and wiggled eyebrows. 'I've got references. Available on request.'

I laughed now. That intense, scared look was gone from his face. I had clearly been more convincing than I had thought I was capable of. *Friendship.* We were back on an even keel, even though my insides felt as though we'd been through a hurricane. I'd held the line and not revealed my emotional fragility. He'd let his condition take the blame and I had let him.

I felt a quick moment of shame about that. 'I'm not saying I don't want to find out what's going on here,' I said, the words slipping out in my relief. 'I'm really not.'

I meant the Fred affair. Of course I did.

'Well, how could you, when I'm so downright adorable?'

'That's not...' I stopped talking. There was a different look on his face now. An expression I didn't think I'd ever seen before, a softening and – something else.

'Cressida.'

I found myself caught by his eyes. He'd got the lid of a Pringles tube in one hand but his attention wasn't on that, it was on me. Full beam, laser-intensity, as though his eyes were trying to concentrate the soul out of my body. 'Cress,' he said again, and it was a breath, a vibration in the air that hit me in the heart and tingled all the way down to my toes.

The lid went down and he raised his hand to tangle it in my hair, slowly, keeping eye contact as though using it to pull me closer, like a magnet. My neck prickled, all my skin rising in goosepimples where his fingers contacted, as though he were ice, while I felt his skin like fire against me. 'Cress.'

He leaned in and his lips were soft, although there was pressure in the kiss that spoke of a longing on both sides. His other hand rose and held me steady. I closed my eyes and let myself get lost in kissing Ivo.

It was like everything I'd ever dreamed, combined with my worst nightmares. Ivo. *Ivo.* His touch, the firmness of his hands holding me in, the feel of his fingers caught in my hair, the familiar smell of him and the implicit promise in the contact made all the bad stuff and the doubts flare and catch light, burning away in the face of what I wanted. What I'd wanted for so long.

We broke apart after a few moments of the kiss. Gulls wheeled overhead, dipping their wings into the wind and staring at our picnic with wickedly sharp eyes, but we ignored them.

'Ivo, I...' I wasn't even sure what I had been going to say. There was nothing *to* say. That kiss had taken all my words.

But he interrupted my ellipses. 'That car down there, just coming into the cove. Isn't that the car that passed us on the track this morning?' His whole attention had moved from me; he was staring over my shoulder and down the cliff to where a white SUV had driven onto the narrow band of beach.

'I don't know. It was just a car, I wasn't looking.' I tried to stifle the annoyance I felt at the interruption. I wasn't sure whether I wanted an in-depth investigation as to whether we could ever work as a couple, at any level, but this change of subject was too abrupt. I needed to breathe and think about this and now Ivo was off on something else. 'React to the moment' seemed to be Ivo's default and I had no choice but to go along with that for now.

'It was one just like it. Can you see if it's got damage to the passenger-side wing?' Ivo had got up onto his knees and was creeping closer to the fence in a kind of all-fours crouch.

'Not from here, no. Why?' I breathed deeply. Switched to 'Ivo mode'.

'The one that passed us did. Big dent down one side.'

'Ivo, I'm sure there's more than one white SUV on the island. And be careful, that fence doesn't look all that safe.'

'Mmm.' He shaded his eyes from the low-level sun that was bouncing the last of its rays off the sea's surface, clearly not listening to me. 'It's the kind of thing I notice, you see. Big dent, how did that happen? Why haven't they had it fixed, clearly an expensive vehicle, so maybe they didn't have time, or didn't want the car to be noted by a garage...'

'Maybe it only just happened, and they haven't had chance yet,' I said, my voice rising in a note of panic. 'Ivo – the fence...'

'The damage looked older than that.' He was squinting into the diamond light. 'Yes, I'm pretty certain that's the same car.' Then he turned and kneed himself back up the slope towards me. 'You're very risk averse, Cress, ever wondered why that might be? Because I have.'

The relief that he'd come back and not plunged over the clifftop accompanied by inadequate fencing made my voice shrill. 'I am *not* risk averse! I just don't want you dying on my watch! Your parents would kill me.'

'Go on, admit it. You are. Just a little bit?' As though he didn't have a care in the world, Ivo reached past me for the little pile of food and began picking olives out of the packet, with oil dripping down the front of his shirt as he palmed them into his mouth. 'And I'm not just talking about right now. You took a week off work to have a cold.'

'I felt wretched!' I could hear the self-justification in my voice as I wailed the words. 'I wanted to sleep it off, not snot all over baby hedgehogs and badgers.'

'How do you feel now?' He ripped open another pack of Pringles, despite the fact that we hadn't started the first one yet.

'Fine.'

'So you could have gone back to work.'

'I *could,* if I wasn't out here in the middle of nowhere trying to help you find out what our man was doing with Fred in his pocket!' The wonderfulness of that kiss was now being completely subsumed under the feeling of annoyance that Ivo could engender in me. I narrowed my eyes at him and helped myself to crisps.

'But it's only been a couple of days. You've recovered quickly, which means the cold wasn't that bad, yet you rang in sick for the whole week – why was that, Cress?'

His tone was very neutral, not accusatory or demanding, just Ivo wondering why I'd seemingly over-reacted, and it took some of the annoyance from me.

'I dunno. Maybe I worry too much about illness. I was a sickly child, I think. Mum used to make me stay in bed for ages when I was ill. I know I had a virus once that made me come out in a rash and she... oh, nice try at changing the subject there!'

'I'm not changing the subject, Cress.' Now he sounded almost – sad? I found myself reluctant to meet his eye and concentrated on the little bits of buttery pastry stuck to my fingers and the lazy drone of a huge bee that was contentedly bumping its way through a tall set of purple flowers right by our picnic. 'I want to know about you.'

'There's nothing *to* know.' The bee had little sacks of bright gold either side of its fuzzy body, where the pollen had stuck. 'You know all there is to know about me anyway. We've known each other for what, eight, nine years? What more do you think there is?' My heart had started to double-time again, thrumming like a generator in my chest. I had no idea how he could manage to wrong-foot me so consistently.

Ivo dipped a crisp in some humous, concentrating furiously. 'Maybe nothing, maybe something.'

'Very enigmatic. Very debating society.'

I was trying to forget about the kiss. Ivo was just Ivo, annoying, captivating, irrational and inquisitive, with his questions and his wavering focus and it was as though he'd never even considered kissing me, never mind actually done it. He could switch conversational topics faster than I could change channels on the TV. 'You never talk about your parents, do you know that?' he asked, fishing broken Pringle from the humous tub with the end of a sausage roll.

The bee stopped buzzing and crawled inside a flower. I wanted to get in there with it. 'No need to,' I said as lightly as I could manage.

'Oh, I don't know. I never shut up about mine, and they're complete pains in the legal and journalistic arse. I know nothing about yours. They didn't come to graduation, did they?'

'They... it's just not important.' I turned around to see if the SUV was doing anything interesting that I could use to distract him, but it was still parked on the edge of the sand. Out to sea, a small motorboat was chopping the waters around the headland towards the cove, but it didn't look as though it would be enough to stop Ivo's train of thought. I tried to put a metaphorical concrete block on the tracks. 'Do you not think I'm posh enough for you, is that it? You want to meet my entire family so you can check out my pedigree? See if they know the right cutlery to use in a restaurant and make sure that they don't think *Loose Women* is the epitome of intelligent TV programming?'

There was a pause while he licked dip off his fingers and the bee set about another flower stalk. The crushed grass around us sent up a cucumber smell to rival the garlic and I fought the urge to lie down and bury my face in the undergrowth, inhaling deeply to stop any further questioning. Perhaps I could pretend to be dead? I sighed, inwardly. I wasn't even sure that death would stop Ivo and his questions.

Finally, and still without looking at me, he said, 'That was below the belt, Cress.'

I knew it had been, and opened my mouth to apologise, but he'd already moved on.

'Besides, I think your feelings may be something to do with your background, like I said, risk averse and, whilst throwing in your lot with me is hardly akin to alligator-wrestling and tiger-petting, it still seems to be a step further than you can easily take. And I wonder why.' Now he looked at me. It was a proper, direct look, an interviewer kind of look, as though my answers were essential. 'Unless both your parents died an untimely and horrible death in front of you.'

I continued to say nothing. Were we still talking about the Fred issue, or... us? When Ivo said, 'throwing in your lot with me', how far was he envisaging that actually going?

And that kiss. I could still feel it, all the way down my body. My brain had opted out of involvement about that.

'Oh, shit, Cress, they didn't, did they? Oh, please tell me they didn't, otherwise I've just come over as the most tactless jerk on the planet – not that it would be the first time, obviously, but I don't like doing it.' He grabbed my hand, effectively preventing me from picking up another sausage roll. 'Cress. Just *tell* me.'

I shrugged. 'Single mum. Dad unknown. Grew up poor, got to Cambridge, met you. That's all there is to it, Ivo.'

He looked down at my hand, and again ran his finger over the raised weals and half-healed score marks. His touch felt different, not the usual Ivo reckless, thoughtless grasp but... just *different*. 'Where's your mum now?'

His hair was flopping down, covering his face so I couldn't see his expression.

'Crofting in Scotland.'

'But you told me you bought your place from an inheritance your granny left? So, you grew up poor, but there was family money, yet your mum didn't access it... I mean, you're called *Cressida*, for heaven's sake.'

'Stop doing investigative journalism on me, Ivo,' I said, but my voice was quiet and a little bit clogged. Beside me, the bee bundled itself into another purple flower, with intermittent buzzing. I looked at it, trying to appreciate its furry stripes and softly coated body, because it was easier than having to look at Ivo. It had wicked looking spurs all along both legs. Soft and sharp. Fur and sting.

'Look.' He gave my hand a little shake. 'Why not just tell me? It will be far, far easier than this "Twenty Questions" thing and you've nothing to be ashamed of, after all. You're amazing! Gorgeous and clever and you're here with me, it's a wonder the world hasn't been blinded by the brilliance of your situation.'

'Big head,' I said, mildly, but he'd made me smile. Which was, evidently, his intention, because now he flicked his hair back with a twitch of his head and gave me the calm, rational expression again.

'Go on,' he said. 'You'll feel better afterwards. Probably.'

'Oh, it's all family stuff, very boring.'

'Try me.'

He was so persistent it was annoying. 'All right. But you must promise...'

'Anything, Cress, my darling, anything.'

'...not to interrupt me. Can you do that?'

He grinned and did the 'shaky hand, could go either way' thing with the hand not holding mine. 'I can try. But, please, please forgive me if I interrupt, I'm just so fantastically interested in you that I may not be able to hold back.'

I stared at the countryside, Ivo only half in my sight. I didn't want to look at him. 'Right. Well, my mum was born into money. Lots of money. Her dad was something big in the army and her mum came from land-owning stock, so she grew up with everything. Lovely house...' I remembered that house, the glowing stone amid the apple trees, glimpsed from the top deck of the bus. 'Anyway. She and her brother were raised with all that and sent away to school. Her brother, Michael his name was, he was quite a few years older, five or six, so he finished school first and followed their dad into the army. Brigadier Captain Sir Umpty Tumpty, something like that.'

Ivo opened his mouth and I gave him a ferocious look, so he closed it and performed the 'zip lip' mime. I switched my attention from the clifftop to the little motorboat that had nosed its way into the cove and was bobbing just offshore.

'Michael was killed in the Falklands. Mum was brought home from school and groomed for marriage to the son of a friend of her father, some bloke in the Guards, apparently. But she rebelled. Went off the rails, ran away to London, met my dad – whoever he was – and got pregnant with me.'

'Hard on the parents, that. Losing a son and then a daughter,' Ivo commented.

'Sssh. Anyway. Mum couldn't manage in London. She was picking up secretarial work but she had to stop when I was born, so she came back. Asked her parents for help and they cut her off. Wouldn't have anything to do with her, or, by extension, me. In fact, they sold up their house and the farm and moved – I don't know, to Wiltshire I think. Leaving Mum to raise me with nothing, in a little flat just outside York.'

I stopped now. That was pretty much it, but Ivo had other ideas.

'Your degree, though. History. And what you do now. Wee bit of a contrast?'

'Mum wanted me to do History. I went along with it to keep her happy. But when the solicitor got in touch to say that my grandmother, her mother, had died and left us money...' I shook my head again. 'Mum had managed to keep in touch with her, somehow. It was Grandad who cut us off and he was dead by then, so...'

'How very Victorian.' Ivo sounded a little sharp. 'Casting you out into the snow, simply because your mum wouldn't marry who he wanted her to.'

'She said she would, when she came back from London. She went home and told her dad that she'd marry the Guardsman now. But he didn't want her, because she'd had me. "Damaged goods" were the words used, I believe.' A flashback to the grimy little kitchen in the rented flat in York, Mum sorting out cutlery while she told me the story. The way her voice had wobbled over the phrase, and how my eyes had flooded at the realisation that, had she *not* had me, her life could have been so different.

'And I don't think my grandfather ever really got over losing Michael.' I'd tried to understand; it had been the only get-out clause I could come up with. 'So it was rough all round.'

'That's very... it sounds as though you've forgiven everybody. Have you?'

No, I wanted to say. *I haven't forgiven my grandfather for leaving my mother to raise a baby with nothing or my grandmother for not standing up to him. I haven't really come to terms with my mother chucking away all her advantages to play at being a hippy chick in London and getting pregnant by some bloke whose name she hadn't bothered to remember. I've even managed to raise a bit of a grudge against Uncle Michael for joining the army and getting himself killed; without that, none of this would have happened and I'd be the daughter of a privileged mum, and a dad who knew his way around Chelsea and Trooping the Colour.*

'Sort of,' I said. 'Mostly.'

'And it does explain why your mother conditioned you to be a low-risk person. Losing her brother and then her parents. In different ways, obviously, but both because of high-stakes lifestyles. I suppose she thought History was a nice, safe sort of degree that wouldn't lead you into dubious behaviour, like getting involved with a bloke with absolutely no mental filter and an inability to cope with life.'

'Is that last bit you?' I asked.

'Yes, that's me. And you're involved with me, whether you like it or not, it's just the level of involvement we have yet to ascertain.'

I laughed. 'I should have known you wouldn't be fazed by a background like mine,' I said. He'd been right. I felt better now he knew.

'Hardly. It's the stuff of melodrama and, I told you, I had a very eclectic upbringing. I'm pretty sure your life story is somewhere in some of those books at my place, only they have added Workhouse.' He kept hold of my hand, curling his fingers around mine and giving a little squeeze. 'Besides. You weren't the only penniless student at uni, but you may have been the one with the biggest chip on their shoulder.'

'I do *not* have a chip!' I said fervently. Now I'd told Ivo what he needed to know, my appetite was back and I was trying to negotiate the stuffed olives one handed. Then I thought about how I'd felt, when my mother had told me her life story, and backtracked. 'All right, maybe I do, a bit.'

'And you can honestly say that it isn't why you struggle with me and my lifestyle?' Ivo took my hand and placed it gently on the blanket, as though it had been a poorly creature he was nursing, so he could use both hands to manoeuvre the crisp tube.

I repossessed my hand and went back to the olives. He was right, again. I'd used his not knowing about my background to shield myself from him and his glamour. After all, how could anyone with his lifestyle ever want poor little Cressida? How could someone who casually ruined centuries-old furnishings even imagine my life back in that flat, with the damp and the mould? I had been so convinced that he would have been disgusted, hadn't wanted the possibility of pity to enter our friendship. So I'd just never spoken about any of it. He had *stables* for God's sake!

'You're "casually privileged". You use the term yourself. How do you think that feels to someone who grew up with silverfish in the larder and juggling money between rent and food?' It sounded harsh, I knew. I wasn't even sure it was the real backbone of my problems with Ivo, but it certainly formed a goodly part of the ribcage. 'I had nothing, and you spill water on Georgian furniture that's worth more than my house.'

'What the hell is that boat doing down there?' Again, predictably, his attention was gone from me. And, while I welcomed the distraction, I had been enjoying, in a weird way, getting to the bottom of my objections to Ivo. It felt as though I finally had words for the poverty and deprivation and what they'd done to me.

'Just floating, I think.'

Ivo shaded his eyes again. 'And the car is still there. I can't see what's going on, the light's too bright.' Then that switch of focus, of intensity, that almost made me jump. 'You're more important. *We* are more important than whatever's happening down there.'

'Is that really true, though?'

His eyes were the fathomless blue of the vast sea below us. When he turned their spotlight on me it was impossible to look away. 'If you asked me to, Cressida, darling,' he said, quietly but with emphasis, 'I would give up this whole thing, run home and become a traffic warden or something.'

Those eyes. 'I wouldn't do that, though,' I breathed.

'I know, and that's part of what makes you so utterly fabulous.' His tone was normal, conversational again. 'You know what I am and you accept it. Well, mostly.'

I laughed again. Everything felt easier now. I wasn't hiding any more and he knew all about me. And he'd managed not to interrupt. Mostly. 'You are an impossible pain, Ivo, and I don't know that I can ever accept that.'

'Good enough for me. Have some of this taramasalata. I only bought it because I like saying it, but it's good, honestly.'

We sat on the clifftop and ate the rest of our picnic while the sun went down behind the hills.

10

The next morning I was up and ready to meet Sally while Ivo was still blearily trying to find his jacket.

'Where's she meeting you? I'll drop you off and head over to try to winkle Tony's secrets out of him before she comes back to spoil my plans.'

I checked my phone. 'She says to meet out on the cliffs somewhere. She's sent me the what3words.'

Ivo shuddered. 'I'll drop you nearby then. I've had enough of cliffs for a week or so.' He'd got lightly sunburned during our evening picnic and there was a red ridge along his forehead about which he was being ridiculously self-conscious. 'When we get back to Yorkshire I'm not going any higher than the third rung of the stepladder. The gutters can take care of themselves.'

He found his jacket, crumpled casually on the sofa, and put it on.

'I can't imagine you ever having anything to do with guttering.' I followed him out to the car. It was strange how our friendship felt easier now that we'd moved on into something else. Or was it easier because I wasn't having to pretend that was all it was?

'Ah, I can be surprisingly practical when I so choose.' He paused for a moment, sliding into the driver's seat. 'I wanted to be a painter and decorator for a while. But then Latin happened, and I discovered that I look dreadful in overalls.'

'Stop it.'

I appreciated his attempts to make me think he had simply shrugged off what I'd told him about my family. I knew it would resurface at some point; there would be questions about my mother, how often I saw her and whether we got on, how I felt about her inheritance of the whole of her own mother's fortune. Lots of questions. But, from Ivo, they'd feel like curiosity. Like wanting to get to know me better. And they wouldn't hurt.

He dropped me at a footpath sign, where a narrow pathway between two hedges led relentlessly upwards, and I trudged amid the birdsong and flappy-stemmed bouquets of wild flowers to where the path opened onto a windswept field, with a far-off view of the sea.

Two men were up there, close to the edge of the cliff, wearing fluorescent overalls and pegging tape like temporary fencing all along the periphery.

Sally was waiting for me, sitting on a half-hearted wall and kicking in a desultory way at the masonry. 'Hi.'

She sounded downbeat. When I got closer, I realised she'd got the kind of abrasion along one cheek that usually comes from a thrown fist. 'Morning. Are you all right?'

'Sure. Yes, of course.' She shook her head as though to cast off memories. I wondered if she'd got an abusive partner tucked away somewhere. The job of wildlife rescue means a lot of strange hours, irregular meals and constant wet clothing. It's not an easy gig for someone who has a suspicious other half who demands their dinner on the table and a body in the bed at pre-directed times. I had a quick moment where my brain tried to wonder what Ivo thought of me living that kind of life. But then, wasn't that the same as his job, only with cuddly animals instead of stolen bikes?

Or had it been irrationally angry Tony? I had a brief, heart-clutching moment of worry for Ivo, who could, right this minute, be driving towards fifteen stone of argument.

I closed my fingers around my phone, itching to text a warning, but not wanting to look rude or dismissive in front of Sally, who'd clearly already suffered enough today. She smiled at me, a little tightly.

'What are those men doing?' I asked, trying to distract her away from what seemed to be irritation.

It worked. Her expression opened as she looked up to watch the men staring down towards the sea, seemingly arguing about the distance at which to peg the tape from the edge. 'We're due a storm,' she said. 'That bit of cliff might go, so they put up warning tapes and signs.' She sighed. 'I wish that we got a tenth of their budget, but it seems like protecting humans is more important than protecting animals sometimes.'

I wanted to debate this point, but her ferocity was off-putting. 'Excuse me a second,' I said. 'I just need to let Ivo know that I've met you all right. He was a bit worried we were in the wrong place.' Then I added, 'He's going down into town to do some shopping for souvenirs, that sort of thing,' in case she suspected he might be going to the rehabilitation unit to disrupt her squirrels and upset Tony.

I didn't want to lie, but then I didn't want to tell her that I thought her co-worker might be a dangerous lunatic. Anyway, Ivo could look after himself, and, if Tony was aggressive, then he'd just get back in the car and drive away.

Sally's been punched. Be careful of Tony today.

That should be enough. I put the phone back in my pocket and gave her my best bright, unconcerned smile. 'There.'

'Our main facility is this way.' Sally began to walk ahead of me. I looked down to my right, where the land gave way to sky, a rapid descent, and then the plunge and rear of large waves, and followed her.

'Are you all right?' I asked again. 'You seem a bit...'

Seemingly unaware, she raised a hand and touched the sore spot on her face. A bruise was forming underneath it, the reddened skin turning blue. 'I'm good,' she said, 'Thanks.'

A bit further on she stopped. We were quite close to the edge of the clifftop here, with no fence to prevent a sudden plummet and the two taping men considerably behind us. I wanted to move back, further into the short-grassed field, which was studded with golden flowers, as though the grass had been fixed down with brass staples. But Sally seemed lost in thought, peering down towards the sea.

'Your squirrel,' she said at last. 'The one you brought back to us. Where did you find him, exactly?'

Her voice was a little tentative, as though she hadn't really wanted to ask the question.

'Up on the moor above Helmsley.' It couldn't really do any harm to tell her, could it? After all, it was just a stupid series of incidents, nothing that anyone could have foreseen. 'The man – the one Ivo showed you the picture of, the guy you said you'd seen with Tony? He'd taken Fred up on the moor and then had some kind of accident.'

'Accident?' Sally didn't seem to be able to look away from the drop. I took half a step back.

'Yes. He'd fallen and hit his head. Died up there. Fred's cage was all smashed up, probably when the man fell or by animals coming afterwards, and Fred had crawled into his pocket. They called me out to look after him.'

'His cage was broken?' Sally seemed incredulous. She half-turned towards me, frowning ferociously. 'You found it?'

'Yes, lying in the woods a little way away. Completely smashed.'

She let out a little sigh. 'Okay. That's... Okay. I'd been... wondering how he was transported.' Her voice still sounded odd. As though she was talking about one thing while thinking about another. I'd got so used to Ivo's ability to switch topics within a conversation that her stilted responses struck me as awkward.

'So were we! It was a bit of a puzzle until we found the box.' I laughed, although Sally seemed very serious about the whole thing. 'All just a bit of a tragedy wrapped around an enigma, really. Well, no, not an enigma, but we still don't know what Mr Williams was doing with Fred all the way up in Yorkshire.'

'Williams? You found out his name?' Sally edged a little bit closer to the point at which the cliff looked decidedly unsafe.

'We took his picture round the local B&Bs.' I put out a hand, almost without thinking. 'Can we go back a bit? Heights make me nervous.'

'And there was nothing... weird about it? Nothing else turned up, nobody asking questions?'

'Only us.' I grabbed at her sleeve, like a child. 'Please. I don't like the edge.'

'It's fine. It's all stable up here. That's why they're marking off back there, you have to know the cliffs to know where's safe.' Sally looked at me now, rather than the several hundred feet of drop. 'Just you and Ivo, then?'

'Sorry, what?'

'Just you and Ivo. Here on the island, trying to find out what happened?'

'We're only curious because of the squirrel.'

To my relief, she took a step back, then another, and then we were secure with several metres of the rabbit-grazed grass between us and the drop. 'I see.'

'And we're pretty much resigned to not knowing, now. It's just been a good excuse for us to come away together and work some stuff out. Fred was incidental, really.'

'You and Ivo, you're...?' Sally let the question hang. She seemed to have relaxed a bit now. Perhaps the person who'd given her the incipient black eye had accused her of having a 'thing' for Ivo, and knowing that he and I were – well, whatever we were, would eliminate that particular threat.

'We've been friends a long time. There might, just possibly, be more, but he's a posh idiot and I've got hang ups.'

Now she laughed. 'Ah, a bit of posh never hurt anyone. If he's got money you can tap him up for funding, can't you?'

I was affronted by the suggestion. 'I don't think so. It's his family that are loaded really, not him specifically.'

'And he didn't want to come and see our unit with you?'

'No.' I didn't want her to even suspect that Ivo might have gone to see Tony. If Tony really *had* been responsible for her blackening eye, then she might stop opening up to me, and I really *was* interested in seeing what they were doing with their rescued squirrels. 'He's sightseeing. Like I said, he went down into town to look around and shop,' I finished.

'That's a shame. Our favourite people to show around are the ones with money.' We were walking downhill, away from the clifftop path and towards a small cottage surrounded by trees and sheds. 'This is our main rescue centre,' Sally said, sounding far more relaxed and conversational. 'Come on, I'll show you round.'

As we looked around the squirrel rescue and conservation project, Sally became increasingly professional and less wound up. There were three other people working there, two men and a woman, who said brief hellos and then kept their heads down. There were a lot of clacketing keyboards and swinging doors as they typed and then dashed outside to deal with outdoor work, then back in to check their emails.

'We're on a knife edge, funding wise,' Sally said, as we raided the kitchen for coffee and biscuits. 'Everything's a bit tense.'

'Everywhere's like that though, isn't it?' I sipped at my cup of cheap instant and restrained myself from dipping into the dubious allures of the biscuit tin, because they seemed to be down to Rich Tea and crumbs. 'We work on a shoestring and our charity status.'

Sally looked at me over the rim of her 'I Heart Red Squirrels' mug, which highlighted the bruise on her cheekbone. '*Really* a knife edge,' she whispered, with a head-jerk to the office, where muted conversation had broken out. 'We're looking at not being able to pay those three next month. Then it will just be me and Tony, covering all bases.' She lowered the mug and then went on in a slightly louder voice. 'There's a couple of fundraising efforts in progress. The holidaymakers do love a good fete, and they'll pay to come and see the rehabilitation unit.' Then, back to the whisper. 'We might manage to keep afloat until autumn.'

I looked around the walls. They were covered in posters about squirrels; care, feeding and handling, what to do if you found an injured red squirrel, and the numbers of local vets, presumably those trained in red squirrel management.

'Fundraising is hard,' I said. 'We do our share too. Donations are good though, if we can manage to get ourselves into the local press, and everyone loves a rescued furry animal story.' Then, remembering the newts, snakes, dumped reptiles and rats. 'Of course, we tend to only publicise the cuddly ones. You've at least got all cute and fluffy on your side.'

Sally was looking around at the posters too now, as though she'd only just noticed them. 'We *have* to stay open,' she almost hissed. 'We *have* to.'

Her expression was one of furious determination. Slightly worrying, from my side, but no doubt her energetic anger was reassuring to her co-workers. I knew what it felt like to be working in a job that could be gone in a heartbeat, and only the fact that I didn't have a mortgage, and that Lilith and Dix were sharing the bills stopped me from having biannual breakdowns over the stress.

Sally's phone rang and I left her to it, wandering into the main office, which was deserted now. Two of the work force were getting into a small car and the remaining bloke was outside, disinfecting transport boxes and screwing replacement hinges. Squirrels could be tough customers; we'd got lucky with Fred.

Sally stayed in the kitchen. I could hear her occasional answers, although I was trying very hard not to listen.

'Yes. Yes, I asked. No. No, nobody seems to think anything of it. Mmmm. Must be what I said, it was taken. No, on her own. Oh, yeah?'

Then she went quiet, seemingly listening to the other end. I flipped casually through some leaflets about IWRSPS and mused that Ivo was right, a good acronym would do wonders, checked my own phone to see that he had read my message but not replied, felt another little burst of warmth in my stomach at the thought of him, and it was only when I heard Sally start speaking that I half listened again.

I had to admit that I was curious. Was she talking to the person who gave her the bruised cheek? There was something slightly apologetic in her tone, she sounded conciliatory, and I wondered why I hadn't asked her outright what had happened. Was Ivo right about my risk-averse nature making me not want to poke a hornet's nest of emotion?

Sally was uh-huh-ing and saying 'but' an awful lot, but the person on the other end seemed to not be letting her get a word in edgeways. I knew how *that* felt. 'I can't,' she said. 'No, really. It's only the two of them and they don't know... it would be stupid.'

And then she said something that made my neck go tight. 'He's in town,' she said. 'Shopping for souvenirs.' She gave this phrase a little twist of bitterness, as though all the souvenirs anyone could ever want to buy should be purchased through IWRSPS and contribute to their funding.

On its own, nothing particularly noteworthy. But it replaced the heat of the day and this over-stuffed office with a tingle of goosepimples and chill.

She could only be talking about Ivo. She'd even used the same words I had, as I'd busily invented a destination for him. 'Shopping for souvenirs.' But, *why*? There was no reason for her, or anyone else, to care what Ivo might be up to.

I shuffled a little bit closer to the closed kitchen door.

'But then what?' Sally was asking, in a voice that sounded slightly tearful. '*Then what*? Do I have to...?' An indrawn breath. 'What do you mean, "leave it to us"? What are you going to...? Well, yes, of course I do, but...'

No further mentions of Ivo. I must have been getting the wrong end of the stick here, perhaps one of her fellow workers had been keen to meet him, or someone else had gone shopping and my phrase had just stuck in Sally's head. It could be anything.

Then she stopped speaking so suddenly that I wondered what was happening in there. Half a packet of dry biscuits and a jar of dreadful coffee weren't enough to provoke the almost sinister silence that had descended. It sounded as though she'd not only stopped speaking, but breathing and moving. She made a small sound, somewhere between a cough and a sob and then whispered something I could only half hear, even though the door between us was uninsulated plywood. 'I don't want anything to happen. They're *nice*.'

Another moment of breath-holding silence and then I heard her footsteps so I dashed back across the office to pretend a close interest in a Save Our Squirrels poster as Sally opened the kitchen door and came out.

I glanced quickly at her face, but her expression was so full of turmoil that I went back to the poster again. After all, her personal affairs were nothing to do with me, and a mention of someone shopping could be me leaping to conclusions. Nothing I'd overheard meant anything to me; maybe I was feeling the effects of being a long way from home with a man who challenged me on every level, not enough sleep and too much roaming around, and I was retrofitting every word Sally said to try to slot it in with my experience because my brain was tired. Perhaps it was, as Ivo would no doubt have brought up, my risk-averse nature, seeing things to worry about that didn't exist.

What could any of it be to do with Ivo and me?

After a moment's lurking in the kitchen doorway, Sally gave a huge sigh. 'I'd better get you back,' she said, and her voice was thick. 'I'll take you down to say goodbye to the squirrel.'

'Ivo said he'd pick me up,' I said airily. 'It's fine.' Then, when I'd turned to see an awful look of conflict on her face, 'Truly. Then you can carry on with your day. It's been lovely to see round the unit, but you must have a lot to do.'

'No,' she said, and her voice still sounded odd. 'I need to go over to the office there, I'll take you.'

After I'd talked up Ivo's shopping trip into town I had to stick to my story now. And she looked so tense, strung out, as though half her mind was elsewhere. 'All right. Thank you.'

'When is he expecting you? I mean.' She shook her head as though correcting herself. 'When is your sailing? You said you were going back today.'

'We didn't really set a time. I didn't know how long we'd be, and I said I'd call him when we were done. He's...' I stopped myself from saying we'd agreed to meet at the rehab unit. Sally hadn't exactly given the impression of being bosom buddies with Tony, and she may not like the idea that Ivo was at the rehab unit without her permission. Red squirrels are highly strung and easily upset and she probably wouldn't want Ivo stalking among them. 'He'll come and pick me up. We thought we'd take a late sailing, and we have to go back to the house, to pack.'

Sally seemed to relax a little. 'Come on then. The van's out here.'

She opened the door and ushered me around to what had evidently been the garden of the cottage, before it had become the headquarters of IWRSPS. Lilac bushes dropped sad brown flower heads onto unmown grass and roses unleashed from domestication scrambled unpruned and reckless amid the saplings and a half-fallen wooden arch.

The van that had been at the rescue unit was parked in the middle of the erstwhile lawn, and Sally clicked it open as we approached. 'Um, would you mind going in the back?' she asked, opening the sliding door to reveal transport boxes, gloves, bottles of disinfectant, maps and tarpaulin all scrambled together on the floor. 'The passenger seat is wet. I left the window open last night and it rained.'

'Sure.' I climbed in. Travelling 'in the back' was pretty much my default anyway. Someone had to make sure that nervous animals didn't get rolled about too much, or that urgent injuries were attended to en route to the vet. As practically the only employee of the rescue centre who didn't get crippling travel sickness when thrust into the boot of an unpleasant smelling vehicle with unsatisfactory suspension, it felt like my rightful place.

'And I know this is going to sound stupid,' Sally went on, 'but could I borrow your phone? I need to message Tony and tell him we're on our way, but my battery's flat after that phone call.'

I scrabbled in my pocket. 'I keep forgetting to charge mine too,' I said, sympathetically. 'Were you on call last night? I sleep with my phone under my pillow when I'm on the night shift, and then forget to plug it in when I get in!'

'Yes, something like that,' Sally said. She seemed to have her teeth clenched and she was jittering like Ivo when he got really excited. 'Thank you. I'll just take it in here...'

'I'll unlock it for you.'

I pulled the phone from my pocket and opened it. The screen burst into life and I saw a notification of a message flash up. Just those first two lines.

> IVO
>
> Ru just called and still hush hush but they think it's murder.
>
> Don't go...

Sally snatched the phone out of my hand and gave me a push. I was already halfway into the van, so the shove sent me tumbling headfirst in among boxes and empty sacks, and the next thing I knew was the sound of the door sliding shut and darkness descending.

'Sally?' I called, but she didn't reply and I heard the van's engine start, felt the thrumming as we moved off over the grass and everything in here with me jostled up to me and away as the vehicle swung.

Sally? Murder? What the hell was going on? What could Sally have to do with the death of a man on a moor three hundred miles away? I banged again at the door, but more in an experimental way than because I expected release. The vans were sturdy and dark, you wouldn't want a squirrel escaping and pelting around inside while you were driving, nor any chance of it getting into the cab or out on the road.

My hands were sweating. Where was she taking me? And *why*?

'Sally!' I yelled against the part of the van nearest the cab. 'Stop!'

But, predictably enough, she didn't and I rolled around like the last pickle in the jar, with my heart suddenly banging against my breastbone hard enough to make my pulse sing in my ears and my mouth dry to a bitter stickiness.

'Sally!' I screamed the words now. She'd got my phone. She was taking me... somewhere. That conversation I'd half overheard, what had she said? Something about leaving it to someone else? Was I the 'it' in this scenario? Why hadn't I listened more closely?

Answer, because until I thought she'd been talking about Ivo I'd had no need to. I'd been so caught up in looking round the unit that I'd never even felt the vibration of Ivo's message coming in – my phone was always set to vibrate rather than ring, because small and frightened animals don't respond well to the sound of Fallout Boy from a pocket.

Bloody hell. I'd only gone and got myself kidnapped. The supreme irony being that I had absolutely no idea why. The possible murder of Mr Williams? What the hell could I say about that, other than I didn't know anything about it, other than he'd had a squirrel on him.

We cornered tightly and a couple of the transport boxes bashed into me again. I caught hold of them to keep them from smacking me in the ribs, and found myself sitting with them on my lap to try to prevent further injury, fiddling with the cage fastenings to give myself something to do other than collapse into hysterics.

I knew nothing. That would be obvious to anyone. This was all a big mistake. Of course it was. Fiddle, fiddle.

The cages were slightly larger than our smallest animal transport; one of them was of the same manufacture as I was used to, the other sturdier. Idly, I turned it over in my hands, wondering why it needed to be bigger. Red squirrels were smaller than greys. Fred had been quite happy in our smallest cage; what did they need the bigger one for?

I held the two cages side by side as we careered along, with frequent jolts that told me we were probably going off-road. The normal one and the bigger one, identical in every way, except one was bigger. But was it? When I looked into the animal compartment, they were both the same size, pretty much exactly. So why was this one...? I turned it upside down, the base compartment fell out, and suddenly I knew.

I threw both cages away from me, leaping to my feet, despite the precariousness of my situation, and being hurled back down again by another sudden corner.

'Shit! Shit, shit, shit!' I banged again at the side of the van, feeling my knuckles split with the impact, but it was no less than I deserved for my stupidity. Of course this hadn't been about the squirrel. It never had been. But I'd been so tied up in Fred and getting him home that I'd never stopped to think about his transport cage.

And what else may have been in there with him.

11

Eventually the van slowed, bumped over some quite violent ruts, and stopped. Then there came a terrible pause. Nothing happened at all, not a door slam, no voices, only the distant sound of birdsong filtered through the metal of the doors.

I huddled down in a corner, trying to stop my brain from imagining a huge wrecking ball swinging towards the van while running through every scenario I could come up with for escape. I could lie down under one of the crumpled tarpaulins and hide – only, it would be pretty obvious where I was, and the thought of discovery made my flesh feel as though it was sliding sideways on my bones. Or... or maybe none of this was what I was imagining, and Sally would let me out of the van down at the rehab unit, full of apologies and offers of tea and cake? Huge misunderstanding, so sorry, never mind, forget all about it, go home...

I'd dropped the cages into a different corner. If I could stick to my 'not knowing anything', then I just *might* have a chance of getting out of this. But Ivo's message – the word 'murder', I was beginning to see how it could all slot together, and this 'holiday to return a squirrel' stopped being a cute deceit. Stopped being a reason to be in Ivo's company, all fun and laughter and ice cream on a beach, and became something altogether darker and more sinister.

I couldn't avoid a kind of sarcastic half-laugh at the thought that it was me, risk-averse Cressida, in this van, when Ivo would have had an absolute field day in here, and probably not have experienced a moment's panic. He would have processed the situation, understood it well before the whole 'get in the back of this van', and probably dug his way out with a spoon and one of the hinges before he'd ever arrived at this destination.

Those final words of his message, 'don't go', cut off by the fact that my phone only showed the first two lines on the preview screen, meant that he presumably now knew I was in some kind of danger. Unless the full sentence would have read 'don't go off the deep end and start shouting until I get there'? Or 'don't go to the beach, I'm on my way to pick you up'?

Because if the sentence had been 'don't go anywhere with anyone, wait for me', then I was going to have words with him about brevity and getting to the point much, *much* faster.

My knuckles were sore where I'd punched the metal wall, and blood was dripping from the scrape I'd engendered. I wiped the blood off on the edge of the tarpaulin and hoped I hadn't broken anything. All I needed right now was to be stuck here, locked in a van with a broken hand. It was all distraction; I knew that from the way my heart would pulse into my throat and all my internal organs seemed to be frozen every time I let myself wonder what happened next and who Sally was meant to be 'leaving things' to. Because if this was what I thought it was, she wasn't leaving me to people who were going to offer me an iced bun and a hot chocolate.

This was serious.

Eventually the birdsong was broken by the sound of another

car engine, coming slowly. It stopped, still distant and I could very faintly hear voices, if I pressed my ear to the door closure mechanism. I tugged, feebly, at the inside of the door, just in case it had been unlocked, but it remained a static, solid wall between me and any hope of getting out of this in one piece.

The voices came closer. One was Sally, I could hear her higher-pitched tones amid the grumbling lower ones of what sounded like two men, but no words. Nothing distinct anyway, until I heard Sally shout, 'No!' and then a male voice telling her, in no uncertain terms, to shut up. There was a note of hysteria in Sally's voice that made me wonder. None of this seemed natural to her. She didn't seem to want any great harm to come to me. And that yell of 'No!', did that mean she was on my side and was here under nearly as much duress as I was?

All this was, of course, purely academic, since she was out there in the open air with, presumably, every chance to get away and I was locked in the back of a van with bleeding knuckles and a terrible sense of impending doom.

The voices faded and came back, as though the talkers were walking up and down. Why? They knew I was in here; were they waiting for me to die of natural causes, or trying to work out what to do with me? Where were we? I'd seen enough of the Isle to know that there were hidden, secluded spots that, even in this high-summer heat, tourists wouldn't venture to, privately owned beaches and tucked-away little corners. My heart went down a little further, allowing my stomach to rise in its place with the knowledge that Ivo would have no idea where I'd gone. He'd be on high alert; I could almost picture him standing on a clifftop somewhere with his head up and his hair streaming back in the wind, searching for me. The pulse in my throat gave a painful double beat as I realised that I was actually hurting at the thought of Ivo looking for me, worrying about me.

Was I in love with Ivo? Being in danger, having him out there not knowing what was happening to me certainly made it feel as though I was. And the thought that he might be in just as much danger as I was gave it an extra twist. And that kiss last night on the clifftop – that had held such promise and all the meaning that we hadn't been able to put into words.

I looked at the transporter box, thought of the implications, and it reinforced the sense of danger. I'd carefully replaced the loose panel that had concealed the large hidden section, my only plan to deny all knowledge of anything. After all, I didn't *know* anything.

But my suspicions were diamond-hard certainties. Someone – Sally, Tony, the deceased Mr Williams, someone I hadn't even met yet – was using the movement of squirrels to cover moving something else. And given the size of this hidden compartment, it could really only be one thing. Drugs. I looked over at the boxes, which I most certainly and absolutely was not going to touch ever again. Yes, you could get quite a few slabs of pure, what, heroin? Or cocaine? Or meth? Something like that, anyway, hidden away in there, with a cute and carefully flighty wild animal ensuring that nobody would risk opening it up. You could move practically *anything* around the country under the cover of relocating squirrels.

So presumably Mr Williams had been up on that moor to hand over a consignment to someone, someone who had got greedy, killed Mr Williams – and I really wished we knew his first name – smashed open the box and taken whatever was in there, with no worries about what would happen to the newly liberated red squirrel. They'd thrown the box into the undergrowth, left Mr Williams where he fell, and disappeared, presumably to go freelance with the spoils and removing any identification that he had on him to slow down any police involvement. They would, I thought, be in even more danger than me right now, but, again, to me that was academic.

And Fred, terrified, half-tame Fred, knowing humans to be a safe space, had crawled into a pocket to await rescue.

Oh, I was in *so much* trouble!

The voices came back, louder and closer and I heard sounds: someone leaning against the van, then the rattle of the door being grabbed. I tried to work on an expression suitable for one who has been unjustly imprisoned in a van with no idea as to why, then realised that I had no idea what this expression would look like and settled for the more natural 'terrified'.

My eyes had adjusted to the dimness inside the van, so the blast of white sunlight hit my retinas and blinded me totally. I put my hands up to shade my face and more blood dripped from my split hand.

Two men stood at the opening. Men I had never seen before in my life, with Sally standing behind them, pale, wearing a new abrasion just above her jaw and with her face stretched with fear. I wanted to speak but my mouth wouldn't work. A kind of horror had infected my voice box and paralysed my lips so that all I could do was sit where I was, half huddled in the tarpaulins, hands to my eyes and unable to move. The freezing of my face extended down to the rest of my body now, so I would swear my heart had stopped beating and joined the rest of my internal organs in one solid mass somewhere in my lower intestine. I couldn't have stood up if everyone had said they would turn their backs and give me a minute to run.

This staring tableau seemed to go on forever, but eventually one of the men turned to Sally. 'Get her out, please. We'll do this in the cabin.'

For some reason, his use of 'please' made me feel better. Surely he was too polite to actually harm anyone? As Sally, still with her expression too wide and her skin too bleached for this brightness, reached in and grabbed my arm, I looked at the two men. Half of me was thinking, 'I need to know what they look like so I can describe them to the police,' and the other half was thinking, 'Don't look at them; if they think you can identify them then you're dead.' So I was trying to look at them without being obvious, while also trying not to be sick with fear and trying to force my arms and legs to co-operate with what Sally wanted me to do. All this attempting to do things was making me twitch like a landed fish; one leg had started to vibrate as if fifty thousand volts was running through my body, and my eyes were flicking over the men, Sally, the van as though I were having a seizure.

One man – the polite one – was smartly dressed, in a 'casual summer yachting' way. He wore blue chinos and a white shirt, with a sweater tied loosely around his shoulders. His hair was neat, he had the cheekbones of a catalogue model and he looked rather bored with this whole thing. The other man looked as though Central Casting was missing its thug. Shaved head, stubbled face, jeans and a T shirt – he was only lacking a set of visible tattoos and he could have stepped straight out of a Guy Ritchie film.

I took all this in and then my gaze fell to the ground, suddenly becoming fascinated by the irregular nature of the grassy surface and the little white flowers that studded it, nodding in the passing breeze as though affirming my glance.

Sally bundled me out somehow, and the two men led the way over the grassy surface to a building. My eyes had adjusted sufficiently to the light now, so I could see that the van, and the white SUV that seemed to be everywhere, were parked right at the bottom edge of a landslip that had subsumed much of a small inlet. The cliff had collapsed in a soggy and defeated mass, leaving a gradient now peppered with attempted regrowth, and right at the edge of all this, having been missed by the slide by a fraction, stood a tiny shack. Into this we went, and the sunlight was cut out once more by the closing of a wooden door.

Sally stood beside me and I could feel her shaking too. The inside of the hut smelled of soggy wood and mud and I couldn't help but worry about the overhang of cliff that towered above it. On every conceivable level, this did not feel like a safe place to be.

'Right.' Polite man turned and looked at us. 'Well. We've got ourselves into a bit of a pickle here, haven't we?'

He was nicely spoken too. Surely he couldn't be involved in drugs? But then I thought of my university associates, some of whom were so posh that they made Ivo look like a down-and-out living under a bridge. *They'd* been involved in drugs. Some of them still were. And they were working in professional jobs, still possessing all their teeth. There was no reason why someone in the illegal drug business should look like someone in the illegal drug business, was there? After all, wouldn't that be counterproductive? I felt hysteria giving my solidified organs a kicking, and made a small squeaking noise of suppressed giggle.

Polite man frowned and then sighed. 'I'm willing to wager you never thought things would turn out this way when you approached me, did you?' He addressed Sally now. Mutely she shook her head and I felt her hand grope for mine as we stood side by side.

'Sorry,' she whispered, and her voice sounded as though her throat was as closed as mine. I didn't know whether she was talking to me, or to him, and couldn't have replied anyway.

'One hell of a way to raise funds,' Mr Polite went on cheerfully. 'Still. Here we are. And you're absolutely certain that *she'* – he inclined his head towards me – 'isn't the one who took the Middlesbrough consignment? They haven't decided to go into the business up in Yorkshire? After all, it's worked so well for you, perhaps squirrels and a couple of kilos of pure Colombian are synonymous now?'

He laughed, and his laugh was decidedly less pleasant than his appearance. He honked.

'She doesn't know anything,' Sally whispered.

Eyes came back to me. 'She didn't,' he observed mildly. 'But she does now.'

Oh shit. There went my plausible deniability.

'It's Halvo's lot.' Mr Thug had joined the conversation now. He also was surprisingly well spoken. 'Told you. Williams couldn't keep his mouth shut. Or maybe he was going to cut a deal with the Durham boys and leave us out of it. Take the money and run, sort of thing.'

'I suspect he's changed his mind since,' Mr Polite said, dryly. 'Tch. There isn't even honour among thieves these days. I don't know what the world is coming to.' He adjusted the sweater around his shoulders, as though he were feeling a chill. 'But I suppose the prospect of a hundred and fifty thousand pounds – well, more once it's cut, that's an awful lot of honour going begging.' Sally made a little noise and he looked at her now. 'Sorry?'

She shook her head.

'When is the storm forecast?' Mr Polite turned to Mr Thug, and the question was so out of context that my brain couldn't make sense of it. From drug smuggling to the Met Office in one sentence?

Mr Thug looked at his phone. 'This afternoon. There's a front coming in from France, heavy rain and storm force winds,' he said thoughtfully. 'That's going to stop the sailing,' he added, in another non sequitur that nearly made my brain bubble out of my ears.

Mr Polite sighed. 'All right,' he said, then stopped as a tumble of earth cascaded alongside the cabin. Rocks bounced and there was a slither as something fell from the roof. 'All right.'

He seemed to be thinking, fiddling with the sweater, which – rational thought told me in a flurry of unwarranted detail that it seemed to be using to distract it from what was actually going on – was cashmere. He sucked at his lips. 'Any ideas?' he asked Mr Thug. 'Because we need to get out of here before the storm comes and brings that entire cliff down on our heads.'

Mr Thug frowned. 'We can't kill them,' he said. My spirits immediately rose several notches, until he went on. 'Even the Old Bill are going to be able to put two and two together if we keep disappearing people. Williams died, they came down here with the squirrel – she turns up dead, then that's one whole line of operation closed down.'

They came down here. They knew about Ivo. They knew that someone had been with me. That someone whose brain moved at a million miles a minute and who had probably put it all together already, was out there on the Isle. I gave Sally a little sideways look. Ivo was in danger.

'We really don't know anything.' I spoke up for the first time. 'Honestly. We're only interested in the squirrels, you see.'

All the eyes came to me now. I didn't dare look at Sally again.

Mr Polite sighed again. 'It really doesn't work like that, you see,' he said, almost sadly. 'Because you *do* know. And I've got an awful lot of money tied up in all this, far too much to let you go.'

He fiddled a bit more as the sound of more earth slithering past us made the rest of us flinch.

'Er,' said Mr Thug. 'I think we're going to need a decision.'

'Yes, yes.' Mr Polite steepled his fingers in Bond-villain style. All he needed was a fluffy cat and somewhere more stylish than an old shed, and he could have carried it off. 'Right. An accident will be fine, it will be believable. This lot' – he looked upwards as another shower of shingle pattered on the roof – 'will be coming down in the storm. The roads are all closed, the place is taped off. What they did...' He tailed off, looking at us thoughtfully. '...is they drove down here to look for... squirrels. They came over the beach, so they didn't see that the area was cordoned off for landslip, and they were, unfortunately, caught in the storm. So they decided to shelter in here, and...' He did a dramatic mime with both hands, artistically expressing the reality of a geographical natural disaster. 'Very sad, of course,' he finished.

'What if it doesn't fall?'

A resigned look from Mr Polite. 'Oh, I think it can be arranged to come down. I'm pretty sure I know people with access to explosives, only in a small way, you understand. If it doesn't come down when the storm hits, we can send someone along to give it a helping hand afterwards.'

'And nobody knows they're here anyway,' Mr Thug went on. 'Could be weeks before they clear the slip and they're found, if we shift the van.'

'Except for her companion.' Mr Polite pursed his lips. 'We'd better get cracking then. Deal with these two and go and find him and perhaps arrange for him to be, what, standing unfortunately close to some very large waves?'

A sudden gust of air blew between the planking, carrying a scent of thyme and sea thrift in a perfumed waft.

'The tide's rising, so we can take both vehicles out the way we came, across the beach,' Mr Polite carried on. 'There's no way out, once the sea's in, unless they go up the cliff, which is too unstable...'

Another rattle of stones illustrated his point nicely. The cabin vibrated in the wind and more earth came down. I heard it slither over the surface outside, but I'd used up all my emotion and couldn't even raise the adrenaline to worry about it.

Ivo is out there somewhere. In danger. Maybe looking for me, which will put him in even more danger...

'Should we shoot them?' Mr Thug asked, almost as though it were an academic point.

'No, no.' Mr Polite took the sweater and began putting it on. We could all feel the new chill in the air, and it wasn't just a metaphorical one. The weather was changing, and fast. 'It has to look natural. We'll just leave them in here.'

My mind ran sudden images, probably gleaned from too much TV as a child. My mother had had to work, and school holidays had been boring as she'd always refused to get a television, so I'd go round to school friends' houses and watch hours of unmitigated delight and unbelievability while being pumped full of crisps and Mars bars by their parents. Everyone had felt sorry for me, I knew. A somewhat ditzy mother who'd carried the air of faded gentility and a lot of the outmoded traditions – like no television or junk food – but without the wherewithal to really carry it off had seen me taken in by various families. I was still in touch with most of them.

Those hours of unfiltered TV watching had led me to believe that villains always tied up their victims, using rope that could be sawn through with a convenient sharp edge. Sally and I might just be able to get out of this, if we waited for Polite and Thug to get clear, untied ourselves and then managed to clamber up the cliff face before the storm took hold.

We could get out of this.

But then Mr Polite hit me very, very hard on the side of the head and I passed out.

12

I had no idea how long I was out for. I came round, feeling sick, with my face pressed half into the planked floor of the shed and half into a pair of jeans, which turned out to be Sally's leg. We were crumpled together in one corner of the wooden building and from outside I could hear the sound of the wind whipping the waves into ferocity.

It was dark inside the shed, even darker than it had been before. My head was thumping and it felt as though my brain had come loose inside my skull as I tried to work out whether the darkness was meteorological, nightfall or because I'd lost my sight. I had to lie very still for a moment before I could even feel my arms and legs through the nausea, and every time I tried to move anything the sickness would flood over me and force me back to immobility.

An extra loud *whump!* as a gust of wind caught the planks, shaking the shed, gave me the imperative to finally move. Grabbing Sally, the wall, my own knees and anything else that was firm enough to hold onto, I inched my way up to standing, even though I had to bend forward and breathe very carefully in order not to throw up on the way. Then I crept my way along the side of the shed, hand over hand, until I reached the door, which I gave a hopeful shove, but it didn't so much as rattle. I didn't know what had been done to it, but it was completely rigid. Outside, the sea sounded close and angry, and from the roof there was a constant plop of things falling onto it.

With a lot of blinking, I managed to force my eyes to focus. Sally was lying, unconscious on the floor, arms flung above her head as though she'd been dragged there by her wrists. She still looked pale, her red hair was tangled up around her face and I had to suppress the urge to give her a hearty kick for getting me involved in all this.

The men would be long gone. Taking, as threatened, the van and the SUV. The sea sounded as though it were right outside the door, the constant gusts of wet, salty air that billowed through between the planks were also a bit of a giveaway and it sounded as though the promised storm had arrived. I looked around for anything I could use, but the shed was empty, apart from the recumbent Sally and me.

She was making little groaning noises now and, as I watched, her eyes flickered open. 'Where am I?' she managed between lips that looked cracked.

'You tell me,' I said, despite wanting to invoke every kind of wrath from any passing deity on her head. 'You're the expert.'

'Oh God.' She gave a little moan and closed her eyes again.

'We've got to get out of here,' I said, as another sharp shower of gravel hit the roof. 'Before everything comes down on top of us.'

Sally groaned again. 'There's no point,' she breathed. She looked as though the nausea was catching up with her now. 'I know where we are. We're on Wanscombe Tip. Most of the cliff came down last winter and it's too unstable now for anyone to go near.'

'That "anyone" excludes us, of course,' I said tartly. I *wanted* to make a plan, wanted to escape, get out of here and, if necessary, float myself to safety on Sally's corpse, but point-scoring seemed to be all I could manage. 'Why the hell did you agree to meet those two here, if you knew it was unsafe?'

Sally struggled to sit up. 'They've been bringing stuff ashore in the bay. You can get across the beach at low tide, so they told me to come here.'

'You could have just driven us to the nearest police station!' I shouted, but it made my head bang. 'Turned yourself in, told them everything and then we wouldn't be trapped in a shed!'

Sally had gone whiter than pale now. Her skin was almost transparent. 'But then I'd go to prison,' she whispered.

'Well, yes, but you'd be alive! As would I, because that seems to be a decidedly temporary state at the moment.' I hit the door with my elbow. It still refused to budge. 'Sally, that cliff sounds as though it's going to come down on our heads in a minute. Ivo is out there and he has no idea where we are. They'll be looking for him, and we *have* to get out of here!'

'But then what?' Her eyes were wide, as though her lids had been stapled to the back of her head. 'The tide's in so we can't go across the beach. Half the cliff is coming down, and the other half is unstable, there's nowhere for us to go.'

Another, and more sustained, scuffle and scatter at the roof and walls made me screw one eye to a gap in the planking. Rain was a curtain now, belting in with the force of the English Channel behind it, and a large amount of Solent for good measure. The sea roared.

'At least we're dry in here,' Sally said, with an attempt at looking on a bright side that wasn't visible with a telescope.

'Dry and about a millimetre thick, if that lot comes down.' I jerked away from my little hole in the wood and looked up. 'Out there we at least stand a chance of not being flattened, even if it does mean we drown. Come on, we've got to get out of here.'

I kicked ineffectually at some of the lower planks, but they were firmly fixed and not as prone to splitting as I'd hoped, and the kicking made my ears whine and my head thump. 'We need something to use.'

'There's nothing in here.'

She was right. The hut was just four wooden walls and a flat plywood roof, which wasn't offering a lot of protection against the elements and was about to offer even less to thirty thousand tonnes of loose earth and cliff face. Whoever had forecast the landslip was right, it was going to fall. It only needed a bit more rain, some powerful waves or the alluded to 'men with explosives' and we'd be the filling in a clay and boulder sandwich.

'Come on. Maybe if we both—'

Sally was searching her pockets. 'They've emptied my pockets. I've usually got a screwdriver.'

I stared at her. 'An absent screwdriver isn't much help, is it?'

'I was only saying.'

I looked at the planking. 'What would a squirrel do?' I mused, absently.

'Chew their way out,' Sally responded, so quickly that I knew she'd been thinking of the squirrels too. 'And I don't really think we've got the right teeth.'

'We're just going to have to try kicking then.'

Cautiously, because, presumably, her head was banging as much as mine, she kicked in a desultory way at the wooden walls. I joined her, trying to co-ordinate our kicks to get enough force to split one of the planks. We were both holding our heads and moaning with the effort and must have looked like a couple of people with hangovers trying to get out of a cupboard.

'That's it. This one's going.' Our joint attempts on one of the planks were causing a tiny crack to appear. It was feeble and might even have been more of a fault in the wood than our kicking, but the renewed sounds of soil bouncing off the shed roof gave us impetus and we channelled all our ferocity into more strenuous attacks on the wall. The wood fractured. The whole plank split along its length and we booted it in ferocious desperation until it dissolved into splinters and shards, leaving a gap about a metre long and twenty-five centimetres wide. We looked at it.

'I don't know if I...' Sally began, and then we heard the rumbling from somewhere above. Some, by the sound of it, quite large rocks hit the roof, and both Sally and I suddenly discovered that we were a lot more agile and a lot skinnier than we thought, squeezing ourselves out through the single plank gap like two miners escaping a disaster.

Hand in hand we dragged one another clear as part of the cliff overhang that had loomed threateningly over the shed stopped looming and came hurtling down in a glossy wet mess, the surface broken with large trees and most of a field. It hit the shed as Sally and I, emitting screams, hurtled a little way further down what had been that white-flowered stretch of grass and was now a sodden, slippery patch of land where the sea was hurling huge drifts of foam and spray as the tide advanced over it.

The wind was fierce, the rain was intense and the sea came at us from the remaining direction. We were instantly soaked, but at least we were alive. For now. There was still an enormous imposition of cliff above us, fraying its edges a little more with every gust, and if it all came down then it would fill the entire space and we'd have no option but to jump into a sea that was boiling and whirling just below. We were either going to be flattened or drowned, with a small possibility that we'd be dashed to death against rocks.

I looked at Sally. Her hair was roped against her head, her shirt was stuck to her skin and her jeans flapped dismally in the wind. I suspected that I didn't look any better.

'I'm sorry!' She had to shout it above the noise of the wind and the waves. 'This is all my fault!'

'You're bloody right there!' I shouted back. A particularly large wave broke nearby and threw spray over us both in a breath-holding chilly shower that made us gasp and grab at each other.

'I just wanted to raise enough money to keep us afloat,' she went on. 'To pay the wages and make sure we could feed the squirrels in the rehab. For petrol and night shifts and – all that.' Her voice petered out. Or maybe she carried on talking and I couldn't hear her over the noise of the storm and the blood lust that was making me want to push her into the water right now.

'You started moving drugs to pay for the *squirrels*?' No, drowning was too good for her. I wanted to shove her face down in the gleaming wet earth of the landslip that stretched like a glossy chestnut-coated beast beside us. 'Do you know how stupid that was?'

We looked at one another again, both of us soaked, barely able to stand upright for the force of the wind, with a mobile landmass at our back and an unruly tide in front of us.

'I'm beginning to get the idea, yes.'

Lightning flickered out to sea, highlighting the navy black of the clouds. More rain was coming and the instability of the cliffs wasn't going to stand another downpour.

'Well, we're not dead yet,' I said firmly.

'But what do we *do*?'

I looked up again. The new landslide was still moving, added to by continual slithers of turf and bits of fencing evidently coming down from the erstwhile cliff edge. The hut was mostly gone, only jutting fragments of roofing material showed where it had been buried under the clay. To either side of it lay the sea. The Tip was well named, it stuck like a boxer's battered nose into the water, and there was no way out except up its unstable face.

'We'll have to climb.'

Sally stared at me. 'We can't. It's clay. When it's wet and moving it's like trying to climb up ice.'

I gave her an evil look. 'What do you suggest then, Pablo Escobar? Building a raft out of the remains of the shack, like the Kon-Tiki?'

She looked at me blankly. Another jag of lightning flicked an angry yellow tongue over the sea. It looked as though we could also add electrocution to the ways we were going to die, just in case the list needed elongating.

'Oh shit,' I said. 'We're going to have to try.'

Sally watched me approach the nearest part of the landslide where it was dusted with small trees and random rocks. The wind howled at me, coming around the cliffs with enough force to make me stagger, and the constant wash of spray from the waves dug at the Earth's surface hard enough to leave pockmarks. The face wasn't sheer, it was loose, clay and soil, wood and greenery all mixed together. Everything drooped, as saggy and tumbled as wet washing straight from the machine.

Sally gave a little moan as I approached the nearest part of the slip and tried to climb up. It looked as though it ought to be no more effort than walking up a steep path, albeit a steep path that kept moving and shifting and was muddier than the average path, but I hadn't accounted for how loose the surface was. I got a grip on a large rock and tried to pull myself up, but sank immediately into the scree and mud until I was fighting to get my legs clear enough just to gain a foothold. Meanwhile, loose stones kept hurtling down and only missing me because they were bouncing off the rock I was grasping, and being deflected.

I'd only just come around from being punched in the head, I was probably concussed, I was *certainly* frozen to the marrow and soaked right through my clothes *and* I'd skipped breakfast to get an early start to meet Sally. It all meant I had to give up the climb less than my own body length up the cliff. As it was, Sally had to come and grab my legs to help extricate them from the slimy, earthen mess so that I could drop back down to the ground and lie, exhausted and covered in mud, like a competitor in a particularly gruelling cross-country race.

We crouched together. The only plus side of the sliding cliff face was that it formed a barrier between us and the wind, and a measure of shelter from the rain and spray, as long as we kept an eye above us for the imminent detachment of the huge overhang.

'If we can wait until the tide drops...?' I asked hopefully. 'We can walk off the beach?'

Sally jerked her head, coils of hair swinging, at the threatening sight of the continuous roll of earth and rock from above. 'That won't last out until the tide turns, never mind until it's shallow enough for us to swim round the headland,' she said, depression in her every word. 'Besides, the Tip's only passable at really low tide; there's gulleys and rips as soon as it starts coming back in. It's not even fully in yet.' She stared at the booming, foaming water, only a few metres from where we crouched. 'And the Tip has been slipping for months. This whole part of the island is a no-go area.'

'Aren't you a cheery soul,' I muttered, sitting down hard again on the urge to push her into the sea.

'That's why I took you over the cliff to the unit. I was checking on the state of the tide, because I was meeting the guys here after you'd gone, to pick up another consignment.'

'Only they found out about us before that,' I added, putting my head onto my knees to try to stop it aching. 'Probably heard from whoever was supposed to receive the drugs that they never arrived and then put it together with you telling them about the squirrel return.' All my energy was gone. Right now, I hoped hypothermia would get me before the cliff or the sea, because I'd heard it was a quiet way to go. I hoped Sally boiled in some randomly spilled oil. 'You absolute *melt*, Sally.'

'I know, I know.' She huddled next to me. 'Drugs. Just say no,' she added, dismally and began to cry.

Everything in me wanted to abandon all hope and join her. A few tussocks of grass bowled down past us, scuttering to a halt at our feet. When I looked up, there was an ominous crack across the cliff face that towered above this little scrap of land and, given the wind, the rain and the high tide, it probably wouldn't be long before it came down and engulfed everything.

'Come on.' I hauled myself to my feet, pulling the still-weeping Sally with me. 'We can at least go out fighting.'

Solemn as a suicide pact, we faced the least ominous end of the land slide and began trying to climb. It went about as well as my previous attempt, but being a few metres off the ground meant that we were at least not swept into the sea or pulverised, when the inevitable happened and the cliff overhang came barrelling down to obliterate the patch we'd been sitting on previously. It did, however, mean that the part of the slip we'd been hanging onto was swept further towards the sea as it came, and Sally and I found ourselves clinging to a few random sods while the sea licked at us like an affectionate dog.

We were plunged up to our waists in loose soil, fighting the sea and the land. I didn't know about Sally, but my head was still banging in a routine that competed with the slamming of the waves against the shore.

But sheer bloody-minded determination not to let my body sink without trace kept me going. The thought of Ivo not knowing, and the need to alert him to what was going on; a desperate, driving urge to get to him before Mr Polite and Mr Thug; the fear that something may already have happened to him – it all kept me going in a blindly instinctive clamber and drag through the mud slide.

I reached a hand back, grey to the shoulder and what few nails I'd had now mere lines of black against my fingertips. We'd made about ten metres, but were now trapped in a kind of quicksand of mud, unable to move any further forward. The ground sucked like treacle and slid like butter. We were exhausted, and the best we could hope now was that we'd get bopped on the head by a falling boulder and it would be over quickly.

Sally found my hand and gripped it. I closed my eyes.

Rocks tumbled. Soil moved in a cascade alongside me and there was a sudden sensation of hands. Hands reaching across me. For a second I thought I was having a near death experience, and that the Other Side was going to involve a lot more groping than I'd been led to believe. Then I opened my eyes.

'Who the fucking hell are you?'

13

The man dangling alongside me pushed a helmet onto my head, gave me a dazzling grin and buckled a final strap.

'Haul away!' he shouted, and suddenly the harness he'd fastened around my body went completely tight and I was yanked out of the mud and dragged along the surface of the landslide with my jeans ripping on the rough edges and my waist and armpits subjected to an incredible force. Metre by metre I bounced and scraped my way along until the gradient meant I could swing free and, suspended entirely by the harness around my midriff, fall up the cliff.

More scraping ensued, but this time it was grass and the occasional cowpat and I was so relieved to be moving in a forward direction that I could barely muster the energy to say 'Ow'. Eventually I stopped, face down, and more hands came around me, this time helping me to my feet and unbuckling the harness so that I could step out of it in a far more dignified way than it had gone on.

Whereupon all strength left my legs and I collapsed against a large piece of whining machinery, which turned out to be an electric winch, powered by a Land Rover parked a judicious way from the cliff edge, just inside some impressive orange fencing. I looked up in time to see Sally slithering up over the edge like a monstrous birth. She was muddy to the eyebrows, a long shape of brown, with occasional flaps of fabric, and an incongruous white helmeted head. I imagined I looked pretty similar, but lacked the energy and willpower to check.

Radios crackled. Strong arms picked us up and supported us over the field and across the orange tape, past some large and impressive '*Danger of Death – Keep Out – Cliff Subsidence*' signs, down to a road that had clearly not been used for some time. Weeds grew out of the tarmac, brambles were blurring its edges, and there, rotating with anxiety and paler than death, stood Ivo and Tony.

All inclinations towards being a Strong And Independent Woman went out of the window and I flung myself into Ivo's arms, buried my face against him and cried. His normally slight body felt steady, secure and wonderfully permanent. It felt like coming home.

I knew he was in shock too, because he didn't speak. Ivo, who never usually shut up, was a silent, solid presence, holding me close and warming me through the mud and wet clothes. When I eventually stopped sobbing and gasping, he put both hands under my arms and supported me over to the Volvo, which was parked in the overgrown roadway, where he sat me firmly down on the passenger seat with my legs out of the door and him crouched on the grass in front of me.

I gave another, stifled sob. 'I'm all muddy.'

'Yes, well, I don't think we'll worry about the upholstery just now.'

Behind us an ambulance bumped its cautious way over the rutted tarmac and two paramedics climbed out, eyes on the cliff edge about fifty metres away, as though we were about to be sucked down into the depths. Nearby I could see Sally being similarly embraced by Tony, and I was glad to see that she was at least as much of a blubbering wreck as I was.

'We're going to have you checked out now.' One paramedic came towards me, while the other went to Sally. 'We'll take you down to St Mary's.'

I clung to Ivo. 'Come with me.'

'Of course. I'm not letting you out of my sight from now on. You can expect stalker-levels of monitoring for at least the next six months.' He gave me a shaky, but bright, grin. 'It was a close-run thing there.'

I looked at him. Today's cotton patchwork shirt was now obliterated by clay smears, his bleached denim flares were soaked to the knee and the ill-advised yellow cravat that he'd tied with such insouciance around his neck now hung in bedraggled soggy shreds down his chest. 'And they didn't get you?'

His knowing what the hell I was talking about was testament to his having put everything together far, far faster than me. 'Evidently not.'

'How?' was all I could ask.

'We'll get to that. Suffice to say that I am a genius, and Tony is running me a close second. Get checked out first though. I'm not going to go through it if you've got amnesia and I have to do it all again.'

Hand in hand we went to the ambulance. Sally and Tony were in there already, and we were driven for what felt like hundreds of miles through the lanes, while I fell into a half-doze.

The hospital was bright and noisy, even compared to a landslide and the sea. My head still hurt, the sounds washed over me almost meaninglessly as I sat wrapped in a blanket and talked to doctors, nurses, watched lights, and was fed regular cups of terrible tea. Sally and I made occasional eye contact while it all went on around us. I was still 98 per cent relieved, but she was obviously having moments of terror as the implications of rescue and having to face some very awkward questions dawned.

'Please,' she hissed at me as we moved from one examination to another. 'Let me tell them.'

'As long as you tell the truth,' I said. 'Just be honest, Sally.'

'It's going to be bad, isn't it?' Her eyes were huge, pupils distended with fear and her skin the yellowy pale of old wax. 'I'm going to prison, aren't I?'

'At least you're alive to *go* to prison,' I said. 'It could have been worse.'

Those big eyes filled with tears again. 'We nearly died.'

'Yes. And I still have to get to the bottom of our rescue,' I said, as I was helped away by a nurse, whose constant monitoring of my pupils was becoming wearing. 'Ivo keeps hinting that he's totally responsible.'

When I was eventually pronounced to have suffered little more than a touch of hypothermia, a wee bit of a concussion and some near-fatal broken nails, I was taken down to the waiting area, where Ivo was pacing up and down and speed-eating a packet of biscuits. Ruined wrappers dotted around on various surfaces told me this was probably not the first. There was a jaded-looking policeman in uniform stretching out over two of the seats and talking on his mobile phone, who raked me up and down with an acerbic look and carried on talking. He had an uneaten biscuit in his other hand, I noticed.

'Cress,' Ivo said, slumping with relief on seeing me. 'Thank heavens. You're all right?'

'Keep an eye on the headache, keep warm, take it easy for a bit is all they've said. I can go.'

He slumped further, as far as one of the chairs. 'I hate hospitals.'

'Then we should go. I'm assuming we've missed the sailing?'

Ivo gave me a very direct look. 'We can't leave the island,' he said. 'For one thing, the police want to talk to you.' He cast a meaningful glance at the extended form of the officer, who was still chatting away on his phone, although he'd now gone as far as eating half the biscuit.

'Ah.'

'And for another, all the sailings are cancelled, have you *seen* the weather?' He stood up, brushed crumbs off his shirt, which caused flakes of mud to fly, and then sat down again.

'Well, yes. I was in it.'

'Oh, yes.' For a second his eyes were very bright. 'It was a wee bit touch and go there.'

'Yes. And that has resulted in me having a *lot* of questions for you.'

He handed me the last biscuit, crumpled the packet and threw it in the bin. I ate the biscuit. It had been a long time since my last meal, and hunger was making itself known with a vengeance.

'Let's go back to the house. I've given it to the police as our address on the island, so we can't really go anywhere else, even if we wanted to.' He moved as though to leave the room, seemingly remembered me, came back, raised his arm and then lowered it again. 'Do you need me to help you?'

'I'm not sure.' I tottered a few tentative steps. 'No, I think I'm all right.'

'Can I just hold your hand?'

I pondered. 'I think that would be very nice, yes.'

With a surprising amount of resolution, Ivo took my hand,

then put his other arm around my shoulders. 'I don't want you to
ever do that to me again, Cressida, do you understand?'

I snorted a crumb-strewn half-laugh half-sob. 'Don't worry.
I'm going to stay away from anything higher than a very small
incline in future. Clifftop picnics are *definitely* out. I don't think
I'm going to fancy paddling much either, for the foreseeable.'

The pressure of Ivo's arm increased. 'Please don't.'

We scuffled past the policeman, who gave us a curt nod,
although what he could have done to have stopped us I had no
idea, and Ivo called a taxi – 'No Uber on the island, Cress,
honestly, it's practically primitive.' – and when it arrived he
helped me shuffle out of the hospital and into the back seat,
solicitously adjusting the borrowed blanket so it covered my
shoulders and also prevented the taxi driver from seeing the state
of my clothing.

We got back to the treetop house with the rain still lashing
down and the wind urging the tide high onto the cliffs below us.
Curiously, the bleached wood and linen now felt far more
homely and cosy, and when Ivo lit the fire in the classy modern
grate, I started to relax.

'You need a bath,' he looked at me appraisingly.

'I need to know what happened out there,' I said, trying to
find somewhere to sit that wouldn't leave mud stains.

'Have a hot bath, get changed, I'll make us some food. When
you're looking a bit more... human, we'll talk.'

I wasn't used to Ivo being so... so *in charge*. But I still felt weak
and a bit stupid from the blow to the head, so I meekly obeyed
and had a long and soapy soak, after which I felt a lot better.
There was still a crust of mud ground into my fingertips, and
parts of me that had never been muddy before had had to have a
thorough scrubbing, but at least I could move without cracking. I
put on a pair of pyjamas and spared a quick thought for Sally.

She may have been a complete idiot, thinking that drug smuggling was a get-rich-quick scheme, but she'd done it with the best of intentions, if anything to do with drugs could ever be said to have 'good intentions'.

'Are you done?' Ivo tapped on the bathroom door. 'Only I've made some food. Well, I think I've sort of made it. I put it on a plate. It smells nice.'

I opened the bathroom door and was confronted by Ivo, wearing a rainbow outfit of a metallic red and gold jacket, a scarlet T-shirt with 'Hello, Sailor' emblazoned across it and a pair of bright blue shorts, from which his legs protruded to end in Nordic knitted socks.

'Good grief,' I said, weakly. 'I think I might have a relapse.'

'Don't. I found these clothes here. I'm not sure if it was someone's wardrobe or the dressing-up box, but they'll do for now. Everything else is wet.'

We faced one another for a few seconds, then we both started to laugh. It was the half-hysterical laughter of people who've been in a life-threatening situation from which they have escaped but are as yet uncertain as to the damage that has been done. We both had tears in our eyes when we stopped.

'Food,' Ivo said, eventually, hooking his hair back and sniffing. 'Food and coffee, in front of the fire.' He looked at one of the porthole-windows. 'Best place to be.'

'Look, you're going to have to tell me.' I settled myself in front of the driftwood coffee table, which stood stylishly in the middle of the room. 'How did you find us? How did you even know to come looking?'

Ivo put down the cafetiere and a plate of leftovers from our picnic. I was now so hungry that I almost fell face down on the plate and just ate everything lower than my eyeballs, but I restrained myself to taking a plate and putting a careful selection of food onto it, watching Ivo as I did so. He was pouring coffee, slowly. Working on his reply, clearly.

'When I'd dropped you off to meet Sally,' he said, 'I went down to the rehab unit and Tony was there. D'you know he does aerial photography? Fascinating thing, he's had pictures on calendars of the island...'

'Shut up, but go on,' I said, folding ham into my mouth.

'I showed him the picture of our Mr Williams. Now, after Sally had told you that she thought he was a friend of Tony's, I was expecting – well, a reaction. I'd got my best ju-jitsu moves to bust out if he got violent.'

'You did ju-jitsu?'

'Until I was twelve. Once I went off to prep school I started fencing instead. With rapiers, I mean, not penning areas of land. Had enough of that from the ancestors, what with the Enclosures Act and all that, and I don't think the peasants ever forgave us. Anyway. There I am, all braced, and Tony just stared at the picture and said that the guy was an old school friend of Sally's.'

'But *she* said...'

'I know, Cressida, darling, and that's what first gave me the heads up that something was amiss. Why would anyone need to lie? It's just a man who took a squirrel, no biggie. So I started to wonder. If Sally lied about that, what else might she have lied about?'

'Or Tony was lying,' I added. 'Trying to shift the blame onto Sally.'

'Either way' – Ivo picked up a sausage roll – 'someone was telling porkies bigger than these rolls. So I chatted to Tony, who was still refusing to allow me to bring out my best take-downs and showing absolutely no animosity whatsoever, disappointingly. I told him what Sally had said about him having anger issues, and he laughed.'

'Presumably not in an aggressive way,' I put in.

'Not at all. He said that he was the last person to have anger issues, and his ex-wife actually divorced him for being too placid. He and I have a lot in common,' Ivo added. 'So, together we worked out that Sally wanted us, that's you and me, not me and Tony, to stay away. Two strikes to Sally, and by now those spidey senses that you told me I ought to develop are starting to twitch. Then I got the message from Ru.'

Ivo pulled his phone out of one of the pockets of the ridiculous jacket and flipped up the message.

RUFUS

Look mate, this is all hush hush so don't go plastering it all over the site yet, but wanted you to be in on the ground floor. Your dead body on the moor has been on the slab and our guy reckons it wasn't an accident. Couldn't have hit his own head, apparently, so we're looking at a deliberate act. Being as it's a murder, and you and your girlfriend are involved with returning the squirrel, best not to make any waves, and just get back home as soon as.

'Girlfriend?' I asked.

Ivo stared at me. 'Really? Seriously? We're in the middle of a murder enquiry, people are lying to us, anyone could have done anything – and your take-home is that Ru called you my girlfriend?'

I hid my face behind my coffee mug. 'Well,' I said. 'It's just a bit...'

'Anyway, you are, aren't you? I mean, I know we're... that we've not... that it's all up in the air, but can we just let that go for a minute?'

I remembered, as I sipped the wonderful hot and strong coffee, how I'd felt about Ivo when I'd thought I was going to die.

How I'd been almost more worried about him than about myself. How it had given me the impetus to hold on and keep climbing.

'All right. Glossing over that for now.' I continued to look at him over the mug rim. 'Now you know it's murder.'

'Yep. So I messaged you, but you never opened the message. There's a little tick, you see, when a message has been—'

'I do know this, Ivo.'

'Sorry, yes, of course. I could see you hadn't read the message. And I'm getting a wee bit worried now, because you've been an awfully long time looking at squirrels, or whatever you were doing, and you usually check your phone pretty often. So I started thinking, out loud, with Tony. There was the SUV, we saw it heading down towards the rehab unit – that lane only goes down to the forest, and then we saw it again down in that little cove.'

'If it was the same SUV.' I licked my fingers.

'Of course it was. It's highly unlikely there would be two white SUVs with identical damage to the front wing. And that little motorboat coming in just offshore – what were they doing down there? Both Tony and I could only come up with one solution – well, no we had a couple, but one involved jet skis – and that was drugs. Once we got that, everything else fitted into place and I knew you were in danger.'

'Jet skis would have been more fun.' I cleared the cold meat plate and started in on the olives.

'You're not online. You're not answering your phone. Drugs have come into the picture and Ru's telling me that our Man With Squirrel is a murder victim. So I did the obvious, and panicked like an *Outlander* fan denied a tartan.' A silent hand came out from underneath a sausage roll, scattered with pastry crumbs, and touched my wrist. 'I really care about you, Cress.'

It was said quietly, evenly, but with such feeling that my heart started the whirlwind impression that I'd only just got it to calm down from after being rescued. 'We'll get to this bit, Ivo,' I said, my voice thick. 'For now, go on.'

'You're missing, there's a storm coming in, according to the office Sally's out somewhere and I don't know what's going on. There is also a high likelihood that I'm next on the list to go mysteriously missing. The first item on the agenda today, is to find you. The rest can, quite frankly, go fuck itself once I know that you are safe and well. So, we set out to find you.'

'How, though?' I felt warm. Not just outside, where the coffee and the fire were doing a sterling job keeping any incipient hypothermia at bay, but inside. Somewhere around my solar plexus a tiny bonfire had ignited and my inner woman was dancing around it, naked.

'I said that Tony does aerial photographs? Well, he has a drone. Keeps it in the office on charge, just in case it's needed to do something squirrely. I have no idea what use squirrels could have for a drone, perhaps they might want to stage a world takeover? But anyway, there was this drone. I *did* experiment with calling him "Droney", but he didn't like that so I only did it to myself. Quietly, when he wasn't listening.'

'Oh!' I said, remembering the weirdly shaped black thing with the glowing green light that I'd seen in the Portakabin. 'That thing was a drone. I thought it was some new design of printer.'

'We had to stay hidden, because we'd worked out that there must be people out there on the island who were looking for me. So we went to Tony's place – he's got a lovely little cottage not far from the rehab centre, actually. We put the drone up and started looking for you. Tony knew where you were supposed to be, over at the IWRSPS HQ, so we started from there. And then I found the van.'

'How did you know it was our van though? There must be thousands of black vans on the island.'

Ivo gave me a look that was almost pitying. 'I recognised the number plate.'

I stared at him. 'You knew the number plate of her van?'

'Of course. Just as well, too, Tony didn't have a clue. I noticed it when we were over at the rehab unit.' Ivo shuffled a little closer to me. 'You forget, Cress,' he said softly. 'My brain doesn't work like yours. I get fixated on details. When I've got focus on something it's like... it's like there's just no room for anything else. I can see detail, patterns, that nobody else would notice. It's shit when I don't want it, when I'm trying to organise something that doesn't *have* a pattern, because my mind tries to impose one and that can cause all kinds of confusion. But, to answer your question, yes. I knew Sally's number plate. So when I saw it on that beach, with the SUV with the dented wing – I put two and two together. You were either there, or Sally had dropped you somewhere and *she* knew where you were. Then the drone saw the vehicles drive off but neither you nor Sally driving, so... And then, when Tony and I found the van parked up on that disused road near the clifftop, there was blood inside it and I'm afraid I rather lost it. Channelled my mother more than I usually like and started barking orders at people.'

'Who were the blokes with all the equipment?'

'Bunch of lads Droney hangs out with. Amateur climbers and cave divers, and very used to hauling stranded tourists up and down cliff faces. Once we knew where you were, Dro... Tony gave them a call and they all downed tools to come and help get you out of there, because they knew the cliff would come down today in the storm. And then it did, and they found you hanging there...' He trailed off, his voice breaking over the words.

'We owe them a bottle. Many bottles.' I remembered that

feeling of having given up, hanging there in the mud and the rain; the weak hopelessness that came with the resignation that we were never going to get to safety.

'We do.'

The fire flickered and Ivo got up to throw another lump of wood on. 'So, you said you worked it out too?' He stayed crouched over the fire, watching the primeval glow.

I explained about the transport cage and finding the hidden compartment. I also explained about punching the side of the van and I even held up my injured knuckle to illustrate my point.

Ivo stared at my hand. There was still a deep gash running across the back, into which mud had worked itself so the wound looked like a satellite image of the Nile delta. His face crumpled for a second, he screwed up his eyes and twisted away.

'None of this should have happened,' he said hoarsely. 'This was all my fault for insisting we found out about the squirrel.'

'Maybe. But you weren't to know it was all some big drugs mystery. It looked like an innocent, fun trip, let's take the squirrel home, all cute and a nice holiday.' I touched his shoulder. 'You didn't know, Ivo.'

It wasn't like Ivo to be defeated and afraid like this. I realised that I could deal with ridiculously over the top Ivo much better than I could deal with deflated and depressed Ivo.

'And you were there for me,' I went on. 'There's me being afraid that *I* would be the one having to take care of *you*, and yet...' My words died in my throat because of the way he was looking at me now, with a heat in his eyes that fanned my inner bonfire still further.

'That's relationships, Cress,' he said softly. 'You take care of each other. I want to take care of you.' Then his voice strengthened. 'Within defined parameters, of course. I don't mind mowing your lawn or cooking you dinner, I draw the line at... at...

actually, I'm not sure *where* I draw the line, but I'm sure we'll know when we come to it.'

He came in closer now. I could see the blond stubble, smell the mud and oil and the indefinable sweet smell of hospital on his hair. 'I do have to point out that you didn't see me when I worked out that The Big Bad could well be after me too. There was a wee bit of screaming, running around in ever decreasing circles and some, frankly unrealistic, ideas of hiring a helicopter to get off the island.' The grin didn't touch his eyes, I noticed. 'Tony talked me down from that one. The bad guys didn't know where to start looking for me, which bought us time.' Now he was right in front of me. 'Can we do this, Cress?' he whispered. 'Can we make it work?'

He cupped my face and looked into my eyes. I watched his pupils grow and absorb the blue until his eyes were almost black with desire and the heat.

'I think so,' I whispered back, almost hypnotised by those eyes, the tracery of hair that wisped down over his brow, the way his lips were coming closer...

'Good. Well, that's settled then.' Ivo let me go and sat back.

'What?' I snatched back the hand that I'd raised to run through his hair. 'I thought we were going to... that you were going to... I mean, I want to...'

Ivo was looking at me with an expression of understanding but also of amusement. He raised his eyebrows and wiggled them. 'Well, of course,' he said, and his voice had lost the weighted tone of desire. 'But not now. Now you're still upset. And while I admit that my sheer sexuality has been known to send women into shock, I'd prefer that they went there from a baseline of normal, not already halfway into hysteria. So, go to bed, Cress.'

I stared at him. My inner bonfire was trying to scorch off

those wiggling eyebrows and my inner naked woman had her hands on her hips. 'You bugger, Ivo,' I said.

'Not really. Now I know that you want to try something with me, I shall sleep far more soundly. Go to bed.'

'Is that you channelling your mother again?'

'Possibly. Possibly. I'm beginning to admit that she quite frequently had a point. Although some of the shouting was a little over the top.' Ivo stood up now. 'I'll clear up. You go and sleep.'

I hated to admit it, but now that we'd told our stories, most of the adrenaline that had been keeping me awake had vanished and I was bone-tired. My legs felt the drag of that awful wet clay again and began to shake.

'Well, all right,' I said. 'But under duress.'

'Obviously.' He began carrying plates back through to the kitchen, so I wobbled my way up the stairs to the little cabin bedroom in the eaves.

14

I fell asleep instantly, but, of course, I didn't stay asleep.

First came the nightmare. The dream of being buried alive under tonnes of earth, slowly suffocating, unable to move, until I jolted awake with my face pressed into the pillow. I turned over, only to fall into dreams of pursuit. Faceless creatures were chasing me over an unknown landscape, my legs were heavy and I couldn't run faster than a slow walk, with my enemies gaining all the time...

'Are you all right?' The voice startled me from the dream. The room was completely dark and I was disorientated. Was this one of the pursuers? Where was I? What was that noise?

Slowly the shadowed shape beside the bed resolved itself into the outline of Ivo, rumpled and with his hair unusually vertical. I was in the cabin room and the noise was the sound of the trees below, frenzied in the passing wind.

'Yes, I...'

'You don't *sound* all right. You sound as though you're dreaming your way through what happened today, which is perfectly natural. And that bang on the head is probably not helping.'

'Nightmares,' I said blearily through lips dried out with too much breathing through my mouth. 'Did I wake you up? Sorry.'

'Oh, bless, you think I sleep. No, I just hang myself up in a convenient spot and do Sudoku until morning.' He sat on the edge of the bed. Rain spat against the little window and I had a flashback to being very young, Mum perched on the edge of my bed reading me stories like *Little Grey Rabbit,* nothing too stimulating, and I felt a momentary grief that I'd had to grow up. 'I don't sleep a lot when things are stressful, Cress,' he went on, in a more normal voice. 'Brain won't turn off, you see. Bit of a curse, but it's great when you really need to get some work done.'

'How aren't you dead?' I elbowed myself up against the pillow and he crouched up to allow me to move, then sat back on my feet.

'I crash every now and then. And anyway, it's not *all* the time. I can keep perfectly sensible hours if I have to. Plus, I have tablets.'

'Which you said you don't take.'

I looked at his profile as he perched. So good looking that he was almost an illustration in a book about dream men, with his classically straight nose, big blue eyes and flopping blond hair. He'd got a good chin too, and a jawline that looked as though it could cut granite. My brain accepted that this was Ivo, scatty, random Ivo of the peculiar conversations and the sudden arrivals and leavings, but my heart told me that this was a new man. Not the tolerated, humoured one that we made slightly irritated allowances for, but a man who had realised I was in danger and hunted for me, then pulled out the stops to rescue me. Okay, much of the actual work had been done by the man we weren't allowed to call Droney, but I had absolute faith that, should Tony not have been around, armed with a flying machine and a Band of Brothers who knew their way around mud, Ivo would have found another way to save me.

'You are brilliant as you are, Ivo,' I said. 'I'd love to say that you don't need the tablets, but you can also be an absolute pain.'

He laughed. 'Tell me about it.' Now he swung himself round, kicked his legs up onto the bed and sat beside me. 'I'm a gift to journalism though, admit it. Shame about the stories of lost bikes and shed thefts, this whole thing has given me a taste for running around the country hunting men with dubious intent.' There was a moment's pause, and then he shifted to look at me. 'Actually, no it hasn't,' he went on. 'It's been bloody terrifying.'

I bumped my head against his chest. 'You won, though.' His chest felt nice, so I left my head there, and he raised a hand and began stroking my hair.

'Not really. Well, yes, in that you're safe and not an unidentified corpse under a landslide. Incidentally, the island is earth over clay, and when the water gets right down to the clay level, that shifts, which is why it's so prone to movement.'

'Thank you. I needed to know that.' I could feel his heart beating a regular rhythm under my ear and the stroking of the hair was nice. I was back in *Little Grey Rabbit* territory again.

'It's all parents, isn't it?' Ivo went on, sounding almost as though he were slipping in to sleep himself. 'We blame them for everything.'

'Unless you have a whole background you haven't told me about, I don't think we can blame the parents for a bunch of guys drug running.'

'No, no, I mean – here's me, trying to compete with my father in a weirdly Oedipal competition...'

That made my drooping eyelids jerk open. 'Hang on, hang

on. Where is this going, exactly? I'm not sure I can take much more in the way of startling revelations.'

Ivo laughed and my head wobbled around on his chest with the movement. 'I just mean, I went into journalism because, subconsciously, I thought I could be better than my father, trying to win my mother's affection probably. Trying to be top dog, all that stupid competitive stuff that happens in families. I've no idea how Ru got out of it.'

'Conforming, probably,' I said. 'He's neurotypical to his fingertips, I presume?'

'He had a worrying childhood thing for construction vehicles, but he seems to have grown out of it.'

For some reason my brain had a momentary flash of tonnes of falling earth, the sound and smell of it, accompanied by the terror as Sally and I had hung onto our temporary piece of ground. I caught my breath.

'You just have to work through it,' Ivo said placidly. 'It will get better. And you hold your mother responsible for so much of your life too, don't you?'

It helped. It really helped. I wasn't sure how, but switching my mind back to thinking about my mother, about our penny pinching, saver-seeking, restricted life in the scruffy flat, where Angel Delight was a luxury, pushed the intrusive terror thoughts into the background.

'Not really,' I said, untruthfully.

But Ivo's thoughts were running. 'If she'd married that Guardsman that your grandparents wanted, she'd have lived a life of untrammelled luxury and her parents' approval.'

'But then I wouldn't be *me*. I'd be some willowy girl who studied Interior Design and features on Instagram,' I said, trying to keep up with him. 'I'd talk about colour drenching and upcycling and I'd be all eco-friendly, while throwing out a perfectly good kitchen every five years.'

'Perhaps.' He shifted his weight. 'But tell me you don't hold it against her, just a little bit? Otherwise, why else would you use your excellent degree to go off and work in wildlife rescue, rather than go into research or the preservation of documents or something? Were you trying to prove a point?'

I wondered why Sally had gone into squirrel work, what her upbringing had been like, and I hoped she wasn't sitting somewhere in a cell worrying about the finances of her unit. The memory of her terrified eyes and the coldness of her hand gripping mine when we thought we were going to die out there on that landslip...

'Just breathe,' Ivo said, steadily. 'The more you let it run now, the faster it will lose power over you.'

'How do you know?'

'It's just therapy-speak. My parents put me through an awful lot of therapy. No idea why, I suspect they thought they could make me slow down a bit through the medium of CBT and raffia-work.'

There was another long pause. I began to drift into sleep. It was surprisingly comforting having Ivo stroking my hair while I lay with my head against his ribcage and listened to the weather frothing angrily against the house and the trees. Eventually, and very quietly, he said, 'Cress, I can't be like other people, but, actually, I *like* who I am. That's why I don't take the tablets. I don't want to be medicalised into being what other people think of as normal.'

I wanted to tell him that it was fine for him, he had money and well-known parents and a ferociously upper-class upbringing on his side. If he'd been at school with me he'd have either been known as 'that little bugger who can't sit still and can't concentrate', or he'd have been put into a class with the other kids who threw chairs and climbed out of windows. Nobody would have been quite as understanding about his desire to be himself, or quite as tolerant of his uneven time-keeping and forgetfulness.

But I was too drowsy, and really, there was not a lot he could do about that now. It wasn't his fault he was posh, just like it wasn't my mother's fault that I wasn't. Ivo was wrong, I didn't blame my mother for my upbringing. She'd lost her brother to war at a tricky age. All the money and class in the world couldn't have saved her from the awful emotional turmoil that must have caused, and running away from home was probably the only way she could express that. The getting pregnant with me was collateral damage.

No, I blamed her parents. Who *could* have welcomed her back, illegitimate baby and all. They could have let her make her own decisions about who to marry, rather than having her potential future mapped out. And cutting her off and moving away when she needed them, needed to raise her baby in a safe and secure place? Well, that had just been cruel.

My mother had read me *Little Grey Rabbit*. She'd done her best.

When I opened my eyes again, convinced that I hadn't slept another wink, daylight was coruscating outside the window in sunlight reflected off sea, and the trees were back to their whispering shivers.

I still had my head on Ivo's chest, and, from the feel of it, he had his head resting on top of mine as he'd toppled slightly sideways. Seagulls were squawking and stamping about on the roof above, and my entire body ached. I shifted slightly and the weight of Ivo's head moved away.

'Hey. Morning. Gosh, I slept well, I sleep better with you,

that's a point worth noting.' He hauled himself upright and my head bounced. 'How are you feeling today?'

'About a hundred,' I croaked.

'Out of how many?'

'Years old, Ivo. Please tell me we can get off the island today.'

He laughed. 'I could tell you that, but I'm not sure it would be truthful. The police need to interview us both, there's an awful lot of admin goes along with drug smuggling, apparently. And don't you want to say your final goodbyes to Fred? Plus, we owe the mud boys a crate of beer and I think Drone... Tony wants to see you too.'

I wriggled. 'What's going to happen, Ivo?'

'Entropy, decay, sun goes supernova, eventual heat death of the universe. Oh, you meant to *us*. No idea, I'm afraid. I can ask Ru about the likely outcomes for Sally if you like. But I doubt we're in any trouble.'

I swung myself out of bed. I hadn't really meant what would happen to us. I didn't exactly know what I *had* meant. There was a whole lot of future out there, stretching away to the horizon in all its multiplicities, but one thing I did know, it would include Ivo. My future would *always* include Ivo.

'I can't guarantee that I won't get really annoyed with you,' I said, continuing my train of thought.

Ivo was straightening the bed. 'What? I mean, annoyed with me, when? Oh! This must be what it's like having a conversation with me – when half of it has already happened in your head and the rest is just infill. Wow. Being on the other side is horrible.' Then he grinned. 'Of course you'll get annoyed. I am a very annoying person.'

'You are.'

Now he grabbed my hand. It was the one with the sore knuckle, but I tried not to wince because he had an intense expression on his face. 'But I am also loyal unto death and I am crazy about you, Cress. I truly will do whatever I can to not annoy you beyond that which you can cope with. I'll even start taking the tablets to calm me down, if you'd like that.'

We stood for a moment, both of us ruffled and slightly stiff from an uncomfortable night. I also suspected that I had garlic breath from the food last night, so I hoped he wasn't going to kiss me.

'No,' I said eventually, watching his expression clear. 'I don't want that. I want you as you are, Ivo, because that's the man I – well, I suspect that I have fallen in love with.'

A pause that lasted a heartbeat. Then Ivo closed up against me, swept his arms around me and we were off, dancing around the small room in a half tango, half waltz. Held against him I could feel the energy crackling from his slender frame, feel the strength of the muscles that held me.

'Ditto, Cressida,' he said quietly against my cheek. 'Ditto.' Then he stopped, looked into my eyes. 'I mean the bit about falling in love, not all the stuff about the tablets. I'll take those if I need to. If… if everything I am gets a bit much for you. They don't make me normal, if normal is really a concept we can embrace when talking about neurofunctioning…'

'Shut up,' I said, equably. 'And your phone's ringing.'

It was the local police. We needed to get to Newport and be interviewed. There seemed to be a seriousness to the phone call that I hadn't expected, when really all we'd done was get caught up in events that were nothing to do with us. Surely we only needed to give a statement?

'Yes, it is rather worrying, isn't it?' Ivo frowned at his phone after he'd finished the call. 'Unless they think that… you don't think they suspect that we were bringing stuff back, with Fred?'

We stared at each other, wide-eyed.

'No. Given what happened, they must know that our involvement was all coincidental, surely. *And* your brother's in the police,' I said.

'That's no guarantee of anything,' Ivo muttered. 'But they can't. I mean, Sally...'

We looked at each other again. 'They would have arrested us.' I blinked at him. 'If they thought we really were a part of all this.'

'Why? They knew where we were. We weren't going to get off the island, unless we fancied rowing, and in that storm we'd have capsized twenty metres offshore.'

This made me think. 'If *we* couldn't get off the island, then do you think Mr Polite and Mr Thug might still be here?' I asked.

'Who the hell are Mr Polite and Mr Thug? Weird names.'

'Says the man who tried to call Sally's assistant "Droney". No. They're the two men who tried, rather ineptly, to get geology to kill Sally and me. We should be a lesson: never leave a geographical fault line to do a man's work.' I thought for a second. 'Get a piece of paper, Ivo. I think we may be able to do something useful before we go to Newport.'

15

Ivo and I were separated at the police station. I gave a statement to a bored young constable, who didn't seem to believe a word of it, and then I asked, 'Have you got Sally here?'

'Sally who?'

'Sally. Who set this whole thing up. You arrested her yesterday, in the hospital, I think.'

'Oh, her. Yes. She's not saying anything.'

I produced the piece of paper from my back pocket. 'These are the men you want. They're driving a white SUV with a dented passenger wing, and Ivo's written the number plate on the back.'

The constable held up the drawings. Ivo had done his best from my detailed descriptions, and, with much rubbing out, we'd produced likenesses of Mr Polite and Mr Thug that were as good as I could do from memory. Ivo really was terribly good at drawing, I thought, looking fondly at the pencil sketches. It had probably been thanks to his art therapy.

'I'm just going to take this to the sergeant,' he said. 'Wait here.'

'As opposed to what?'

I got a cold stare. 'Well, I haven't handcuffed you to the chair.'

'Not yet,' I muttered. 'And could you ask him if I could talk to Sally?'

Another cold stare and I was left in the little interview room, which smelled of people who smoked too much and cold coffee. There was a large damp stain down one wall, and ceiling tiles made of that dotted plastic that always looks as though it's going mouldy. I wondered where Ivo was. I wondered what the hell was going on, and why we hadn't been given a pat on the head and sent on our way.

Eventually the door opened. Bored Constable was there with Irritated Sergeant, who looked as though he'd only just missed having a TV series written about him. He was jaded and tired looking, unshaven, and I would have taken bets on him having a failed marriage, an alcohol addiction and a child who refused to communicate with him.

'This yours?' he grunted, holding up the sketch.

'Yes. Well, not exactly, Ivo drew it. Those are the two that put us in the shed.'

Another grunt. It was like being interviewed by a gorilla in a man suit. Then, 'And the car? You're sure about the car?'

'Absolutely.'

Grunt. 'We got them trying to board the ferry.'

A silence. I wasn't sure how I was supposed to react to that. Delight? Horror? I certainly didn't want to run into them any time soon. If they realised Sally and I were still alive, they'd know everything was over for them, and I didn't think they'd be rushing to send us cards of congratulation on our intrepid escape and boxes of chocolates. Ivo, of course, they'd missed out on giving a creative death too. Presumably his escape would be another reason they were so intent on getting off the island.

'But we need everything you can tell us about them, about the operation here.'

'Operation Dovetail, sir,' put in the constable, helpfully. 'That's what we were calling this investigation.'

'Really? Not Operation Red Squirrel? I'd have thought that was more appropriate,' I said. 'And I've told you everything I know. You need to ask Sally for details, she was the one sending the stuff out in the transport cases.'

A double grunt this time. 'She's not talking.'

'I expect she's terrified.' I leaned forward across the table that separated us, putting my elbow on the drawing of Mr Polite's face. 'Let me talk to her. I want to know what the hell was going on, probably more than you do, and she'll talk to me.'

The constable and the sergeant looked at one another. 'Are we allowed to do that?'

'Course we are. We're the bloody police, we're in charge. Don't let this young madam make you think otherwise.'

Young madam? I bristled, but it didn't seem politic to wade in while they were making a sensitive decision. 'If you record our conversation,' I said, delicately, 'then you might just get your evidence.'

The sergeant harrumphed and I upgraded him to being happily married but having an uncomfortable relationship with his ageing parents. 'True. All right. Think they're a bit sick of her down in custody anyway, she won't stop crying.' He pushed his chair back and I furtively checked to make sure he had both legs. 'We'll see what we can do. Stay there.'

While Constable and Sergeant went out, not giving me time to ask what the alternative was again, I leaned back in my chair and looked at the drawings they'd left behind. I supposed there must be CCTV at the ferry port and they'd managed to nab these two trying to get off the island. I frowned down at the sketch, which had Ivo and I arguing over whether a monobrow was really an identifying feature, and shook my head. Ivo's particularly focussed memory had saved us. He'd recognised the van, and the SUV, because they'd caught his attention and been worthy of memorising. He'd been right; sometimes, just *sometimes*, it looked as though his brand of butterfly mind could come in very useful.

The door opened and Sally was bundled in. She was wearing what looked like a police-provided tracksuit, her hair was still dreadlocked with mud and salt water and she looked as though she'd spent the last twenty-four hours crying solidly. As soon as she saw me, Sally crumpled and had to be held up by the officers, one to each arm.

'I don't know what to do!' she wailed. 'Everything's gone! I've been so stupid!'

'You're not hearing any disagreement from me,' I said, somewhat curtly, but then I *had* had a disturbed night. Oh, and nearly died. 'Look, sit down and you can tell us all about it.'

We were shuffled towards the little plastic-topped table, screwed to the floor, I noticed. I sat directly under the brown stain and Sally, after some hesitation, sat the other side of the table. Everyone except Irritated Sergeant left, and he went and stood in a corner, being as inconspicuous as he could, but it didn't really seem to matter. Sally wanted to talk. I could only assume that she'd been paralysed with fear at the whole situation and seeing me had made things feel more normal.

'They came to me,' she started, making it sound as though she'd been recruited by a supernatural brigade.

The sergeant cleared his throat and gave me a meaningful nod. 'These two?' I took my cue and flourished the drawing. Sally picked it up.

'Yes. Well, just this one.' She tapped the sketch of Mr Polite.

'He told me to call him Simon, but I know his name is really Nate because that's what the other guy used to call him. He came to me one day when I was trying to get extra funding – I was *desperate*!' She turned pleading eyes on me. 'I was rattling a bucket in town!'

I nodded. Those bucket-rattling sessions were the worst. Being ignored by shoppers while getting soaked and frozen and trying to look upbeat and friendly. Horrible.

'He asked me if I wanted to make some money.' She snorted. 'I was standing in the middle of Cowes, with a plastic bucket of 2ps, so it was a bloody stupid question when you think about it.'

She sounded a little calmer now, a little more like the down-to-earth Sally I'd first met.

The sergeant coughed again.

'And it went from there?' I was beginning to enjoy this. Maybe I should join the police force? I'd got visions of myself as the maverick cop who does things unconventionally and Gets Results. Then I remembered the punch to the head, the fear of dying and looked again at the big brown stain down the wall and decided to stick to rescuing animals.

'They came up with the idea of pretending to take the squirrels around the country and gave me the special boxes. Adam – that's Adam Williams, he was a friend of mine at school, bit down on his luck at the moment – he came in to do the actual travelling and meeting up with people. He'd take the squirrel – it was usually Swoop, because he's pretty tame – in a special box with a couple of kilos of… of the stuff, and he'd meet up with someone to dispose of it. They'd transfer the money, swap it for the drugs, give Adam a lift to the nearest station and come back with the squirrel and the cash. But this time it looks as though whoever he was meeting decided to have the drugs *and* the money.' She sniffed. 'He used public transport. Said it would be less easy to track him that way.'

She stopped speaking and dropped her head. Her hair, weighted with mud, fell forwards over her face.

'How long?' I half whispered it. She looked so defeated, so downtrodden. 'How long has it been going on for?'

'About six months.' Then she jerked her head up and her eyes were angry. 'And you know what really pisses me off? Him' – she jabbed her finger at the sketch of Mr Polite, getting him right in the eye – 'saying that it was hundreds of thousands of pounds a time! They were giving me ten grand! Ten grand for use of the squirrel and the cover story. Ten' – and she stabbed her finger down again, emphatically with each word – 'measly… grand!'

I could only hope that, somewhere in another custody suite, Mr Polite was now wondering why his vision had gone blurry.

'Would you be prepared to stand up in court?' The sergeant sounded surprisingly gentle. 'Testify? Give us everything you know about these two and the operation? Any names, dates, further details?'

Sally snorted. The anger seemed to have re-energised her. 'Course I will. I'll personally set them on fire if you want.'

Another cough. 'Yes, well, I don't think *that* will be necessary.' A pause. 'Tempting, but not necessary.'

We all looked at one another for a moment. 'What will happen to me?' Sally's voice was small again. 'Only the unit will close. There's no funding unless I keep at it, and everyone will lose their jobs, and the squirrels…' She swallowed a small sob.

'Oh prison, that's a given, I'm afraid.' The sergeant poked thoughtfully at an ear. 'But for full and complete co-operation, transparency, maybe some useful info – you'll get a reduced sentence.'

'I know a high-court judge,' I offered, helpfully. 'Well, Ivo does. If that's any use.'

'Maybe, maybe not. But we'll do what we can, given the severity of the offence.' The sergeant eyeballed Sally sternly. 'What the hell were you *thinking*, girl?'

'I don't know!' She was back to wailing. 'I just wanted to keep IWRSPS going!'

She pronounced it Eye Warsps. I made a note to tell Ivo.

'Bloody stupid way to go about it.'

'I know. I know.' She hung her head again. 'I'm not going to get involved with anything stronger than paracetamol from now on.' A deep breath. 'And I'm going to be giving that a swerve if I can.'

'And Tony?' I had wondered about the absolutely-no-anger-issues-at-all man. 'What was all that about him knowing Mr Williams?'

I got an approving nod from the sergeant for that.

Sally snorted. 'I got scared. I was trying to throw you off. I knew Tony had seen Adam around the place sometimes. I tried to only hand over the squirrel and the boxes at night or when nobody was about, but people keep coming and going and it's really hard to keep a secret on an island. So I thought, if I told you Tony was a bit... well, that he had problems, it'd put you off asking him anything. He's going to wait for me, you know.'

The sergeant and I frowned at one another. 'What, now? Is he outside?' I asked, confused.

'No, no, I mean, for me to come out of prison. He says he doesn't care what I did, he knows it will have been for good reasons. He's actually quite sweet.' Sally looked as though this had come as a revelation to her. 'And he's very good with the squirrels.'

'Which is what really matters,' I said, somewhat weakly.

'Well, yes.' Sally looked as though this should go without saying. Then she squared her shoulders. 'I was bloody stupid,' she said, and now her voice held strength rather than self-pity. 'I thought I could raise a bit of money for IWRSPS and I sort of kidded myself that they were just renting a squirrel for a while. I managed not to think about it being, well, basically, drug running.'

'Did you know?' I grasped at the feeble straw.

She dropped her eyes. 'They didn't tell me, not directly. But I knew they weren't moving duty-free cigarettes or anything, it was a bit obvious.' She sighed. 'I am a good person, Cressida, really.'

'Tell that to the judge,' said Irritable Sergeant, who then slapped himself across the forehead. 'Sorry. Too much *Law and Order* in my formative years.'

Sally stood up. 'You can take me away now,' she said. 'I just wanted to explain to Cressida why she nearly died, and to tell you that I'm really sorry.'

The sergeant stood up too and went to take her arm to hustle her back to the cells, but she stopped again in the doorway and looked back over her shoulder at me, in a scene worthy of the best TV detective drama. 'Look after the squirrels, please,' she said, with her eyes full of tears. 'I couldn't bear...'

Anything else she said was lost in the noise and general bustle once the door was opened. The corridor outside was full of people moving and talking, there was laughter and a crackle of radio, and it was evidently lunchtime, because there was also a smell of cottage pie and the distant noise of plates clinking.

I wanted to stop her. I wanted to ask her how the hell I was supposed to look after the squirrels. I could hardly package up and ship all the orphans and hand-reared creatures from the rehab unit to Yorkshire, which hadn't seen a wild red squirrel in decades – and what about the other unit? The one that dealt with fundraising and public awareness? What would happen to them without Sally and her, albeit sometimes misguided, fundraising attempts?

Ivo was waiting for me in the small plastic reception area near the doors. He was jiggling about, pacing the floor and reading the unenlightening posters about stopping crime and locking your car. When he saw me, he grabbed me into a hug and drooped all over me.

'Thank heavens! I thought they'd arrested you and bundled you off in a van covered in a coat!'

'Ivo,' I said indistinctly, giving him a bit of a push so I could breathe. 'Why would I have been arrested? I haven't *done* anything. And who would be covered in the coat, me or the van?'

'Oh, you know, like on the news, when you see someone covered in a blanket, although that's to protect their identity isn't it, and they wouldn't do that for you because you haven't been found guilty yet.' He loosened his hold but didn't let me go.

'What do you mean, *yet*? I was talking to Sally, to get her to tell them about her involvement. She's an idiot,' I added. I hadn't got over that precarious time on the landslip, and I wasn't sure I ever would. But then I remembered her red-stained eyes, her blotched face and general air of abject misery. Sally was making *herself* suffer for her stupidity, she didn't need me to join in.

'I gave Mum a ring.' Ivo slung his arm around me casually, but it felt different now. He'd always been a hugger, given to random physical contact, but now his touch had more certainty to it. As though he knew I welcomed it, rather than regarding it as something casual. 'Obviously she can't say much, she doesn't know the ins and outs of it all, but she said Sally won't do too much time.' He gave me a sideways look and grinned. 'See, there's me with all the lingo now.'

I laughed. Some of it was at his evident pride at his brush

with the law, but some of it was relief that we were walking out of the police station without a backward glance. A shiver vibrated my spine for a moment as I realised, again, that it could all have been very different. 'How long could she be in prison for?'

'Maybe a couple of years. If Sally's got a completely clean record, and she talks up being persuaded into it by a guy who's liable to violence – with a good legal team, she may well be out in a year to eighteen months.'

We walked out into cool air. The storm had swept the last of the lazy heat from the day and replaced it with briskly moving clouds and the smell of the sea. I stopped at the car and looked around, filled with relief that I was able to stand here, watching the traffic and seeing the uncaring crowds pushing through the narrow streets. *It could all have been so different.* I wasn't sure that I had enough lifetime left to process all the possibilities.

Then I thought about Tony, labouring alone in the squirrel rehab unit, and the three workers at the other location, whose jobs might not last out the month. What was going to happen to them all, now that Sally wasn't around? Who would push for the funds, fill in the paperwork, raise their profile? Who would make sure that they got the publicity to bring in the public who brought in the funds? Would IWRSPS close down?

What would happen to Fred?

'Can we go back via the rehab unit and say goodbye to Fred, like we were supposed to be doing?' I asked Ivo as we strapped ourselves in. He was being uncharacteristically quiet, allowing me time to process what had happened, I supposed. I'd caught sight of my reflection as we'd got in the car, and it was not a pretty sight, even though I didn't have Sally's excuse of being in a cell all night, crying. I still had red-rimmed eyes and an unnaturally pale face. And, despite the bath and the scrubbing, there were still traces of mud in my hair and around my ears.

'Mmmm.' Ivo didn't seem to be listening. 'Cress...'

'Only I've got a horrible feeling that the whole IWRSPS thing is going to have to be wound up while Sally's in jail.' Actually saying the words, 'Sally's in jail' made everything seem more real and dreadfully inevitable. 'I can't see that there's anyone else who could step in to help keep things on the rails, is there?'

Again, Ivo didn't seem to be listening. He was driving normally, slightly faster and slightly less conscious of any white lines than most people, but his gaze wasn't wandering as much as usual. On country roads he could be easily distracted by an unexpected view or an unrecognised bird cruising overhead, which made journeys interesting, if somewhat hair-raising. Now, though, he had both hands on the wheel and a concentration so ferocious that I was slightly surprised it wasn't scorching a groove in the tarmac. 'Are you all right?'

I got a distracted smile. 'Yes. Yes, of course. I'm just... thinking.'

Despite the fact that the car was warm, I felt a chill over my shoulders now where his arm had been. Was this Ivo having a rethink about him and me ever managing to have any kind of relationship other than the superficial? Last night he'd been so sure. *I'd* been so sure. None of our differences mattered enough to keep us apart, we cared about one another. Could his tendency to overthink be causing him to second guess our future?

Given Ivo's variable focus, I didn't want to ask. Not while he was driving, anyway. But I did feel a chilly grip take hold of my insides. *Ivo and me.* All I'd ever really wanted. Ivo, with his velvet trousers, his horrible shirts, his liability to come down to breakfast looking as though Beau Brummell had found William Morris and the pair of them had discovered Rihanna. We'd come this close. Surely he didn't want to back out? But then, fear of death changes people, and perhaps he had decided that landslides and crazed drug traffickers were the thin end of the wedge?

Oh, this was horrible. It was my familiar Ivo at the wheel, but his set jaw and straight stare made it feel as though this was a new man, a man I didn't really know at all.

'I'm going to miss our Fred,' I said. I tried to inject jocularity into my tone, but found I couldn't. Anything to distract me from the way my brain was cycling through thoughts. 'We hardly had him for any time at all, but he's my first ever red squirrel and he made quite an impression.'

'Yes. He was adorable, wasn't he?' But Ivo sounded vague, as though his thoughts were back up in Yorkshire in the comfortable agedness of his gatehouse. I gave a tiny, guilty start at the realisation that I hadn't thought about my place at all. I'd been so lost in the character of Ivo's home and the magazine-style luxury of the house on the island, that I hadn't given my tiny house a second thought. Did this mean I was getting above myself? An admonishment of my mother's that hadn't meant anything, until I'd found out about her life, her past. She must have struggled, raising a child with a casual acquaintance with Latin, whose early reading had been Greek myths and tales of battles and history, whom she knew would never have the advantages that she had grown up with. I wondered if I'd ever have the nerve to ask her about that guilt.

Again, we had to leave the car where the forestry ruts began. It must have been my imagination, either that or Isle of Wight vegetation contained some ruthless genetic make-up, because it already seemed that the unit was a little more overgrown, the Portakabin a little shabbier. As though decay and a kind of *Sleeping Beauty*-vibe had already set in. Which was ridiculous; we'd only been here two days ago.

'Tony has gone to Shanklin to borrow some money from his

parents,' Ivo said, still in that curiously tight voice. There seemed to be a lot of words that had backed up inside his head and he was trying to find the right way to let them out. Like sheep, penned together in a barn that had to go into the field one at a time, I thought, and then cursed myself. This was no time for Ivo's whimsy to be catching. Not if he was about to give me the 'I've had second thoughts about us' speech that I suspected was clotting in his throat and stifling his movements.

He led the way around the Portakabin, where I could swear paint was already beginning to peel, to the huge enclosure behind. He still didn't speak and my stomach had the feeling that I'd recently eaten a lead sandwich. *Ivo. All I've ever wanted since I met him that first day of university, where he'd stuck out so far that I'd feared life would try to hammer him back in to make him fit. Charming, breezy, flighty, gorgeous Ivo. My friend. And now... could I go back to being friends? Forget that kiss, and the way he held me all night to keep the nightmares at bay last night?*

'Cressida.' He stopped as we got through the second door of the escape-proof enclosure and I had to squeeze past him in order to close the door and make certain that we didn't allow all the hand-reared squirrels to ping off into the countryside.

'Can you just budge up a bit, please, Ivo?' I nudged against him to make room for the door to swing shut.

'What? Oh, yes, sorry, that's thrown me now. I had it all ready to say and I've lost my... thing.'

He still looked so serious that I wasn't sure I wanted to help him find it. Ivo and serious didn't go together, it was incongruous, like seeing a horse in high heels, and my heart already felt as though it had a series of tight elastic bands wrapped around it.

I tipped my head back and stared up into the trees: mostly beech and hazel, with pine rearing their evergreen darkness further into the enclosure. The leaves were brilliant emerald in the sun, fluttering coquettishly in the whisper of breeze that tickled through them. Fine grass wove a green mat where the light was strongest and in the shade tiny white flowers I didn't know the names of glowed as little highlights. There were no squirrels in sight.

Ivo couldn't give me the 'it's not you, it's me' speech while the world was so beautiful, he just *couldn't*. It would ruin summer forests for me forever, and that would be too cruel.

'I can't bear to think of all this closing down,' I said. It was true, but I was putting the words out there in the way of anything he might want to say. *Give me a few moments longer, please. Let the sun and the shadows be enjoyable, just for now.*

'IWRSPS could recruit someone else. Someone to hold it together until Sally is allowed out,' Ivo said, almost conversationally for someone who'd had 'portent' in every previous syllable.

I shook my head, still looking up into that green-sky world, knowing that there were squirrels up there doing their best to hide from us. Not so much as a fluffy tail-end was visible. 'They're on a shoestring. I got the feeling she was doing a lot of her work unpaid, to make sure everyone else got their wage. And the printers don't work, they're spread over two sites, so there's travel costs. She was bucket-rattling to raise funds, and that's desperation territory.'

Ivo came in close. Out of the corner of my eye I saw him tip his head back to look where I was looking. His hair fell back, leaving his face bare and pale. He looked like a da Vinci angel who's been forced to Earth to work in retail. Beautiful, careworn and a little cynical.

'You could do it,' he said.

My eyes dropped from the trees to Ivo. '*What*?'

'No, you could. Right up your street, in fact, thinking up new ways of fundraising and juggling everything all at once. It's what you do now, only with fewer species.'

'Ivo, I'm just a rescue worker! I go out and pick up injured animals, stick them in a box and make sure they get to a vet. I don't *run* anything!'

Now he was right in front of me. 'But you could,' he said, gently.

'No. No, I couldn't.'

Ivo sighed. 'And *this* is what I mean by risk-aversion, Cressida, my darling. This is your chance to show the world of small furry animals what you can really do. Organise, recruit – I am absolutely positive that you could make volunteering for squirrel rescue the next 'must do' vocation. They'll be queueing up! And you're wonderful at raising money, look at how you've learned to keep life on the road without a penny to your name!'

I stared at him. His eyes were shining with the kind of zeal that was usually only inspired by a potential story. He had his arms raised to the woods as though to indicate that this was my natural territory, and a faint and traitorous wind was blowing his hair back. He looked like the final scene in every disaster movie ever.

Was this Ivo's way of getting rid of me? If I moved to the Isle of Wight, well, he couldn't be expected to have a relationship with anyone that far away, could he? No one would blame him for immediately meeting and marrying a Classics graduate with a part-time modelling contract and a family with a little place in town, would they? Only I would blame him until the end of time...

'But I've got a house in Yorkshire,' I said, carefully 'And a job.'

'Let it out! I'm sure Lilith and Dix can find someone who wants to take the second bedroom! And your job will still be there when you get back – they're hardly inundated with people who want to get covered in mud in the middle of the night whilst being bitten, for a pittance, are they?' Now he was standing so close to me that I could feel his excited breathing, past the sheer magnetic pull of Ivo himself.

Above me, there was a flick of branch, caught out of the corner of my eye. A squirrel had emerged to sit in a willow fork, staring down at us. The sun glimmered on its fur, dappling it with leaf-shade and the dancing twist of twig-shadow, so it seemed hardly there. An ethereal, tree spirit, waiting for my answer.

I just knew I couldn't condemn all this to fall into decay. For the upkeep to be more than Tony, even should he want to carry on working here, could manage. The wire would rot and split, the squirrels would escape out into the wild where, hand-reared and fed as they were, they wouldn't survive for long. Rats would take any young they might have, or they'd starve over winter. And the rescue programme that was run from the little cottage in the cliffs? Those busy three people who'd mended and dashed about – they'd all go off to do other things, or move to the mainland and not be replaced.

I knew how to work a recalcitrant printer, and organise fundraising events.

'I could, I suppose,' I said, sounding more reluctant than excited.

'Yes, you could,' Ivo said, far more decisively than I had. 'Here, you can show the world what Cressida Tarbet can *really* do!'

At the expense of you, I thought. But then, hadn't my mother always drummed into me not to live my life based on what a man wanted? Stained and scarred by her family's rejection, them cutting her off from the life she'd been born to, all because of grief and some silly mistakes, one of which was me, she'd become fiercely independent. She'd had to. I had a choice.

'Yes, you're right,' I said, and my voice sounded firm. Strong. 'The place needs a shake up anyway. I can make it successful, and then hand back over to Sally when she's released.'

This was where Ivo should insert, 'And I'll be waiting for you in Yorkshire when you come back.' I left a little pause, but he was gazing upwards into the canopy again, at where the little squirrel was now grooming its fur.

'I'm sure that's Fred,' he said.

Everything in my risk-averse nature wanted to glide over the uncertainty, not say anything, not hazard my heart. But I'd stared at death down the barrel of a few thousand tonnes of unstable earth, and the ferocious hungry sea. I could take Ivo backing out gracefully, of course I could. It would hurt, but I'd heal.

'What about you, Ivo?' My voice had more strength than I thought I was capable of, and I was glad. 'If I stay here, that's it for any chance for you and me, isn't it?'

He looked at me, and his expression was total astonishment. 'What? No, Cress, don't say that! I mean, I've made arrangements, there are things in place... what on *Earth* would make you think... please don't tell me you've had a rethink! I know I'm terrible and awful to be with and I'm unreliable and everything but – darling Cress, please reconsider.'

I wondered if my bafflement was showing on my face to anything like the degree that his confusion was on his. His eyes were wide, their pupils huge and his skin had acquired the taut look of someone facing horror.

'*What*?' I said, for the second time in as many minutes.

Ivo's expression changed. His eyebrows came together in a ferocious frown and his mouth twisted. 'Er,' he said. 'I *think* we may have missed out a conversational step here, Cress.'

I was beginning to feel that I'd missed an actual physical step. My insides had jolted hard enough to remind me that I'd not eaten for most of the day. 'Please can we back up and go over it again, then?' I said, with, I thought, commendable evenness. 'Because, to me, it sounds as though you're leaving me here on the island.'

A new spark came into his eyes now and I was rushed into an embrace that I didn't want to start to enjoy until I knew what was causing it. 'Sorry, sorry, I've done it again. I've had the conversation in my head so often that I've forgotten to actually have it in real life! I'm so sorry, Cress.'

'Shall we have it now then, for the sake of argument?' I asked, encouraged by his turn of mood. Maybe things weren't quite as grim as I'd thought.

'Events, shall we say, of the last few days, have brought home the point to me that I'm not really cut out for this investigative journalism thing. Far too dangerous, and that's me saying it. So I was thinking, maybe, of moving down here. I've got contacts...'

'Of course you have,' I muttered faintly.

'...on Radio Four. There's the possibility of my making some programmes about the reintroduction of our native species; bustards on Salisbury plain, that sort of thing. It would keep me busy for, oh, the next couple of years or so.' I got a wide, innocent, Ivo-smile then. 'I thought I'd mentioned it to you. Obviously not.'

'Oh, Ivo,' I said, and I wasn't sure if I meant my tone to be happy, understanding or so bloody annoyed that I was only two steps away from throwing wildlife at him.

He shrugged. 'Life with me, Cress. It's how I am, I can't keep saying sorry. I *won't* keep saying sorry. It's tough being with me, but you ought to try *being* me.' A look of momentary sadness crept into his eyes. 'I think too fast. I miss out stages. I can't cope with overload, but I overload myself all the time, I can't help it.'

Then a sudden switch and there was that mischief back. 'But, you know, I saved your life and so there's that.'

'Oh, *Ivo*,' I said again, and this time it was happiness. Definitely happiness. A *teeny* bit of exasperation, perhaps, but I could deal with that. As long as he was trying, as long as he was aware of his difficulties, I could deal with that.

'And I didn't say anything, because I wasn't sure, but Ru messaged again.' He stopped and began fumbling for his phone. Today's trousers had too many pockets, and there was a good deal of poking and prodding.

'Oh? Have they got the person who killed Adam Williams?' I asked.

'What? No, not that. Ru reckons it will have been the person sent to collect the drugs on the moor that night and we may never know. But if they've tried to steal from their own people and go freelance, they've got the life expectancy of a mayfly.' A vague smile and more pockets were discovered. 'See, I've got the animal lingo down. Ah, here it is.'

He opened his phone. It occurred to me that mine was gone. I'd have to borrow Ivo's to see if Lil and Dix wanted to stay in the house and to tell work that I was staying on the island. Then, the sudden clutch of panic again – but where would we live? Were there houses to rent, that I could afford?

'Ru has had a word.' Ivo looked at his messages. 'As long as we're prepared to move out for Cowes week and two weeks in November, when there's a film shoot, we can have the house. Peppercorn rent, to keep it occupied so that burglars and drug dealers don't move in.'

'Stop it.'

'No, Cress, you have to admit it, there *are* benefits to being with me.' Now he came in again, and this time there was nothing fraternal, nothing everyday, about the way he put his arms around me. 'In fact, there are benefits that you know nothing about yet, but I have the feeling that we might be exploring them really quite soon.'

He slid a finger under my chin and, as I looked up, he kissed me. It was a hard, hot kiss, and there was a degree of roaming of hands that heated things up even further. I was slightly surprised that some of the nearby branches didn't catch fire and set the entire compound alight, as Ivo backed me up against a narrow sapling, mouths connected and fingers sliding in a most pleasurable way.

So, thankfully, it was a few minutes later that the squirrel dropped out of the tree and landed on Ivo's head, because it would have quite ruined the mood.

ABOUT THE AUTHOR

Jane Lovering is the bestselling and award-winning romantic comedy writer who won the RNA Contemporary Romantic Novel Award in 2023 with *A Cottage Full of Secrets*. She lives in Yorkshire and has a cat and a bonkers terrier, as well as five children who have now left home.

Sign up to Jane Lovering's mailing list here for news, competitions and updates on future books.

Visit Jane's website: www.janelovering.co.uk

Follow Jane on social media:

facebook.com/Jane-Lovering-Author-106404969412833

x.com/janelovering

bookbub.com/authors/jane-lovering

ALSO BY JANE LOVERING

The Country Escape

Home on a Yorkshire Farm

A Midwinter Match

A Cottage Full of Secrets

The Forgotten House on the Moor

There's No Place Like Home

The Recipe for Happiness

The Island Cottage

One of a Kind

LOVE NOTES

LOVE IN EVERY CHAPTER

WHERE ALL YOUR ROMANCE
DREAMS COME TRUE!

THE HOME OF BESTSELLING
ROMANCE AND WOMEN'S
FICTION

 WARNING:
MAY CONTAIN SPICE

SIGN UP TO OUR
NEWSLETTER

https://bit.ly/Lovenotesnews

Boldwœd

Boldwood Books is an award-winning fiction publishing company seeking out the best stories from around the world.

Find out more at www.boldwoodbooks.com

Join our reader community for brilliant books, competitions and offers!

Follow us
@BoldwoodBooks
@TheBoldBookClub

Sign up to our weekly deals newsletter

https://bit.ly/BoldwoodBNewsletter

Printed in Great Britain
by Amazon